Galaxy Girls:
Wonder Women

Galaxy Girls:
Wonder Women

S T O R I E S

ANNE WHITNEY PIERCE

Winner of the 1993 Willa Cather Fiction Prize

HELICON NINE EDITIONS
KANSAS CITY, MISSOURI

All rights reserved under International and Pan-American Copyright
Conventions. Published by the Midwest Center for the Literary Arts, Inc.,
P.O.Box 22412, Kansas City, MO 64113.

THESE STORIES ORIGINALLY APPEARED IN:
American Fiction, Number 2, The Chattahoochee Review, The Chicago Tribune,
Cimarron Review, Crosscurrents, Kansas Quarterly, The Massachusetts Review, The
North American Review, The Southern Review, and The Virginia Quarterly Review.

Cover photo: Anne Pierce
Photo transformation: Linda White

Book design: Tim Barnhart

Partial funding for this project has been provided by
the Missouri Arts Council and the Kansas Arts Commission,
state agencies, and by the N. W. Dible Foundation.

The author extends special thanks to Al, Sofia, Anna, Natasha,
Olive, George, Zoya, Seymour, Janie Simmons,
Linda White, Ann Collette, and Mameve Medwed.

Library of Congress Cataloging -in-Publication Data

Pierce, Anne Whitney, 1953-
    Galaxy girls : wonder women : short stories / Anne Whitney Pierce.
    -- 1st ed.
        p.   cm.
    Contents: Sans homme - - The twins - - Abeyance - - Lucy - - Empire beauty
    salon - - The gumball man - - Remarkable - - J*E*W*E*L - - Star box - - Lost in
    Casablanca.
    ISBN 0-9627460-9-6 : $12.95
    I. Title.
PS3566.I38157G3   1994
813' .54--dc20   93-8411
                                                                       CIP

Manufactured in the United States of America
HELICON NINE EDITIONS

For Natasha, Anna, and Sofia

CONTENTS

SANS HOMME

I once heard Mrs. Applebaum, an old busybody who lived in our apartment building, talking about my mother in the park. It was an autumn day and the trees were bare. I was kicking a stone through the leaves, and I heard Mrs. Applebaum say to Mrs. Yee, "Lily Minneker, you know, is never *sans homme*." I was eight at the time, in the third grade at P. S. 10. My teacher, Mrs. Shumway, thought that children should have a smattering of all things—hygiene, Mozart, nature, and French, and so, although I didn't understand exactly what Mrs. Applebaum was talking about, I did know that *homme* meant man.

I never considered the fact of my mother's many men friends to be a flaw, only part of her description, like her poetry or her love of avocados or the way she made the beds so tight. The men came without fanfare, because my mother would stand for no fanfare—appearing for dinner one evening, and then again, offering to help with the dishes or my homework, later playing soft music and laughing with my mother after I'd gone to bed, at which point I knew it was only a matter of time before I might pass them half-naked in the night, in the hallway on my way to the bathroom, or in a dream.

In the morning, the dream men were always gone. My mother woke me with a shake and a kiss, fresh and alone at my bedside, smelling only of soap and herself. At breakfast we'd talk about things we'd done or things we'd do, as if no one had ever intruded, looking as far into the day as we could. And then my mother would walk me briskly to school and wave and wave and blow kisses until I'd gotten inside the door safely. She never did any of these things for the men.

Slowly, in a reverse sequence of hospitality, the men would disappear back to the places from where they had come—my mother pleading fatigue after dinner one night, or no food in the house the next, sometimes saying that she needed to spend more time with me, but only if it was true. Finally, the man was invited for one last meal—an elegant, candlelit dinner of misunderstanding, with all of his favorite foods. On these occasions, my mother would be at her most lovely, her kindest and most charming, truly happy in this ritual of severance, loving the man best at that last moment in a tender way that made him love her more than ever, unaware that it was all a prelude to rejection.

After these dinners, I'd be put to bed, and then I'd listen at the door while my mother told the man it was over. She never told any lies, simply saying, usually over a glass of wine, that the thing had run its course, that it had been lovely, what they'd made together, and that she would never forget him. And although she did none of these things with the intention of cruelty, I will never forget the confusion or the anger or the pain in these men's faces when she told them, the change in their eyes, the wine glasses raised in hand. And although it is not a good thing to watch a spirit crumble, I will remember these last evenings as happy ones, because of the good feeling with which they began and the way we made them celebrations, Lily and I—the eves of those times when my mother was *entre hommes,* when I slept knowing that I would have her all to myself, at least for a while.

* * *

My father, my mother told me, had been the best of all men—fine, handsome, intelligent, not a bad gene in his line, which somehow featured Italian royalty. He'd seen my mother walking on a New York street and pursued her in a limousine, then kept her in a penthouse while he jetted around, for as long as she would be kept. She'd loved him madly, she said, for almost a year, then asked him for a child, without mentioning that the request did not include the usual accompaniments— marriage, family vacations, company for the twilight years. From what I gather, he took the news quite well, only pointing, my mother said, to his good judgment. My father had been sensible, a trait she valued in both him and me, she said, to help her make me and then go about his business, which was the business of fine wine, and one that made him heaps of money.

I first met my father when I was nine, and he was struck with the urge to know me. This was to be expected, my mother said, though surely it had never been one of my expectations. He wrote from Rome, where he lived, to say he was coming for me on a Saturday. Lily let me buy new black patent leather shoes, which my father never noticed. He was fabulously rich and handsome, but very fidgety, and sad. He flew me on a private plane to Rome, where he took me to a carnival, which except for the loud Italian voices, might have been anywhere in the world, and then flew me right back in time to get a good night's sleep for school. And because this was the only real adventure of my life, my only real claim to glamour—a moonlit plane ride and riding a ferris wheel while "*Amore*" boomed from the loud-speakers—I stardusted the memory of this trip and this father, telling my friends at school that I was sort of a princess and that I'd been to a magic kingdom. This, along with the fact that my mother was the most beautiful mother in the world, made me a figure of some envy, an envy I kept coveting, although I did not really know what to do with it once it was mine.

Those who did not love my mother did not much like her. She was too much of everything, I think—too beautiful, too hon-est, too unafraid, too unconcerned about the things which kept other people humble and occupied—crime on the streets, the evils of TV, and the crumbling public school system. Not, of course, that Lily was in favor of any of these things; she just didn't see the point of dwelling on them. No one could tell her anything about herself that she didn't already know, good or bad. And that left people defenseless and at a loss. "I talk too much, of course," she'd say. Or, "You probably will construe my ardor as arrogance." Over the years, I heard Lily called many things. A hedonist. A genius. A vixen. A beatnik. A slut. A goddess. A bard. A temptress. An atheist. An enigma. People reached deep for ways to describe my mother, needing somehow to imprison her in a word. She listened carefully to everyone, weeding out the truth, she said, and chucking the fiction. What no one understood was that Lily forgave them all, that she real-ly liked people.

"Thank God for you, Francie," she used to tell me. "If they couldn't see how well you've turned out, they wouldn't give me any credit at all."

I don't know how my mother turned out to be what she was—beautiful, passionate, self-strong—maybe, she sometimes mused, from the same genes that had made her Uncle Thomas a black sheep. Uncle Thomas had left his wife and family for a Cuban mail clerk and his causes; they'd stayed with us for a while when I was small, on their way to somewhere underground. Certainly, Lily was not a likely product of her parents—dour, hardworking people, who'd never really forgiven her for being an only child and not a boy. They'd despaired early of her bringing any credit to the family, and then died young.

* * *

The first of Lily's men that I remember was Lloyd. It was the middle of the 1950's and I was about four or five, not yet in school. We lived in Greenwich Village; no point in living anywhere else, my mother said. When the weather permitted, we packed up our lives—books and papers and crayons and dolls and Lily's thermos of coffee—and went across the street to Washington Square Park. It was the best education I could get, Lily said, watching so many slices of life in one pie, sitting under a tree and breathing in what was good of the air. And what wasn't good, she said, we'd learn to weather.

Lloyd was one of the men who sat hour by hour playing chess in the shady north side of the park, oblivious to everyone and everything but cold and darkness, until he looked up one day to see my mother's face peering down at his chessboard.

"I'll play the winner," Lily said.

"Then I'll make sure to win," Lloyd said.

Win, Lloyd did, and then he sat down to a game of chess with my mother. He was at first amused, then puzzled, then affronted, then aroused, and finally defeated by her skill and quiet beauty, which was not a fleeting thing at all, but quite relentless—the creamy skin and speckled eyes, the full lips and black, black hair.

I know all of this, not because I remember the details, but because my mother liked to make a story out of each man after he'd long come and gone, sometimes two, three years later, when she had it all etched in her mind the way she wanted it to be remembered, and then she'd say, maybe at the dinner table or before bed, "Remember Lloyd, Francie? He wore that red bandanna around his neck, and he just couldn't believe that a woman could snooker him at chess."

What I remember of Lloyd, besides how his face changed that first time when he looked up into Lily's eyes, was a red beard that tickled and the stories he made up for me at bedtime, most of them about a cowboy named Bob and his sidekick jack rabbit named Peco. I liked that word, sidekick, though the stories were not all that good. Lloyd was not unkind, or not anything, really, just always preoccupied, in the way of chess players. He was the first person I ever saw bewitched by Lily, the first man to step deep into our lives. Even then, as young as I was, I was not sad or threatened, because he did not make my mother change when she was with me, because he made her happy for a while, and because he never came to our apartment until it was dark, when I couldn't be sure if he were real, anyway.

"Francie comes first," my mother would preach a sermon to all of the men, first thing, right after they'd met, like telling someone before he even sets foot in your house that he must wipe his feet, that dirt on the rugs and floors simply is not tolerated. "This gets understood," she'd say, "before we even pass go."

And the man would nod his head, more times than was necessary, willing to do whatever it would take to get my mother alone in a dark and willing place, or a ring on her finger, sure— even before he'd touched her—that Lily was (as my father told me on the plane), the perfect woman.

"Everything else but Francie," my mother would overdo it a bit, "is really worth very little."

And having been made precious and unhurtable in this way, I could look the man in the eye and smile and shake his hand off my head without malice or mixed feeling, and skip ahead of him and my mother on our way to Beeman's Grocery Mart to buy French bread and spaghetti, which was almost always the first dinner fare. The first nights were almost as gay as the last ones, my mother glowing with good humor and anticipation, the smells of garlic and perfume and oregano in the air, the man melting with his desire—to have my mother and to please me. After dinner, Lily would pull out the Monopoly game, a sort of ritual test of character. She would rate the man by his style of play. A few, who had no patience with my indecision or my passion for neat piles of cash, those who coveted Boardwalk and Park Place, or would not give me money when I went broke from my wild hotel-buying sprees, were not asked back again.

* * *

When I was eleven, my father, who was going through some sort of mid-life crisis, my mother speculated, appeared unannounced at our door. Lily said afterwards, that this second visit, too, was to be expected. This time my father came to say that I, Francesca Minneker da Ramon, could no longer be raised in this so-called fashion.

"What so-called fashion?" my mother asked. (Lily said that he spoke almost perfect English, but had no feel for the idiom, which for a long time, I took to mean idiot.)

"Slovenly. Uncivilized. Look at this place. Trash all over the place."

"Books. Papers. Things we use," my mother said quietly. "None of it is trash. What so-called fashion?"

"Really, Lily," my father said. "She lives like the protégée of a high-class hooker."

I did not know what he meant at the time, but I knew he had made a mistake when I saw the speckles in my mother's eyes grow black. "Ramon," she said, "that is the worst thing I have ever known you to say."

"Go ahead, Lily," he said, "why don't you slap me?"

"I don't hit people," she said. "Violence is uncivilized. It hurts."

"Damn it, Lily," he said, pacing up and down the room, and I realized then that he had not come for me, this time, but for Lily. "There's no melting you, is there? Forever, you will get into my skin."

Forgetful of me, my father shook my mother down on the couch then and nuzzled his head in her lap. A softness came into her eyes—not love, I think, but kindness. She asked me if I would mind going into my room for a while, and then she took my father next door to hers. Although I woke and wandered several times in the night, I did not pass my father, though I knew he was there, heard the whispers and the creaks of the bed through the wall. And though Lily continued to speak to me highly of him as a father, I never saw him again.

* * *

It was soon after this, when I was about twelve, that Dusty Uptown came into our lives. Upton, really. Lily sang a song about an "uptown, down-beat man." There was something different about Dusty from the start—something about how he came into our apartment with reluctance and no grand plans, how he politely declined both spaghetti and the chance to play Monopoly, saying he didn't much like games and didn't eat red meat, even if it was just little bits of hamburger in the sauce. Dusty lived in Brooklyn and jogged over the bridge every morning into Manhattan and all the way to Washington Square Park, where Lily often sat, taking care of household business and writing the poems she sent around in purple envelopes, the same kind of envelopes that came back to our apartment addressed to Lily in her own handwriting, the "so-sorry letters," she called them.

Dusty always made one last lap around the pigeon fountain before heading back to Brooklyn. Lily asked him once how many miles he ran. He said he didn't count them, but it was more than all of the fingers on both of her hands. He was a restauranteur, he called it, waited on tables all night in a fancy place on the Upper East Side called *Chez Moi*. He did his miles and miles of running just after the dawn and then slept for most of the day. Once a year, in April, he went to Boston to run the marathon. It was only the facts of Dusty's odd hours and odd ways that gave me a chance to know him better than the rest.

By that time, Lily had been working for a few years. I was eight when she got the job; she thought it might be good to have something regular to do, since I had so much regular stuff in my life by then—school, friends, judo lessons on Wednesdays at the Y. She was tired of doing a circus act, she said—juggling, finagling, sleight of hand, high wire investment—with the small amount left to her when her parents died and the little bits of money she made on her poems. The money my father sent was religiously reserved for me. Lily bought very few things for herself. Most of her pretty things came from the men, though she never accepted anything of value, and was very strict about what she'd let them give me.

She'd scoured the classifieds in the park for weeks, until she found just the right thing for us—a bookkeeping position in a bookstore from eleven to five. It was perfect, she said, because she still had time to make me breakfast and get me off to school, to do some writing in the morning, and then see me all evening. That left only two hours, she figured, when we would have to be apart. And when she asked me if I could handle that, I said, sure I could handle that. And though Lily's work turned out to be boring, I think she liked the job, liked riding the subway and dressing down, and cleaning up her desk by five o'clock. I think she liked the smells of ink and paper and books, even making coffee for her boss, though as one of her men later said (an angry one, Clem, I think his name was)—Lily could have run the whole shebang. And when Lily was down and neither I nor a man could cheer her up, she'd be late coming home sometimes and I'd walk down to the bookstore and find her sitting like a Buddha in one of the aisles, lost in some book or another.

Before Dusty came, I used to spend those two hours after school before Lily got home downstairs at Mrs. Biondi's apartment. She made me sugar cookies and anise tea. She was just about deaf and we watched the soaps together, but when her hearing aid was on the fritz, she'd shout, "What'd that nurse say?" and I'd shout back, "She said the baby was born without his thumb!" and then we'd cry together. We were both in love with the same doctor on "General Hospital," one whose fan mail was slipping, we read in the *TV Guide*, because he was growing bald and stout. In return for her kindness, Lily and I did things for Mrs. Biondi. We took out her garbage and did her taxes in the spring. Sometimes, when her bursitis got bad, she called me down to rub her feet.

But when Dusty started slipping into Lily's bed in the early mornings after his runs, my mother said I could stay with him in the afternoons, that we didn't have to bother Mrs. Biondi for a while. On the mornings when I knew Dusty was there, I'd get up and make myself breakfast and walk to school with Ellen Morganstern. I knew Lily would not get any work done on her poems on those mornings. All day in school, I'd think about Dusty, sleeping there in Lily's bed all tangled up in the lavender sheets. Tall. Naked. And after eleven o'clock, when Lily went to work and I had math class—alone.

Dusty usually woke up soon after I got home. He did yoga exercises on the living room floor and wouldn't talk until he'd done his salute to the sun and drunk his egg potion. After Dusty showered and dressed, he would come into the kitchen, naked to the waist, his torso almost as long as his legs, sweat pants hanging low on his hips, and a line of blondish hair rising up from his drawstring to his navel. We'd eat toast together and talk about what I'd done in school or something that had happened at the restaurant the night before—like a bug in the soup or a cash register thief—until I could see that Dusty was getting antsy, and then he'd ask would I like to go out and do something and I'd say sure and off we'd go, on foot, as Dusty always did. My feet got sore after a few days running with Dusty, and he up and bought me some fancy running shoes for $23.99, which was a lot back then to pay for just sneakers. I didn't know what to do besides take them, when Dusty said, "If you're going to run, Francie, you've gotta have good shoes."

And so we'd run in fits and spurts to wherever it was that we were going, to the park to study the eating habits of pigeons, or to the library to watch the Dewey decimal system in action, to the health food store, where Dusty would try to tempt me with carrot juice and wheat germ cookies, where no matter how good the things looked, they all tasted like bad medicine, and I'd say, "Forget it, Dusty. Don't try to make me eat that stuff," and he'd say if I ate too much more sugar, I'd crystallize. When we ran, the taxi drivers yelled at us for being weird and taking up too much room on the streets, this being long before jogging became something New York had gotten used to.

And although I'd lived in the city all of my twelve years, it was not until Dusty bought me those red sneakers with the white lightening bolts on the sides, that I came to make sense of the grid of numbered streets and the big cross avenues, to know which direction the Empire State Building was from the Hudson, and what days the museums were closed, what time Angelo put out his day-old rolls.

Whatever we were doing, we'd never be late to meet Lily back home at 5:15, when the three of us would have dinner together. Dusty ate mostly vegetables and pasta, the yin and the yang, and sometimes chicken, which Lily roasted up from time to time for him. And whenever Dusty and I did the wishbones a few days later, I always got the big part and Dusty would say, "Well, it looks like you're the lucky one again, Francie."

After dinner, the two of them would go off to Lily's room, while I watched TV or did my homework. At 6:30, the dinner hour of the leisurely-suited, Dusty called it, he'd shower again and put on his tuxedo and comb back his hair, then ask us how he looked. We'd tell him he was gorgeous, as he sat down and put his good shoes, newly polished, in a bag, and his sneakers on his feet, ready to run off to *Chez Moi*, at which point my mother, still soft and rumpled from their lovemaking, would look sad and say she wished he could stay *Chez Lily,* and then she'd turn brisk and whisk me off into the bath, asking how on earth I'd gotten so dirty. And then Dusty would follow her and take her protesting in his arms, and squeeze her so tightly she'd ask for her breath back and point to me and push him away, saying "Francie's here," but in a way that made both of us know that she liked it.

And when Dusty was gone, off to serve snails and sweet-breads to people who only pretended to like them, Dusty said, or to sip at the not-good-enough wine that got sent back to the cellars, my mother would ask me, while we did the dishes or sit-ting on the edge of my bed, what Dusty and I had done together that afternoon, where we'd been and what we'd seen. And I'd tell her, leaving out some of the parts, like when Dusty sort of smiled at me, or called me Ensign Francie, how he didn't care if I said damn or hell, because they were expletives and had a legitimate place in the English language. And I never told her about the sneakers, taking them off on the stoop when I got home and changing back into my regular shoes, which I hid on the fire escape in a box.

One thing Dusty never did was talk about my mother with me. And he never treated me like a kid. When I got tired of running, we'd stop and walk along and play what-would-you-choose-if-you-had-to from this or that store window. Sometimes, but not always, we'd pick something for Lily, too. Our favorite window was Maxwell's Army and Navy Store window, where our choices never changed. I always picked the deluxe Swiss army knife, the one with the fork and spoon and scissors and can opener and ivory toothpick. And Dusty always got the inflatable raft, which he planned one day to take down the Mississippi. We never picked anything for Lily from this window.

* * *

One rainy day, when I got home from school, Dusty was already up and dressed. He'd been around for a long time, a couple of seasons, at least, because I remember when autumn was over and he changed his shoes to ones with spikes on them that did better on snow and ice. Dusty and I went for fish and chips that day. He said everyone needed some grease from time to time, to keep the old body lubricated. And then he burped, long and loud, and said why didn't we take a ride on the Staten Island Ferry, before they raised the fare to a dime, like they were talking about doing.

Dusty and I had been on the ferry together before, and in my dream, this was where he told me that it couldn't be helped, but it turned out that he loved me even more than he did my mother, but that we could never tell her. In this dream, he gave me the kiss. He'd come so close and hold me so tightly, that I'd have no choice but to fall forward into his arms. Only in my dreams could I not be strong enough to push Dusty away, to betray my mother so.

We leaned over the railing and squawked at the gulls and caught raindrops in our mouths. The drizzle hung in little drops on Dusty's hair. His profile showed a long forehead and pointed nose, a dimpled chin and hair that sprang away from his forehead. The broad shoulders and the blond-haired arms, the pack of Camels tucked under his rolled-up sleeve, made him handsome like a guy they'd haul off the range to smoke cigarettes in a TV ad.

"It's been good, Francie," Dusty finally said, as we passed by the Statue of Liberty.

"What?" I asked. "The fish and chips? Riding the boat in the rain?"

"Yeah," he said, not quite as handsome when he turned his face front to me, a face where old, old pockmarks dented the surface of his skin. "You might call it all a boatride, Francie. These days we've spent together."

"Yeah, a boatride," I said, as he turned sideways again. "You might call it that."

"I think there's something that ought to be said to you," he said. "And it might as well be me who says it." He coughed then, to punctuate everything. "You should never worry, Francie," he said.

"About what?"

"About your mother . . . who she is . . . trying to be like her . . . or not like her."

"What do you mean?" I thought then that Dusty was telling me that I shouldn't care about not being as pretty as Lily was, which I already knew. I had always understood, in some funny way, that Lily's looks were as much of a curse as a blessing.

"There's no point in making another Lily," he said, tapping a cigarette out of the Camel pack. This was the only time I'd heard anything close to wistfulness in his voice and it vanished as quickly as it had come. "One Lily is just about all this planet can handle," he said, lighting up one of his three cigarettes a day. I still didn't know what he was getting at, took one puff of the cigarette, which was all Dusty would ever let me have.

"She did a good job of raising you," he said, talking more down to the water than to me by then. "You turned out your own good self, Francie," he said. "You should always remember that. Being Francie is a pretty good accomplishment right there."

"I know," I said, and although I often only pretended to understand the hard things Dusty talked about, this time I really did.

The kiss came and went, nothing like I'd imagined it, just a soft peck on the forehead and no words, but nonetheless magnificent, the touch of real lips conjured up from a dream. Dusty bought me popcorn then, which was too salty to eat, and we threw most of it to the gulls as the boat headed back to the pier. We jogged home and Dusty waited on the stoop until I'd changed my shoes and Lily had buzzed me in, before he jogged away and said, "So long, Francie."

When I got upstairs, I saw Lily dressed in a white blouse and purple velvet skirt, with dangly earrings and combs in her hair. The table was set and lit up all beautifully and I smelled roast chicken—Dusty's favorite—cooking in the oven. I lost the breath inside me for a minute. Lily lit the candles and asked, "Where's Dusty?"

"He didn't come up," I said. I went to wash my hands for dinner and stopped into Lily's room to peek into her closet and see if Dusty's tuxedo was gone. Lily came into the room behind me.

"Francie?" she said.

"What?" I said. She came closer and we looked together at the empty wooden hanger.

"Where did he go?" Lily asked, reaching out with one hand to swing the hanger back and forth. The smells of her smoky perfume and Dusty's chicken swirled around me and I said all that I could, that we'd gotten wet in the rain and that I didn't know. And as Lily sat down on the bed and I saw the speckles in her eyes fade, I knew that we'd both been left *sans homme*.

THE TWINS

J ust across the causeway onto Coombs Island, where the smells of bay leaves and salt and low-tide mud mingle in the air, stands the Twins' Gas Station and Garage. I see it from a distance as I cross the narrow bridge, the first and brightest spot on a green Maine island splattered with soft browns and granite greys. The garage is freshly painted, red with blue. I remember the inside from long-ago summers when Ellie and I got out of the car to use the bathroom marked GULLS while our mother filled the car with gas. Peeking in, I'd see the gleaming rows of wrenches and screwdrivers and the stack of oil cans by the door—always a perfect pyramid. I loved the dark neatness of the garage, the smooth rhythm of industry that I was sure had something to do with the magic of their being twins.

It's been seventeen years since I've been back to Maine. This is my vacation, I suppose, although this year it feels more like some kind of aimless pilgrimage. At 29, I have just become the kind of person that takes vacations alone. Before my mother went to the old-age home last December, I spent vacations with her. For years, we rented a cottage in Cape Cod in a forest of shrub, away from the shore. Before, when my sister Ellie was alive, the three of us came here to Coombs Island for two weeks every August.

There's no point in wondering how we all would have been different if my father hadn't disappeared when I was two. That was just the beginning for me, of a life in a family of women that had been left without a man. But I often wonder what I was like before Ellie died that summer in Maine, just younger, I've decided, but no less complicated. I was 12 at the time, an age people called impressionable. After it happened, my mother and I took a small plane home from Bangor. I never knew how Ellie's body got to Boston; I did not like deserting her that way. After the funeral, people gathered in our house near Beacon Hill. My mother bustled around with cold-cut platters and cool drinks as if it were a summer party. I'd grown over the summer and wore a brown dress of Ellie's, one she'd hated.

16

As the day got steamy, the air filled with chatter and all the dark, stiff clothes started to wrinkle and unfurl. The room slowly billowed with the relief of a permission to stop being sad. My mother bestowed it, with a smile here, a press of the hand there, a slice of cake. "We'll be just fine," she said, and people believed her because people always believed my mother. I remember what was said of me, words started by Mrs. Peco, my piano teacher, and passed on quickly like unwelcome guests—"She's so fragile to start with . . . that child . . . so fragile."

I went over to the food table and poured myself a tall glass of gingerale with chipped ice. In a moment of confused celebration, I found myself painfully happy about who I had just become—my mother's only, fragile child. Mrs. Peco came over then and told me not to slouch, that I would have to work on the minor scales even harder now. The gingerale bubbles stung my nose and I ran into my room to make sure no one had been snooping around trying to find Ellie's cowboy jacket. There were, even in the midst of all the arrangements, some questions asked about it, why she had been wearing it in the water. They said it must have weighed her down. The jacket was there; in a box under my bed, along with Ellie's shellacked bugs and the letter to President Kennedy about letting girls go into space. Later, I buried the jacket and the bugs next to Paul Revere in the Granary Burying Grounds at Park Street, and sent the letter to the White House.

"Describe yourself," the woman at the dating service said to me last June, more a dare than a suggestion. The whole thing was my friend Sally's idea. She led me breathless to that airless room, with pictures of happy couples on the walls, no different than a doctor's office, really, where people go with hopes to cure their maladies. I fled the office at those words, but I've since made this self-description an exercise in my mind, practicing the words that mean me in a nutshell, in case anyone who might really like to know should ask.

"I'm a person who gets things wrong with too much trying," I would tell a man the bad things first. "I break things."

"Oh?" he'd ask politely. "What kinds of things?"

The list is long. Bottles of hypo in the darkroom, my leg once in a fall from a low tree (just after Ellie died), umpteen rules of thumb, dates that Sally fixes me up with.

("It's not like you're ugly or anything, Paula," she tells me. "Why don't you try breaking a few hearts?")

"But I am not without substance," I would go on, maybe more courageous after a glass of wine. The man and I would sit in some cafe in a warm, sleepy country. "Or without virtue!" I'd say. "I ride the subway and pay the rent on time. I take in stray cats. I love my mother."

I should be more specific, tell him what I do, what I've done. I am a photographer. One of my pictures hangs in a permanent collection at the Museum of Modern Art in New York. It's a fine picture of a man sitting on the bank of a Cape Cod cranberry bog, looking out over the sea of crimson, his big arms draped around his knees. But I still think they took the photograph out of an inexplicable kindness that I never earned, that if I die or go far away where I can't check on it from time to time, they will take it down.

Finally, I might tell the man, so that he might spare me later when we knew each other better. "I am short on courage."

It's taken me all the years since Ellie died to make my way back to Coombs Island. Up until that summer when she drowned, she and my mother and I rented a red cottage called The Shoe, which sat high on a ledge above the old stone quarry, not far from the Twins' Garage, I think, though my sense of geography is not very good. We loved The Shoe, not because it was comfortable, with its ripped screens and broken pump or the mosquitoes that bred in a puddle outside our door, but because of its murky past. It was said that in eighteen-something-something, a miser had been murdered while he slept in the upstairs bedroom. Ellie and I took turns on a dare sleeping in that room, usually lasting only one half or one quarter of the night. That room smelled like a dead old miser.

On the bridge, I stop my car by the side of the road and lean out the window toward the ocean. It is cool for an August morning, with the eerie stillness of winter. The water around the island is too smooth, etching a clean line where it meets the rocks. The salt air trickles inside me, stirring old senses. I remember the look of the rocks and seaweed at half-tide, the squawk of the gulls and the revving of the lobster boat engines. I remember the echoes of voices bouncing off the quarry walls, and the summer games Ellie and I used to play.

"Let's pretend we're twins, El," I'd say. "We do everything together, everything alike. . . ."

"That's impossible, P." Ellie read a lot and searched always for the right word. "That's impractical. That's incorrigible. That's exasperating!"

"Let's say you go to Florida on a business trip with your husband."

"What do I do for a living?"

"You're an astronaut," I'd say, trying to win her. "One day you're at the space center training how to eat upside down, and suddenly you know that something terrible has happened to me and your legs go all tingly and you rush out with your spacesuit on and fly home on a plane to make sure I'm all right."

"What happened to you?" Ellie would ask.

"I broke both my legs," I'd say. "In a terrible car accident. I'm paralyzed for life."

"No." Ellie would flip her braids over her shoulders then. "That's stupid, Paula."

I pull up to the Twins' gas pumps. Softly closing my car door, I wipe my palms on my pants and walk to the mouth of the garage. Inside are the Harmon twins, bending and stretching in their work, unchanged to my eye, in green jump suits and brown shoes. Music plays softly out of a radio, an old fifties song about a girl named Donna. A framed picture of Elvis hangs by the door. The oil can pyramid is still perfect.

"Help you?" asks one twin, emerging from under the hood of a car. He wipes his hands on a clean rag. The other twin sweeps no apparent dirt over the inkblot oil stains on the cement floor.

"My car is overheating," I say. "Could you take a look?" This is a sham. My car is tended in the city by a man named Mac

Somebody and has never overheated. I won't tell Mac about this visit to the Twins, but he will know the minute he lifts the hood, the way a hairdresser knows when someone else has fussed with your hair and yanks with the comb ever after.

"Bring her in," the first twin says—Earl, the patch on his suit reads.

"I'm Paula Blake," I introduce myself. "I used to come here in the summer."

"Earl Harmon," he says and points to the sweeper. "Over there's my brother, Homer."

"I'm a photographer," I go on. "I'm thinking of doing a photo documentary story on twins." The idea which has been milling in the back of my mind comes to life of its own accord. "Would you mind if I brought my camera down some day and took some pictures?"

The twins shrug together, the rise of one's shoulders following the other one's fall. One of them, I forget which, says, "Why not today?"

I look around—at my watch and my car and down at my feet—but there are no reasons for delay. As I get my camera equipment out of the trunk, the old fear of anomaly washes over me. I am too rash, too plump, too oddly dressed, for the first time in my life, maybe too pretty, with my father's chestnut hair and full lips. My scent is swallowed as I step deeper into the garage, and it is only after I load my camera and advance the film a few frames, cradling the cool black metal of my Leica in my hands, that I remember what it is I do.

Earl pops open the hood of my car. Homer keeps sweeping. I snap a few pictures of the garage—of the tools and the tires and the cars, while parts of the twins flash in and out of the frame— Earl's bent leg or shoulder, Homer's earnest face and fine hands. Through the lens of my camera, I get my life bearings. My friend Sally says it is my way of hiding from the world. The light meter barely registers. I will have to try to hold the camera still while the shutter clicks at a fifteenth of a second. The pictures will be blurry, like all the rest. I am not good at clean images, sharp lines.

"Pretty busy in the summer?" I begin the leading chatter of

my trade.

"Depends," Earl says, diving in and out of the engine of my car. "Need a wrench, Homer," he calls out. Homer puts down his broom and starts over with a wrench, then veers off course. I see him coming through my lens, a blur of green chest and the orange wall behind. I snap the shutter. When I ease the camera down from my eyes, Homer is near, staring at me, or the camera, I can't be sure. It is a curious, uncomplicated stare, the kind I am no good at. He is near enough to smell, too close really to see. For a minute he smells like Ellie used to—of sweat and sun and red licorice. But no, those are kid smells, and this is a grown man.

"I like cameras," Homer says, and then he makes a barking noise. I hold the camera out as an offering, but he is already on his way back to Earl with the wrench, dancing to Sam Cooke's "You Send Me."

Time twirls around the twins. They have not aged. Is it because instead of growing older, twins grow only more alike? But identical is not the right word for them, although feature by feature the roll call is the same—brown eyes, long noses and straight black hair. Earl, the mechanic, has the look of a kind, over-taxed vampire, with deep-set almost black eyes and one extraordinary tooth, a fang really. The features work better on Homer, the sweeper. He is handsomer, younger somehow, with eyes and lips and hands that move with grace. He has hair like Elvis's, though less of it, parted to one side and flipped up with some grease.

Earl fiddles some more with my car. "Not much wrong with it," he pronounces finally, and moves back to the other. Homer keeps order, retrieving tools and cans of oil for Earl, sweeping and rearranging. Outside, as the cars pull in, he pumps the gas and cleans the windshields with care, speaking to every customer with the attention of a good *maitre d'*, about the weather, or a sick uncle, or the price of lobster. He checks in with me from time to time.

"How 'bout one of me and the tool chest?" Homer asks.

"Sure," I say. Homer poses next to the shiny red box and

makes the barking noise again. I bring my camera down to see if I am expected to laugh or listen more, or pretend that I am a dog too. But Homer's face has not changed. Nor has Earl's.

"How 'bout one of me right here next to Earl's feet?" he says. "Biggest feet on the island. Size 13 triple E."

I take all of the pictures Homer has in mind, find out later they are some of the best of the lot.

At 12:30, Earl says "lunch." He takes out a store-bought fruit pie and a green can of something and keeps working. I follow Homer outside. He perches on a pile of old tires and offers me a bite of his sandwich.

"No thanks," I say. "I don't each lunch."

"You've never eaten lunch?" A piece of lettuce falls to the ground.

"It's been so long," I say. "I don't remember when."

"Funny thing," he says. "I don't think I've ever missed one."

"What's it like being a twin?" I ask him.

Homer shrugs, the broad shoulders lifting up gently, then melting down into the hunk of his chest. "Guess I have a better idea of what I look like than most people," he says.

"They say that twins are as close as two people can get," I venture. "That they have ESP and feel responsible for each other."

"Earl don't need a keeper," Homer says. He finishes his Coke. "What do you do up there in that city, Paula?" he asks.

"Down," I say. "Isn't it?"

"Down is up around here," he says.

"Oh," I say, not really understanding. "I work, go to the movies, read. I take care of my mother." I look down at my pointed shoes. "How about you?"

"I do pretty much whatever," Homer says.

Leaving Homer on the tires, I cross the road and walk down to the shore. The new moon has drained the cove to a point where the mud turns a rich, loamy black. The sour smell of seaweed and muck rises up from the pit below me. There is no wind.

"Bad smells mask good things," my mother once told me somewhere on this island. In the old days, before she lost her marbles, she often spoke in home-spun proverbs.

"What's so good about smelly mud flats?" I asked her. I liked the coves when they were brim full and sparkling and postcard pretty, all the mud and broken shells and clam holes hidden. It was the quarries I loved, with their crystal clear waters and the salamanders that swam in a friendly manner by your feet.

"Those mudflats," my mother rose indignantly atop a rock, "are home to thousands of crabs and mussels and starfish and barnacles!"

I miss my mother at that moment, as I sit down on a mottled rock, the person she used to be when I was young and she was not old. I miss the way she slapped her knees when she made up her mind about something, and the scent of the rose perfume she wore, never for any man after my father, but only for herself, and the doughy pies she made. She knew things and people by their smells. "Alice Peele's in the hallway" she'd say. Or, "Garbage truck must be coming down Beacon Hill." I wonder how she would defend the bad smells she is making at the end of her life if she knew, with her food-stained clothes and dirty feet.

My mother did not *go* to the old-age home. I sent her. Because in the end, when it was her turn to be fragile, I didn't really know how to take care of her. In the last days we spent together, we became friends, and I could not betray a new friend. So afraid of losing her, I couldn't insist that she brush her teeth or go to the bathroom.

When her memory started to go, I moved her out of the old house and kept her in my apartment in Cambridge, hoping with my stubborn, sometimes angry love to keep her from getting any older, any odder. For that short time, we played together as children do. We dressed up like Salvation Army ladies and rode the subway to Columbia Point. We made bundt cakes and watched "I Love Lucy" reruns at noon.

"You were so busy being a kid," my friend Sally later scolded me. "You didn't even realize your poor mother was going nuts." She was right, I suppose. Sally usually is. But it occurs to me as I sit on that rock looking down on a kingdom of muck, that Sally never tells me anything that makes me feel good.

When my mother started to make small fires in the corners of the apartment to keep warm, I had to put her away in a place outside of the city called The Emerald Shores.

"Where are the emeralds, Paula?" she asked me in tired accusation the first time I went to see her there. "Tell me, Paula, where are the shores?"

And so, like a mortician, I am now a person who has put someone else in a box. Though I visit my mother twice a week, I can barely stand to see her there, all the spark and wisdom gone from her eyes, the bite from her tongue, the backwards johnny stained and all askew. I went to see her a few days before I left. We sat on the lawn, which had been kept mysteriously green in an August drought.

"Did I tell you about the apples in the snow, Paula?" she asked me. My mother looked well that day, dressed in blue pants and a clean shirt for my visit. She'd tried to comb her hair and called me by name.

"What apples in the snow, Ma?" I asked her.

"Apples! Bushels of them, crashing down from out of a box. I nearly got crushed." Her eyes were steamy and yellow.

"What apples, Ma?" I knew then that she was not really with me. Still, I wanted so badly to have that conversation about the apples, to finish it. "Red apples or green, Ma? Where were we? At the market? On Cape Cod? Who was with you when the apples fell, Ma? Was it me? Was it Ellie?"

"No," she said, annoyed. Ellie's name no longer brings a ripple of pain to her brow. "I was with *Carmen*." I know of no such person named Carmen. Nor, to my knowledge, does she.

"I'm going back to Coombs Island, Ma," I told her. "Just for a day or two. Just one time."

"Carmen and I made applesauce," my mother said, looking out over the emerald lawn. "It was the only sensible thing to do."

The image of my sister Ellie is clearer in my mind than any other, because it's frozen at that moment just after she died. I picture frost on her blue lips and icicles clinging to her hair, though there was neither. I remember the freckles strangely clustered on only one side of her nose, the black braids, her strong body just a little overweight. I was picking blueberries in the field when the man who pulled her out came up to "The Shoe" house to tell us. I ran down ahead of my mother and looked over the granite cliff and saw her lying still on the rock. Up close, Ellie didn't look so dead, just cold. I took off her jacket and hid it in a crevice as people came running from all over, people who had been hidden just the moment before.

It was odd to be the one left alive, to be suddenly wearing Ellie's clothes (though younger, she was bigger than me), to be sleeping in our room alone, to have too much dinner (my mother never stopped making enough for three). I had always thought that because I was a year older than Ellie, I would die first. But then Ellie always seemed older than anyone, even Ma, because she didn't need anyone or anything, and that's how I measured maturity in those days, by dependence. Ellie liked to be alone. The fact that Ma and I shared her life was just a mild cross she bore with her even nature. I thought that was unfair. I was bossy and unkind, and when I wanted to ask, "How much do you like me, Ellie?" I told her that she had snot in her nose or that she was in love with Anson Beery, the weird boy at school who clucked like a chicken.

"Anson Beery," she once informed me, "has read every book in the library by authors whose names begin with Z."

There are three things I have never forgiven Ellie for: the first is for having no use for an older sister; the second is for dying; and the third is for cutting off some of my hair one night before my tenth birthday while I slept. She knew that my hair was special—long, shiny, the color of a chestnut in autumn, Ma said. She knew that Ma would take out the big shears the next day and chop it short and even all over. Even now, I am not sure about the order of those three things.

"Don't you have enough pictures yet?" Earl asks when I come back from the shore with my camera, not unkindly, just matter-of-factly. The twins still look crisp and impeccable in their uniforms. I like my clothes better for a Coke stain and some wrinkles, newly dampened by the sea air.

"Just a few more," I say, though I know too that I've taken all of the photographs I need of the Harmon twins, all of the shots I will ever get of Homer and Earl. Elvis knows me for a liar too. He smiles down at me with moony eyes and I take his picture to silence him. I am not ready to leave the garage, to venture any further onto the island. "I was wondering if I might take a few shots outside of the garage," I say to Earl. "Homer tells me you live next door."

"Why don't you take her over to the trailer, Homer?" Earl takes my cue. "Show her the garden."

Homer heads outside in almost a skip, beckoning to me like a mime. Something about him disturbs me, seems to bother Earl too, whose directions are careful, whose watchful eyes never stray far. It is not the barking or the tics of the head, or the sudden long, vacant stares. I'm used to all of these things. Anson Beery used to make animal noises in class. He had some disease that sounded something like a tower. But there is an incongruity to Homer—so much gentle wisdom mixed with naivete. He stops to pee on a tree as he leads me to the trailer, turns around when he is finished, not with embarrassment, but only to see if I am still with him.

Ellie, who thought it was a big fat gyp that girls couldn't pee into the air, once tried to pee standing on her head. It was Ellie's opinion that there were all kinds of injustices to being a girl, like not being allowed to ride in rodeos or go into space or be president. I wanted to have such opinions of my own, but the ones that came to mind floated away again, not important enough to really anchor anywhere.

"Maybe," I once said to Ellie as we grumbled our way into snowsuits, mittens, and caps, "it would be good if there were no winter."

"Gotta have winter," Ellie said. "Otherwise, spring wouldn't be so great."

Ellie wore blue jeans every day until Ma sighed and said, "Try looking like a girl, Ellie, just for today." And so she'd put on a skirt and muss up her hair and throw on the Roy Rogers jacket in revenge, tugging at the fringes until it was not much more than the pile of shreds she wore into the water that day.

As we walk, Homer tells me about his dead pets—some hit by cars, some struck down by leukemia, some found stiff as boards in the woods. All of them are now buried behind the trailer in the pet cemetery. He describes their funerals—the fur-lined shoe boxes and the wood crosses that Earl carved, the depth of the loss. The toad was not missed near as much as the cat. He speaks in hushed tones, the tones of the people who called me fragile. Both Ellie and Homer know more about death than me. Both Ellie and Homer are as old as they will ever be.

The garden is orderly, with neat puzzle patches of cucumbers, carrots, tomatoes, and other obedient shoots I cannot name. Dotted rows of stones crisscross the patch, making narrow passageways for walking and weeding. Homer gives me the tour, stepping with the graceful high step of a deer. He picks a cucumber and snaps off a chunk with his teeth. I take a picture of him posing with his one pumpkin. Then he takes off with his cucumber toward the birch wood.

"Where are you going?" I call out.

"To the quarry!" he yells back. "It's just through the woods."

I run after him with my camera clutched tightly in my hands. I haven't really run in years; my feet have only made the tripping steps which chase papers or buses in the streets. My heart pounds and my shoes are all wrong. I have to stop. Homer waits for me at the start of the path. We walk in silence. He pulls back branches and steers me around puddles of mud. I hear rustles in the trees, but see no animals. Nuts and leaves and twigs drop to the forest floor. Suddenly the quarry is before us, a world of square granite blocks and clear water, tall grey walls and sharp silences. It is one of three quarries on the island, all of them now no more than swimming holes and homes for moss and newts. Homer and I sit on a granite slab. I take off my red shoes and dangle my legs in the water.

"Some pretty," Homer says.

"It's lovely," I say.

Homer hugs his knees, just the way the man in my picture at the museum does. I do not like the way that man intrudes into my life through my photograph, the way I am beholden to him.

I try to think of him as just some Mr. Anybody, not someone who used to come around the Cape house to see my mother, sometimes staying late into the night.

"Have you and Earl always lived together?" I ask Homer. I want to know why there are no signs of any other people in the twins' lives—a mother, sisters, brothers, children, women—why, like me, they have so few appendages.

"Except for the time when Earl went to Vietnam," Homer says.

"You must have worried," I say. It is understood that Homer did not go too.

"Not much of a worrier," Homer says, throwing a rock into the water. "Anyways, had a gas station to run back here." He finishes his cucumber and throws the butt end behind him. "What's the best thing that ever happened to you, Paula?" he asks, parrying all of my questions about earth and people into whimsy.

I haven't the slightest idea and tell him so.

"Think," he says quietly.

For a moment, I do. "I guess when the museum took my picture and hung it on that big, white wall," I say. "How 'bout you?"

"I met Elvis once," he said. "I went to visit Earl in boot camp. Down in Memphis. Elvis was in the drugstore, buying some soda. I wouldn't have thought he'd have to go to the drugstore. Would've thought he had someone to do that for him. Would've thought he had a whole mountain of soda cans at home."

"Me too," I say.

"He had that pretty, pretty wife," Homer says. "Maybe she was thirsty." He runs one hand over the speckled granite. "Earl was married once," he offers. "To Ruby Weed."

"What happened to her?" I ask.

"She came and went," Homer says.

"You ever think of getting married, Homer?"

"No," he says. "I'm not good husband material. With the barking and all."

"It's a terrible question, isn't it?" I say.

"Not so bad."

"You know what I tell people who ask me that question?" I say.

"What's that?"

"I tell them I'm thinking of becoming a nun."

"How do they take it?"

"They either think I'm being funny or rude. Either way, it works out."

"Doesn't mean much," Homer says and reaches for a flat rock by his side.

I follow the course of his stone as it skips and slithers out into the middle of the water. Jumping ahead of it, my eye travels to the quarry's opposite shore and climbs up the granite wall to where the meadow grass starts. In the distance, I see a red roof, the red roof of the house called "The Shoe."

"I think I used to swim here," I say.

"Better swimming across the way," he says. "Deeper water, better diving rocks."

"Is there a big rock over there?" I ask him. "In the shape of a bone?"

"Bone rock?" he says, then swallows in a "yep."

"I used to lie on that rock," I tell Homer, "trying to make freckles."

He looks up at my pale face.

"It never worked," I say.

"Something happened over there," he says.

"Yes," I say.

"A little girl drowned," he says. Ellie wouldn't have liked to be called a little girl. "It was just a fluke."

"Flukes happen," I say.

"Then we live with them forever after," Homer says.

A breeze picks up. My hair drifts from the front of my shoulder to the back. I am glad about the wind because the stillness and the familiarity of this place ache—the water lapping at my calves and the cool granite under my thighs. Homer bends his head down into his knees. I snap his picture, stealing something private from him, but too greedy for what I'm taking to stop. I take a picture of the nape of his neck and the razor-edged line of hair. I frame his hands as they run over his forehead and through that dark hair. And suddenly I remember those fine, wide hands, gesturing in helplessness as he explained what had happened, that he'd seen someone struggling, but had swum out too late. He'd been just a swimmer that day; we did not know him outside of his garage. I wonder if my mother knew that it was Homer Harmon who'd pulled Ellie out of the quarry. Had anyone ever thanked him for trying to save her, or only blamed him silently for failing?

Homer takes off his shoes—sensible shoes, my mother would call them—sturdy and scuffed. He stands up and lifts his head to the sky. I take pictures of Homer standing tall on the rock, after the anguish is gone. He folds his arms and tells me stories about a heron's nest and a church supper, about Earl's preference for canned spaghetti sauce over stuff made fresh from the garden.

As clouds cover the mid-afternoon sky, Homer takes off his garage suit and stands still and nearly naked on the rock. He has a smooth, lithe body, a brown back with wings that stick out like a boy's as he wraps his arms around his chest to keep warm. I make guesses. It is an ageless, untouched body—one that has not gone hungry or to war, a body that sleeps many hours soundly every night and has never made love, a body that will last a long time, perhaps long after the mind is willing.

"Tell Earl I'll be back soon to help him with Martin Rice's car," he tells me. It is too cool, really, for August swimming. I reach out to touch his arm just as he dives into the water with a smooth, strong stroke, he heads out towards the middle of the quarry. I take the roll of film out of the camera and slip it carefully into my pocket with the others I have taken, then head back through the birch wood to the garage, where Earl waits with my car.

ABEYANCE

My four daughters plan to become a rock and roll group some day, like the Chiffons or the Shangri-Las on my *Wonder Women: History of the Girl Group Sound* albums. They practice down in the basement, which my husband Perry has sound-proofed in the name of parental tolerance, although he still rolls his eyes whenever the muffled, discordant music comes up through the heating vents to make ripples in his coffee. "It's pablum, Karen," he tells me. "Pure pablum." The girls dress in striped mini skirts and carefully-ripped T-shirts. They dye pink and green streaks in their hair and draw saturns on their cheeks, bedecking themselves in jewels and slippers from Woolworths. Combination bag ladies and ice skating queens, voices strong and bittersweet, when they are not our daughters, they are the "Galaxy Girls."

"We'll be rich and famous, Ma," they tell me. "We'll buy you a gorgeous house with a tennis court and blue satin shoes. And a guy who gives you a backrub whenever you want. What's he called?"

"A masseur," I purr back. "That would be nice." Their dreams only annoy Perry, who goes so far as to say that he hasn't shelled out eight grand on piano lessons, girls, to subsidize some schlocky, Salvation Army rock and roll band.

"You won't have to support us for long, Dad." The girls become indignant, withdraw their offers to him of rare books and fancy cars and exotic vacations—all of the things for which Perry has a weakness. "We'll pay you back ten times over," they say, stiff-upper lipped. "And we'll always love you no matter what."

"It's not a question of love," it's like Perry to say dryly.

"You're hopeless, Dad." The groaning verdict is always the same.

"You just think we can't make it because we're girls," our oldest daughter, Mary, once challenged him quietly. At sixteen, she is both Perry's dearest ally and one of his few worthy opponents.

"Women," he corrected her with a sharpness not like him.

"Whatever happens, Mary, make sure it has nothing to do with your being a woman."

Perry considers himself a champion of women, although I'm beginning to think that he misunderstands this to mean savior. As a lawyer, he often rallies to the cause of our sex, upholding the rights of injured factory workers, women denied maternity benefits, victims of job discrimination. He will not have us underpaid, overworked, exploited, belittled, scorned or undermined. He is brilliant and passionate in the courtroom and will defend us to the death. But his victories seem more like his than ours, and in the end, we are beholden.

Perry has made a name for himself in this town—as a wise man and a great defender. For so long, like so many others, I've taken his word as some kind of law, or at least the base of truth. But in the last year, I've become wary and weary of him, no longer able to think of him as anything in relation to me—husband, lover, or friend. I don't really believe anything he tells me anymore. Perry, too, seems changed, watching me in unguarded moments, short with affection and patience, criticizing me in ways that suggest I badly need improvement.

"You should cut your hair, Karen," he tells me out of the blue at the dinner table one night. The girls have spun out of their chairs, leaving them all askew. More and more, Perry and I find ourselves alone with one another.

"I thought you liked long hair," I say. Like a child scolded for some unwitting crime, I almost start to cry.

"I do like long hair," he says. "But short hair would make you look . . . older . . . more. . . ."

"More what?"

But Perry never finishes the sentence and we never finish the meal. We drift into the living room with books and magazines. Our daughters leave the house one by one—first Mary, then Lark and Lee, the twins, almost fourteen, and finally twelve-year-old Michael. We send them off with curfews and kisses and read silently in separate corners until we are tired.

All along, Perry has steadfastly denied that it matters that we have only daughters. "I like girls," he's always told people, with a dark gleam in his eye. But when the man from *The Globe* comes to interview Perry about his book the next day, I sense a change. "Regular harem you got here," the man says, as Michael thunders down the stairs and Lark does a cartwheel across the living room floor. "No one to throw the old baseball around with, eh?"

"My twelve-year-old could whip the mitt from your hand," Perry tells him, making the man's busy eyes and pencil pause. "But, no, I have no sons." The gleam falls from Perry's eyes then, leaving them vacant. He doesn't go on to say, as he usually does, tongue half in cheek, that it has clearly been our task in life to populate the world with intelligent, beautiful, women, implying, of course, that there are not nearly enough of us on the earth. As Perry's wife I've had to include myself in this small minority, not always sure that I belong.

"Perry and I have left suns to the sky," I pick up Perry's broken gleam and toss *The Globe* interviewer one of our old retorts, embarrassed the moment it has been said. Perry takes back his gleam then and aims it at me. Not for the first time, as I head for the kitchen to make coffee and the man goes on with his questions, I feel at fault to be the maker of only daughters, as if having no sons makes Perry more of a man, and me somehow less of a woman.

We live in a starting-to-crumble Cambridge house, which we bought thirteen years ago when I found out I was pregnant with the twins. Perry was made a partner in a small law firm that year, giving us the mistaken impression, which we've dragged along in a battered suitcase with a string handle ever since, that we are rich. In truth, we are only richer than we'd ever thought to be—both uncomfortable with money—its vagaries, its complexities, its arrogance. Our money has always controlled us, not the other way around.

I am starting to look back to see if I have always been controlled by other people and things. I am Karen Daily Hart, almost forty years old, mother of four daughters and wife of eighteen years. I look my age but not bad for it. Not that I am pretty. Everything about me is far too undistinguished. Beauty may only catch up with me when I am old, when time has given me edges and then made them ragged. I bore my children without much ado, liking my pregnancies because they brought me kindness and admiration and in the end great gifts. Pregnancy excused me from the lofty goals of womanly perfection—thinness and grace, stoicism and unflagging energy. Big with child, I was exempt from the leerings of construction workers and stances at steel poles in crowded buses, from the impatience of people in supermarkets, even from taking out the garbage sometimes, when Perry would notice me stooping and straining and say, struck by a pang. "Let me do that, Karen."

I am a nurse, and have worked the graveyard shift in a Boston hospital ever since Mary was born. Perry has always been the night-parent in our home, taking on the dark hour tasks of water-fetching or blanket-replacing or nightmare-soothing. But I have always been home by early morning, frumpy in my wrinkled uniform with the smells of sickness and medicine still on me. I've always been there at the breakfast table when my children come thundering down the stairs, with offerings of cut-up grapefruits or treasures I've found in the night—a pack of peanut butter crackers from the hospital cafeteria or an earring dropped in the parking lot.

My children have always come first. This is my credo, a clear one, unclouded. But I begin to think that this, like so many others, was Perry's idea at the outset, and not mine, that all along I've been told, even instructed, how to be a good mother. I've begun to think that all of my ideas are really only Perry's in a second life, that he's been transplanting things, information, opinions, into my brain, slipping a tape recorder under my pillow and attaching electrodes to my temples when I sleep. You're right. This is not mere contemplation, or even discontent. This is suspicion, bordering on paranoia. And I must try to hold this last in abeyance.

Abeyance. I first read the word the evening after *The Globe* interviewer has come and gone. The girls are watching "Hub Star Search" on TV in the living room and I'm reading a novel in the corner. Perry is out playing squash.

"Let's hear it for Contestant Number Three!" The show host's voice booms my way.

"Turn it down, please," I say. But no one hears me.

The girls clap and whistle. "All right Number Three!"

A girl in a taffeta gown and a tiara comes onto the screen. "I'm Darlene Wannemaker from Mattapan," she says. "And I'll be singing 'The Impossible Dream.'"

"Aye, karumba," Michael says.

"Well, Darlene," says the host, "if your voice is half as lovely as your smile. . . ." Darlene launches into a flat and lurching vibrato, staring comatose, but not afraid, into the camera's eye. My girls rise out of Buddha twists to their feet and bounce up and down on the couch as they bellow into the microphones of their fists, "This is my quest! To follow that star!" Jealousy gnaws at their bare, painted toes, which twitch with an ache to leap into Darlene's star-studded shoes. "No matter how hope-less! No matter how far!"

"I can't believe she actually got up on that stage," Lark says.

"I can't believe she's actually singing that song," says Lee. She puts her hands, fingers spread and nails bitten to the skin, over her face, peeking through the slits of her eyes.

"Her mother probably made her do it," one of them says. I look up from my book. In that voice, I hear both accusation for the pushy mother and reproach for me, who has never pushed any of my daughters in any direction in which she has not already chosen to head herself.

"What are you blaming on mothers?" I call out from my corner.

"Nothing, Ma," Michael is kind enough to answer.

"No one can make you do anything you don't want to do," Mary says. "And it's harder than you think to get up in front of all those people and have those TV cameras shoved in your face."

"How would you know?" Lark asks her.

They all chime in for the wailing, wavering crescendo, hands to heart and reaching up to the sky, finally collapsing in a pile on the couch, a tangle of belly, leg and hair. "The un-reach-able

DREAM!"

"Dream on, Darlene," Michael says.

I go back to my book. I've taken to reading with a pad and pencil, having decided that almost forty is not too old to be taught new tricks, or at least a few new words. Abeyance is the fifth word in as many pages over which I stumble. The heroine of my novel is "wallowing in a bed of abeyance" after a nasty divorce, unable to get on with her life. This seems to describe me these days—a wind-up toy slowly grinding to a halt at the edge of a table. I scribble the word in my notebook and go to watch "Hub Star Search" with the girls on the couch. Michael crawls into my lap. Her stocky twelve-year old body still fits there somehow.

"Hi, Ma," she says.

"Hi, Mikey." I wrap my arms around her and kiss her temple, wondering for the umpteenth time if we did her wrong by giving her our unused "boy's" name. She puts her thumb in her mouth as she has always done, right from the moment when she was born, in moments of contentment or anxiety, which I guess is what her position in the family affords her most.

The host introduces a brother-sister act in sequined outfits from Braintree. I stare at Michael's noble profile for a while, full lips and broad nose, almond eyes, something of the Eskimo about her. All of my daughters have a bold, careless elegance that makes me doubtful sometimes that they are mine. I circle Michael's thin wrist with my fingers, feel the hard bone and soft flesh of her. It seems impossible that I have made her, that she has grown, that she speaks and walks and plays the piano, that she says things like, "dream on, Darlene."

Act Number Five doesn't have much over Darlene. The brother plays showtunes on the piano while the sister twirls a baton. Perry comes home from his squash game then. He plays twice a week, although he doesn't like games, if only to remind us that he is ageless as well as wise. He swings his racket hello, making a popping noise with his tongue on the roof of his mouth, not a trace of sweat or strain on him. A neat, handsome figure Perry always cuts, but especially in his white shorts and T-shirt open at the throat, which show off his lean frame and golden, untugged-at skin.

"Did you win, Dad?" Michael asks.

Perry nods. He almost always wins. As he puts away his racket, "Hub Star Search" comes to a close. The contestants cluster onstage to sing a song about how they will always reach for the rainbow and how they hate to see us go. Mary jumps up to turn off the set.

"Hi, Dad," she says, looking over at Perry with something akin to indulgent apology. She is the most her father's daughter, in her deep-rooted seriousness and disapproving mouth, her fierce devotion to fairness and honesty and right. She is perhaps the most officially beautiful of our daughters, with Perry's lovely black eyes and hair, my long torso and pale skin and a strong delicacy which is all her own.

"Dad! Dad!" The twins jump up and attack Perry as he puts away his racket with the sloppy affection that has always annoyed him, speaking in alternate and flowing sentences.

"Can we go to Calloway Sports Camp this summer?"

"Please, please?"

"It costs 600 dollars for each of us."

"It'll be the experience of a lifetime. Says so right here." Lee waves a brochure in Perry's face.

"Come on Dad, old pal."

"Say yes."

"Be a nice guy." They start to peter out and then Lark delivers the punchline.

"Mom says it's probably okay."

Perry gives me what the twins call his Dracula look as he peels them from his waist. "Your mother and I will discuss it later," he says.

The twins turn to me with pleading eyes. "We'll let you know," I say.

"Ah, crap," Lark says. "We'll-let-you-know is death."

"Lark!" Perry says sharply.

"What?" she asks, starting to pout, until her eyes meet Perry's. "Oh, I mean, ah, darn."

"Ah, sugar," Lee joins in darkly.

Perry smoothes his hair as the twins run upstairs in a conspiratorial funk. He is getting stuffier and more authoritarian as he gets older, less and less recognizable as what my father called "that skinny socialist you married." Perry made headlines in the seventies by taking on the case of a nuclear activist who'd injured a policeman in self-defense at a demonstration. Since then, he's been something of a local hero—the "Dr./Mr. Spock of Law," as *The Globe* interviewer is later to label him in the book review, "for there are shades of both the pediatrician and the space voyager in Perry Hart."

"We're looking down Easy Street," Perry told me recently. He's just been paid for the rights to his book; imagine being married to a man whose memoirs are of interest to the world. For once, we can afford to send the girls to all the summer nooks for which they yearn. At Perry's firm, if not tender insistence, I am even taking the month of July off from work. In March I went for a check-up after five years, scared by a lump in my breast. "I'm falling apart," I told the doctor. "My back hurts and I get bad headaches and I'm always tired." The lump was nothing, as it turned out, but I was badly anemic and clearly exhausted. Was I overextended, the doctor asked me. Was I trying to spread myself too thin? "Thin?" I said vaguely. "Well, I haven't been eating much lately." Serious rest, she concluded, was the only cure for all that ailed me.

"Serious rest?" I said to Perry when I came back from the appointment. "She's got to be joking. There is no such thing."

But Perry pressed me. "You've got to take better care of yourself, Karen," he said. "You really need to. . . ." His eyes drifted somewhere far away where I was not welcome.

"Why do you leave all of your sentences unfinished these days?" I asked him. "Why are you picking on me, Perry?"

"I'm trying to *help* you, Karen," he said. "If you know your limits, you can maximize your inner resources, get the most mileage out of yourself."

"What is this?" I sputtered. "Some kind of marriage check? 40 years or 40,000 miles? You make me sound like . . . like a mop!"

"Like a mop?" Perry looked bewildered and it was then that I realized that I was beginning to make him crazy, just by being me. "That doesn't even follow from what you said, Karen. If you'd said carburetor, or fan belt. . . . But mop? That doesn't even make sense."

"Well, that's what I feel like sometimes," I said. "A mop."

After a squash game, Perry is always serene. He pats us all solemnly on the tops of our heads and goes upstairs to take a long shower, one which outlives his sweat and his irritation and even the hot water supply. I know Perry will not say no about the camp. He's just mad that I've been the one to give Lark and Lee first hope by offering them a "probably" which he can now only second. I have let the bacon sizzle before he has even brought it home, and he wants me to suffer a little, even if the girls have to suffer along with me. I try to make up later in bed, thinking it a silly quarrel and truly not of my invention. "I didn't make any promises, Perry," I say, reaching out a thin, freckled arm to touch his.

"In a child's mind, Karen," he says, keeping his eyes glued to *The Nation*, "it's not far from a probably to a promise."

"Oh, Perry," I sigh, swinging my legs to the floor. "Don't be such an old fart."

"All this reading you're doing is really paying off," Perry says.

"*Ancient* fart, Perry," I say, flouncing out of bed with all the drama and petulance of the twins. "*Prehistoric* fart!"

I go downstairs to find the dictionary. The word is there on the third page, nestled between *abet* and *abhor*. "Abeyance: temporary suspension, as of an activity or function; a state of not having been determined or settled."

A good description of my life with Perry, which began in 1969, when I was twenty-one. A group of tenants in my roach-infested Inman Square apartment house were meeting in my kitchen to organize a rent strike. Perry was a friend of a neighbor of mine, from whose door always wafted the odors of dirty socks and dope. Fresh out of law school, Perry came to advise us, asking for nothing but our cause, and maybe one small ounce of glory. I thought his a noble, selfless gesture, and I was big on noble, selfless gestures. He sought me out after the meeting and

I was flattered. He was handsome and dignified, and I thought instantly of the beautiful children we could make together, though I pictured them boys, four or five of them at least. He was strong, yet passionate, stomped on sleazy landlords as he shed tears for the families of war-torn countries. These were, to me, rare finds in a man, traits lacking in the men in my family. After three months, I married Perry, mostly because I could see no earthly reason to refuse. I admired him and perhaps confused admiration with love. When, from time to time in those hazy days before our marriage, I groped in the muddy puddle of my incipient feelings for him, I came up with nothing better than a dripping sliver of an answer, something about how if I didn't know what love was, this might as well be it.

A disturbing thought floats in and out of my mind. Did I re-seek my own father in Perry? They say this is a daughter's unconscious quest. At first glance, the two have nothing in common. Part of Perry still lives in the sixties, a decade my father chose to discredit altogether. Perry keeps his graying hair long, holds it back in a ponytail with household rubber bands, the thick ones that come on broccoli or junk mail. He still won't eat white sugar or white bread or white rice and gives lectures on nutrition to supermarket clerks who've never heard of tofu, let alone eaten it. He wears only breathing cotton and the sandals that a leather maker friend made for him in 1969. He still loves the sandals, but no more the friend, who has strayed into a Wall Street investment firm and a life of fast cars and cocaine. People think of Perry as an old, over-dedicated hippy. Funny. I'm beginning to see him as a middle-aged man growing brittle with his bones.

On the outside, my father was all spit and polish. What he was like on the inside, I have no idea, for he chose to give us no clues. An uninspired banker from an old, but not a distinguished Boston family, he was suspicious of ambition and undercooked food and democrats alike. He more or less disowned me when I married Perry, not in any dramatic kind of way, but just by putting a final mile between us. My mother, who'd always closed lesser gaps between us, died just after we got married, of nothing special—hopelessness, I've always thought. She came alone to our City Hall ceremony, fidgety and haggard in a new dress, with a toaster and some rice. She said right from the start that she couldn't stay long, as if the minutes she spent with us represented the chances she gave our marriage. My father, she said, was waiting for his dinner.

"That's my father in a nutshell," I sputtered to Perry later that night, with an anger that made our first lovemaking more passionate than it would ever be again. "He's never once made his own dinner! Believe me, he's not hungry! You're just not what he had in mind. Not proper son-in-law material!"

"Let it go," Perry said soothingly. "If we let him get to us, we help him make his point." He undid the buttons on my white, cotton dress and stroked my back with his long, tapered fingers as he led me to bed, where we made love, partly in the name of tolerance. For it was tolerance we'd both decided to champion in our adult lives, separately and long before we'd ever met, the one thing we hoped to uphold in our marriage and give as a gift to our children—the one thing we believed might save the humans from the humans.

Summer comes and the girls fly the coop. Mary goes off on a trek to Italy. The twins head for the Calloway Sports Camp in Something, Minnesota, to flip away the days on balance beams and gym floors and etch endless figure eights on the ice of a skating rink. And on the last day of June, I drive eight hours to plunk Michael on a Maine island where she will scale granite cliffs and swim in frigid waters, where she will eat breakfasts at dawn made of things that come straight from the land and the sea.

All of a sudden, I am alone. I vow to dedicate the summer to my health and my reading and to our marriage. I know there will be no better time, perhaps no other time, to lift old, unanswered questions and nameless feelings from the muddy bed in which they've lain for so long, no better time for Perry and I to become acquainted. I think of questions that I will ask him, such as, does he really like ratatouille, or does he only eat it out of loyalty to me and the eggplant. I will ask him if he likes his work, or is only dedicated to it, as I sometimes feel to mine, if he honestly feels that he is some kind of chosen person. I will ask him how he would define love and if he has any regrets, like the one I sensed when the interviewer asked him about not having a son. He's even got me going. Maybe a son would have been the missing link. Maybe a son would have demystified the male myth for me, given me more courage with Perry. By making a man child, I might have been brought out of my womanhood. Out in the world, boys and girls run amok at a near-fifty-fifty ratio. Here, in this household of women, Perry is, as the doctor who delivered Michael put it, "outnumbered, man." So why do we—the girl group—so often feel ourselves to be the lesser force, the weaker voice, the minority interest in this family?

I'm finally too warm and lazy to be lonely, or to make brave, long-overdue gestures. I've been tossed back into a childhood summer, where time, method and reason lose most of their meaning, and certainly their urgency. Perry is working a lot. I'm on a mysterious vacation with myself. I grew up in a small, spotless house. Now I've been let loose in a big, messy one, ghost-filled without my children. I wear the same clothes for three days in a row, let the dishes pile up in the sink, dance naked in front of the mirror. I sleep and eat when I please. I let the telephone ring and ring. I listen to the "Wonder Women" records over and over again. The girl groups are tireless and keep me going in my tasks. DOO WAH, DOO WAAAAH!

Perry and I pass like hotel guests on the stairs, courteous to an extreme. My questions go unasked and unanswered and the road of good intentions simply dead-ends. I try to plan things for us to do—picnics and candlelit dinners and excursions to the Arboretum. But Perry is endlessly, hopelessly, thankfully busy. And being alone is so much easier, so much more restful. He barely leaves traces—no crumbs or dirty socks, only mysterious drops of water in the shower that lead to nowhere. Maybe he has a secret towel somewhere. We still sleep in the same bed, but this no longer seems like intimacy, just custom. We are careful not to brush one another, as if touching were synonymous with hurting. I wonder if Perry and I are, without knowing it yet, parents who are staying together for the sake of the children. We used to look down upon such couples as hypocrites and cowards, those who postponed the family blast until a point in time when they deemed the innocent strong enough to survive the devastation, in blindness forgetting themselves to be as vulnerable as all the rest.

Only in clearly-written notes of goodwill do Perry and I reemerge as husband and wife.

"Library tonight. May be late."

"Leftover tofu and noodles in the fridge. Good with sesame oil dribbled on top."

"Hospital called. Paycheck being sent out today."

"Letter from Lee on front hall table. She's desperate for some David's Chocolate Chip Cookies. If you pick some up," I write to Perry, feeling the need to bargain with him, to divide equally even the smallest of tasks, "I will mail them."

Misogynist is another word I've learned in my reading. Maybe that's what Perry is. The author of the novel I'm reading denounces the misogynists of the world as "the earth's most dangerous enemies, for they are at war with half of it." I don't know. The same could be said of the man-haters, too. Poor Perry. Maybe I'm just looking for places to put these new words I'm learning—pinned on his lapel, tatooed on his smooth forehead, branded on his manhood. Maybe I'm getting old. Maybe I'm bored. It's true that I'm lonely. I miss the girls terribly, my nest emptied for the first time. I miss the hospital, too, the sick bodies and faces that call me, the time that rushes by, the steadfastness of illness, and the regularity of my tasks. Alone at home, I create my own sicknesses. I get rashes on my chin and the underside of my knees. My back is the worse for bedrest. I wake up sweating in the night with no memories of dreams. The rest I'm getting is serious, but I can't be. I am thinking too much; my mind is full of muck. My sadnesses—regrets, I guess they are called as they age—come rising and bobbing and colliding to the oil-slicked surface of my life like gasping fish. And all I want to do is swim past them to clearer waters. And drift and drift and drift.

When Perry is sick in bed one day, I go out to the Store 24 to buy him soup. Remembering only that cream-of-something is his favorite, I stuff a bag full of all the cream soups I can find on the shelves.

"Soup lady," I say, poking my head into our room, where Perry sits naked from the waist up, a pile of books at his side. I settle on the edge of his sickbed, at a distance I never keep, even with the most ill or ornery of my patients at the hospital.

"Thanks," Perry says, peering into the grocery bag full of cans. He looks up at me with troubled eyes and puts a hand on my arm. "It was nice of you to go to the trouble."

"No trouble," I say, pulling my arm away. Whatever is in those eyes scares me. "What would you like? I'll heat some up for you."

"I'll pass," he says, as the tender moment shrivels away. "It's really too hot for cream soups, Karen."

I get up from our bed with a shrug. There is nothing I can do for Perry anymore. I can't give him a shot of pain killer or even the smallest doses of affection. I won't fluff his pillow or his ego anymore. I can't make him soup, and it's too late to make him a son. He's out of my reach, just as I am out of his. I suppose now, as Perry and I stop going to parties and the grocery store together, as we begin to cross like ships in the night, people may think that we've agreed amicably to have fallen out of love, without considering this a sorrow or a crime.

In the end, as my sweaty palm sticks to the bedpost and a great weariness comes over me, all I can do is agree. "You're right, Perry," I say. "It's much too hot for cream soups today."

On a steamy day in late July, I wake at dawn and drive to a bakery in East Cambridge to buy fresh rolls and coffee. Then, I head north on Route 1 past the strip joints and the hamburger palaces to Plum Island. The beach is all but empty, still half asleep in stillness and light. I roost on a striped towel in a valley behind a dune, ducking into the ocean when I get to feeling fried. I lie with only the bottom of my bathing suit on and bare my breasts to the sun. For the first time in my life, I have something like a tan, and some meat on my bones. I am ravenous. Endless avocados and cheese sandwiches fill the empty pockets in my knees and my cheeks. I feel of a heft I've only ever known before when I was big with child, when the feeling of substance was only transient, and not really mine.

One day, a man peers at me from behind the dune, whistling softly, some kind of bird-like trill. I ignore him fiercely as I pull on my shirt, lying indignant and embarrassed for the rest of the morning, shuffling papers and glancing often to see if he is really gone. Later, when I'm dusting the mica-specked sand off my feet in the parking lot, waiting for the air to blow through my hot car, I wonder what might have come after the whistle in the man's wooing if I'd looked his way, if I'd beckoned.

By one o'clock, I'm back on the empty road, passing the incoming beach crowds, soon home in my cool kitchen squeezing lemons for lemonade. I spend the afternoon writing letters to the girls and futzing in the garden. It's odd not to be working, as a mother or a nurse. I find an extension cord and put the stereo on the kitchen windowsill. The Wonder Women keep me company in the yard; "Sally go 'round the roses. . . ," sing the Jaynetts. I can hear Mary's voice in that haunting refrain. All at once, the weeds are too strong and my back aches and the voices of the wonder women are too sure and shrill. I collapse in the dirt of my garden plot and try to cry. Some days, idleness comes too easily. Some days, not easily enough.

In the late afternoon, as clouds cluster and sprout soft summer rain, I fall asleep on the couch, having read two pages of my novel and scribbled the words "tumescent" and "visceral" in my notebook. "Fat" and "gut," respectively, are my guesses. I have a dream about the man at the beach. He creeps from behind the dune as I sleep on my stomach. Except for a stocky build, he resembles me—pale and bland and hairless, like vanilla pudding. After blindfolding me, he rapes me, all of him scratchy with shaven hair and sand, and me soon filled with his sticky stuff. When the weight of him is sprung and his smell only lingers, I whip off the blindfold and watch him as he scuttles off like a crab over a dune, eyes flashing, back rounded low, his bony hands spread to balance himself in the sand.

I awake on my couch, heart racing, and book still open on my chest—thirsty to the dusk and disturbed. The disturbing part was how I let myself be taken in the dream, how I didn't struggle or scream or run to tell anyone afterwards about the rape. I wish that Perry were next to me, so that I could reach out and touch him in a way that would make him touch me back, if not in passion, at least in comfort. But of course, Perry is working and I am alone. What would a rapist see in me? Nothing? Or plenty? And which would scare me more?

"Can women be misogynists, too?" I scrawl in my notebook. "*May* they?"

I put on shorts, a T-shirt and flipflops and head for Bartley's Burger Cottage, where Perry and I have always gone in our carnivorous phases, which seem to coincide with the crises of our lives. A few years has not much changed the Cottage, only made it more so. Painted hamburgers still sail across the greasy, chipped walls like phony UFO's against a creamsicle orange sky, their fillings bulging out of their middles like planetary rings. The booths are dark and deep, back to back, slashed and pock-marked, but made smooth with endless coats of varnish. Taking one against the wall, I slide in all the way, butting up against a wall jukebox. I flip through the titles. My galaxy girls sing these songs. I put in a quarter and play some Tina Turner. Tina Turner must be well over forty by now. And she can still put on quite a show. I remember Perry once saying that she was so sexy it was almost scary. I wonder how Tina and Ike managed in a marriage now gone sour—who made breakfast and who went to bed first, who loved whom more, who got the kids, who's crying now. I notice none of Ike's songs are on the jukebox.

A waitress comes to take the order of the person sitting in the booth in front of mine, plucking a pencil from behind her ear. She's been here all these years, this waitress, well preserved by grease and purpose. I am still trying to decide what I want, when I hear Perry's voice say, "I'll have a swiss mushroom burger with a slice of tomato and extra cheese."

"And to drink?", the waitress asks.

I mouth silently along with Perry, "Black coffee, please. No sugar."

"And what'll you have?" The waitress moves on to me.

"I'll have the same," I find myself saying. "Coffee in the

sugar, though. I mean. . . ."

"I know what you mean, honey," she says. "You take it sweet."

When she's gone, Perry and I emerge from our booths at the same time, nearly knocking heads.

"Fancy meeting you here," I say. We handle this first moment as adults will do, civilly and with a little stab at humor.

"Just taking a break," Perry says. He left a note on the kitchen table in the morning, something about working late.

"A body has to have some dinner," I say. He goes on about taking in a movie in the Square with a friend. I don't really listen; I just watch. Perry is beginning to look like a wizened emperor, with a wispy beard and mustache and crinkles at the corners of his eyes. Only the torn Celtics T-shirt and sports socks under sandals mar the imperial image. I have never known Perry to wear a ripped shirt before. And his squash shorts have a stain, I remember, from the last load of laundry. This unkempt Perry is an almost-scary thing.

"What brings you this way?" Perry asks, looking over at the door.

"Hunger, mostly," I say. "Thought I'd get out of the house for a while. It's such a nice night."

He nods. He understands. We've said these things to one another before in more ordinary moments. This part is so sad, really, this telephone wire of silly caution at which we tug. We're unable to talk about this festering thing right here and now. It's not that we care about making a scene, which has long been Perry's business and my acquired way. We just don't know what to do with one another anymore, how to avoid the saying of something that won't prolong the awkwardness or embarrass us further—maybe do irreparable harm—something like, "Let's cut the crap," or "Why do you treat me like one of the girls?," or "Why do we keep looking at that door?"

"Well, I'm off," I tell Perry.

"But you haven't eaten," Perry points out.

"Not hungry after all," I say, reaching into my pockets for some money.

"Shit," I whisper, finding only holes. "I forgot my wallet."

47

"Here." Perry hands me a ten dollar bill. I can't help feeling that it's a bribe. I end up eating at a Burger King a few doors down, where a slab of unmelted American cheese droops over the edge of my meat, if you could even call it an edged thing. Still hungry and not ready to go home, I buy a milkshake at Baskin Robbins and walk towards the heart of the Square. The shake is so thick that the straw does not lean. I've read they're made mostly of lard.

In summer, Cambridge storefront alcoves become stages. I sit on a bench near Baileys and listen to a skinny boy who can't carry a tune hammering out "Just Like A Woman." Bob Dylan couldn't always carry a tune either, but he surely brought something else to that song. Pulling myself up out of a slouch, I put down my milkshake for a disdainful dog and get scolded for littering by a man pushing a shopping cart piled high with scraps of foam rubber. Retrieving the half-full waxy cup, I toss it in the trash and walk home, trying to sum up what my mother would have called my "lot." I am lonely, but I am not alone. I am only and just temporarily severed from all that makes me me. A job waits for me across the river. My four daughters, soon to be a famous girl group, are about to come prancing back into my life like kenneled puppy dogs. Their din will course through the air pockets of our uncertainty, drowning out siren strains of discontent. They will open cereal boxes and dirty the sheets and turn on the TV and make us a family again.

This thing with Perry and me. It must be some kind of transition, some rite of passage no one warned us about. Change always brings upheaval. We've survived worse crises before. We'll give up meat again and clean the attic, cry a little in a slight embrace and take a trip to the cottage in Maine. Perry will chop wood and I'll clear a path to the shore. Out of city and context, we will remember what drew us to one another in the first place. Snakes that we've become, we will shed our malaise. Neither of us is one to throw away years or hearts or the well-being of our children. We've never been afraid of the hard or the serious. We're just tired, it seems, of being so busy and so right. We've ignored the small us in the larger we, and now we must dig for answers to questions we've never asked through layers of rock hard shale. Perry and I must bother to find out exactly what is simmering between us, or not simmering, this amorphous problem which is pushing us up against cracking, creamsicle walls, making us feel incompetent, foolish, awkward, ugly and at a loss—all of fourteen all over again. What is the point of intimacy and struggle and years spent, if they only land us back in gawky, uncertain adolescence again, when we have neither the energy nor the desire to weather or even survive it, when we must believe that we're better beings—more intelligent, stronger, wiser—that we've made some progress, that we're finally grown-up, more at peace, more in love . . . happier?

It's almost midnight when Perry comes home. I'm sitting cross-legged on the couch, knitting.

"Hello," he says, in the low, purring voice that means he's been drinking.

"Hi," I say sharply.

"Knitting in July?" he says. "Good title for a bad movie."

I give him nothing—no retort, no glance, no smile—suddenly aware that I've spent the past few hours knitting up a fury, as well as a shapeless something. "It is a bad movie," I say.

"What?"

"Our life."

"I ate your burger," he offers, with hands lifted and a half-baked smile. I sit in steely silence, letting him play the first fool, sure that my turn will come soon enough. "Well," he says, easing himself into an armchair. "I guess it's time for a showdown."

"Showdown?"

"You know, don't you?"

"Know what?" I ask stonily. I don't know anything at all.

"About Jill."

Jill. For a crazy moment, I think that he's referring to one of our daughters in some way that I've forgotten about, a term of affection or a lost middle name.

"Who's Jill?" I ask.

"Jill," he repeats in an irritated voice. "My lover."

"Your . . . lover?" For those who don't have one, the word

doesn't come easily. But by now, I've gotten it, and my breath has left me slightly. "You have a lover." I say. "Of course. How stupid I am." I joust foolishly because I don't know what else to do. "I'm so happy for you."

"I thought you might be." Perry has a sarcastic side, too, which he keeps confined as best he can, like a slightly damaged relative. "And no doubt you'll find it in your heart to forgive me," he says.

"I'm not so sure."

"Good," he says wearily, as the drunkenness moves slowly from his voice to his eyes. "I'd rather not be forgiven." He stands up and goes over to the window, turning his back to me.

"What am I supposed to do, Perry?" I ask him.

"Do whatever you have to."

"No words of wisdom from the great Perry Hart?"

"Forget it," he says, head cradled in the fingers of one hand.

"Forget it?" I ask. "That would be nice for you, wouldn't it?"

"None of this will be nice," he says. "It's late, Karen. Maybe we should talk about this tomorrow."

"It *is* tomorrow, Perry. For Christ's sake, turn around so I can see you!" Never before have I summoned Christ for anything. But Perry will not turn around and his bent and narrow shoulders drive me to a rage. "Turn around!" My hoarse scream turns Perry to stone. I come up to him from behind and yank the rubber band from his ponytail. He whirls around, looking both older and younger than I've ever known him, his graying hairs hanging in his face.

"What are you doing?" he sputters.

"I've always wanted to do that," I say. "Stupid rubber bands! Stupid pony tail!"

Perry takes one step forward and slaps me across the face. Once, and then again. There is an empty moment, of numbness, I guess, after which I put my hand to my stung jaw and rub. I feel strangely empty, but enervated, purged. "Oh, my God," Perry says, eyes filling with tears as he wrings the violent hand with the other.

"You hit me," I croak.

"You make me crazy, Karen," he says desperately. "You do

such childish things, sometimes."

"And having an affair is so very grown up, isn't it?" My lips and my legs are trembling, but it's important not to give in to either, not to crumple or fall.

"No," he says wearily. "Try to understand, Karen. Jill is just . . . incidental."

"Accidental?" I wipe my eyes with the back of my hand.

"No, she was no accident," he says. "She's just a by the way. I mean, there's more to all of this."

"More women?"

"No," he says. "This has to do with me, not Jill."

"Talk to me in plain English, Perry. What do you mean?"

"I don't even know," he says. "I'm just not happy."

"I'm not either. Was it hard?" I ask. I wonder how near we've been to the brink of violence, how close Perry has ever come before to striking me.

He looks at me vaguely. "Hard to have an affair?"

"No. Hard to hit me."

"No," he says, too long steeped in truth to speak anything else.

I figure I might as well ask all the questions that tomorrow will forbid, when, the war begun, we creep behind our lines in self-defense, when we raise hackles and swords. "What's she like?"

"Oh, nothing like you." Perry says. "She's not very smart, or nice, or . . ." he even uses the word, "tolerant. Jill is really just . . ." He throws up his hands to finish. "Out of her mind." His private, warped smile pains me. Even close to out of my mind, I've never come, and of this more than anything, I'm jealous.

"What does she do?" I ask him.

"She fancies herself a jazz singer," he says. "And she makes bread at an all-night deli." Again the twisted smile forms on Perry's face, as private memories dance, maybe of kissing Jill's flour-dusted face, being kneaded by her pasty hands, making love on a slab table near a hot oven. Perry and I have never made love anywhere except in a bed. How sad this strikes me at that moment.

"Is she young?"

"Not so young."

"Pretty?" I cannot seem to stop.

"In her way," he says.

"Do you love her?"

"It doesn't really matter," he says finally. "The truth is . . . Jill doesn't like me very much."

Nor at that moment do I. But I can't hate Perry as I'd like to do, for hate, at least, would burn and cleanse. Here, finally, is my husband disarmed. The naked, beaten Perry is a stranger to me, gone to that far, unreachable place where live the men of dreams—men who've moved you and touched you and changed you in some way, but slowly dissolve upon waking. I am not triumphant before Perry, only tired. I am calm and more lucid than I've ever been before. I am almost in awe of the will power it has taken Perry to be Perry over the years—Perry, the husband and father of daughters, Perry the admired and the trusted, Perry the keeper of fairness and goodness and peace and all things right. I see how I could have loved Perry if I'd caught him at more moments like this, if he'd ever let himself fall. But one such moment in eighteen years is not enough, and the price for the moment has been far too high.

The kitchen faucet drips double time. A cat moans in the back yard. Loneliness is more complicated than scary, it seems. How will I take care of a house which is aging more rapidly than I am? I don't know where the fuse box is, or how much the mortgage payments are, or Bill the plumber's last name. If I work longer shifts, I'll have less time with the girls. They will have to give up things—skating parkas and sports camps and the endless ice cream cones we eat all over town. But Perry will suffer more, as he lays himself down—the adulterer—to be trampled upon. He will have to answer to everyone—to the girls and to me and to old friends and to the law, to Jill and all the Jills to come. He will be whispered about and mistrusted and scolded, and he will be told when and for how long he can see his children. I feel almost lucky to have been wronged and am angered by the feeling. I do not look forward to pity or loneliness or sainthood, but I will not lose my daughters.

In the end, our marriage has gone the way of so many others.

I'm perplexed to find that I'm more curious than angry. I don't want to kill Jill; I want to meet her, feeling the same misplaced curiosity I had about the man in the dunes. I don't want to punish Perry or make him suffer or bend to my will or change or repent or beg for forgiveness. I just don't want to have to see him any more. I stand before my cheating husband with a tumescent belly full of lard. Perry cries silently. I feel a visceral sadness, a skewed pity for both of us, a trace of fear. I wonder if forgiveness is strength or weakness, if my lack of pain speaks finally of the lack of love.

"I'm sorry," Perry says helplessly. "Not just about Jill."

"I believe you," I say. "I'm sorry, too."

"The girls will never forgive me," he says.

"They're your children," I say. "They love you."

"They may even hate me," he says. It is no longer a conversation, just clashing chords of lamentation.

"You're not a misogynist," I say.

"Of course that was the chance I took," he says.

"You're just a fraud, Perry," I say. It comes to me then that Perry is an imposter, not of a good man, but of a great man, and that the burden has just grown too hard to bear.

We hear a car pull up, the clip clop of shoes on the sidewalk. Someone turns a key in our front door. We stand, wax statues of parents, for it can only be one of our daughters, come home early and unannounced. I don't even stop to consider that maybe something is wrong—that Lark has been sliced in the face with the blade of an ice skate, that Mary has been molested in Rome, that Michael has fallen off her Maine island into the cold sea. Only later when Perry has moved away, when I've started the day shift at the hospital and toss restlessly in my bed at night, do the tragedies of my children fill my dreams.

The door creaks open. Perry and I glance at one another, the saddest, most laden glance we've ever exchanged, but maybe the most tolerant. Mary peeks her head inside the door, tanned and taller and almost too painfully beautiful to bear.

"I came home early," she says softly, still hiding most of herself behind the door. "I was getting kind of . . . homesick." This, for Mary, is tantamount to mush. Perry and I stare at her, then back at one another.

"It's okay, isn't it?" she asks.

"Of course, honey." I rush over to give her a clumsy hug.

"Dad?" she asks.

"Come on in, Mary," he says.

Mary steps inside and closes the door softly behind her, looking all around her, sniffing the air for danger or change. With a pained look, she sinks gracefully and straight-backed down onto the couch. I understand then that Mary knows all about Perry and me and maybe even Jill, that she has seen with clear eyes what's been been blinding us for so long.

"Is everything all right?" she asks dully.

"Fine," Perry says quickly.

"How was your trip?" I try to sound cheerful, but cheerfulness is at best a fraud. In a family game we play, I cut right to the quick. "Tell us the best part," I say.

"I sang with a band one night in Milan," Mary says. The Cassandra look of doom lifts momentarily from her face. "I was at this club," she says. "This guy I knew pushed me up on the stage. The lead singer wanted me to stay and join the group. He said I could be the next Aretha."

"That's high praise," I say.

"Yeah, well. There's only one Aretha. And the band wasn't so great." Mary brings her legs up under her in the lotus position and folds her arms across her chest. She wants nothing from us now—no gifts, no kindness, no false praise. "Anyway, I think he was just after my ass." A month alone in Italy has given her license to use such words with us.

"You're a talented musician," I tell her. "Right, Perry?"

"You're good, Mary." Perry leans his head against the window. "You know that."

"Yeah, but could I ever hit you down deep with my music?" Mary wants to know. "Would you drive a hundred miles to hear me?" She gets up from the couch and starts walking towards her father. "Would you pay money to see me, Dad?" Perry bangs his head gently against the window pane. I have never been one to let a silence die its own, slow death or to leave a daughter hanging. I follow Mary, step for step, until she reaches Perry and stops. We stand a sad family train, faces to backs, and me the caboose.

"I'd pay money to see you," I tell Mary, reaching out an arm to touch her shoulder. "If I had any."

LUCY

Lucy Madison's refrigerator tells a tale. When it's chock full, her life is too crowded—too many photo shoots and too much noise and too many dolls to fix. When it's filled with junk, her head is full of junk too—crusty memories and sweet dreams and useless fears. Grapefruits in the bin mean that bitterness has dripped in through the faucet in the sink. Mold sprouts on those days of foggy stillness when Lucy forgets that she's supposed to go out and be part of the world, when she misses appointments and picks up the phone just after the last ring, when she can only sit amongst the broken dolls, mending limbs and sewing chins to necks, braiding hair and painting on eyebrows.

Today, on a hot August morning, Lucy finds spider-web mold on the tomato sauce that she made three days before and only ever tasted in the cooking of it. She pours hot water into the pot and watches the mold break apart and float in pieces down the drain. Next to the sink is the window that lets in whatever sun is spared the city and looks down upon a street on which there are fourteen flower shops and six bakeries, if you follow it all the way to the river. Officer Marvin has just called to say that he is on his way over. He will put beer and bottled water in Lucy's refrigerator, chasing, as he does, one bottle of the first with one bottle of the second. Officer Marvin is not so much handsome as splendid, in his blue uniform and cap with a badge. He is a tall man with baby smooth skin, and has become a person that Lucy can't say no to. Dr. Metz used to say that she must learn to say no to people, and it has occurred to her that maybe letting Officer Marvin come over so often is not such a good idea.

Still, Lucy likes Officer Marvin, and she will let him come. Some people down at the station say, watch out, Lucy, that Marvin has a screw loose and that his mind wanders with that left eye of his, that he has not been the same since he chased the boy who fell on his gun and died. But why, Lucy wonders, should anyone be the same after such a thing? One cop even told her that Officer Marvin is crazy. Loco. Missing a few screws. Lucy thinks it may be so, but then again, people have said that she is crazy, too, although you will misunderstand if you think that this is why she likes Officer Marvin. If Lucy is crazy, it was all those years on Dr. Metz's hard, orange couch that made her so. Before, she was just a person who did things that other people didn't think to do.

"Like what?" Dr. Metz asked her the first time Lucy's parents sent her to see him. He was a thin, frail man, lost always in a shapeless suit and a mope, not nearly a big enough person to answer such important questions as, "Is so and so crazy?"

"Like . . . ?" There was never anything for Lucy to do but describe the things she'd done that brought the swampy look into her French mother's eyes and made her say, "*Que tu es surement folle*, Lucille." Surely crazy, that's what her own mother thought of her.

"I covered a wall once with whipped cream," Lucy told Dr. Metz. She thought of him as a kind of box, a container for her thoughts, which, if not caught, might run wild. "And I like to play the radio for the mice in the kitchen. Mice have ears, don't they?"

"Certainly do." Dr. Metz would take notes and Lucy would wait politely for him to stop scribbling before she began again.

"I screamed so loud yesterday, it actually sounded soft," she told him. "And I ate a raw egg to see if I could taste the chicken in it."

"And could you?"

"I could," Lucy told him. "But I think what I was tasting was how bad I felt for the chicken who got eaten before it even had a chance to be born."

"Might have been." Dr. Metz rarely spoke in whole sentences. "Anything else?"

"Well, let's see. I have x-ray vision."

"X-ray vision?" Dr. Metz perked up at this. He had a yellowish hue to his skin and fingernails. Although he never smoked in front of Lucy, the office always reeked of stale cigarettes. "Tell me more about the x-ray vision, Lucy."

She told him about the bald mermaids rising from street puddles and the wiggling fences and the lizards she saw scaling the walls of bank buildings and the way a laugh began in a person's stomach, with a gunshot and a squiggle. Things she'd chosen to see, that she'd brought to life with her eyes, wondrous and harmless things, was what she couldn't make anyone understand. On one visit, when she was fourteen, Dr. Metz gave her a Brownie camera and told her to start taking pictures of the things she saw. Soon after, Lucy stopped going there. Afterwards, she took lessons—ballet and arts and crafts and carpentry for young ladies.

If Lucy is crazy, she isn't dying of it. She is twenty-four years old and lives in a warehouse loft in the flower district of New York City. She still has the camera that Dr. Metz gave her and now three others—a Minolta, a Nikon, and a Pentax—all better names for goddesses, Lucy thinks. They have been like goddesses to her—Minnie, Nikki, and Pen—because they have put to use the only power she has ever had—the power to see in a special way. With her cameras, she can perform great and normal tasks. She has a job taking photographs down at the police station, of objects used as evidence in criminal trials. They say she has an uncanny sense of angle and light. They say it's eerie, how she brings the things to life. The officers put on filmy gloves and place the things on a white cloth. In the right hand corner of the cloth they put small white identification cards with numbers on them, which are the starting points for Lucy's pictures. Some of the things she photographs are beautiful—jewels and rugs and a Ruisdael painting once, of a mill in a forest—a hundred different shades of brown and green all closed up in a gold frame. But more often, the things are ugly—steely guns and knives and frayed rope or stained bits of clothing. Sometimes these things make her hands shake when she's holding the camera and she has to do the shoot all over again. Back in her loft, she processes the film in her darkroom and makes 8 x 10 prints—ninety seconds in the developer, thirty in the stop. The images appear slowly like black magic and she turns them to stone. She delivers the photographs to the police station on 83rd St. Attention: Forensics. She pictures a man with big muscles, and a scar.

Lucy has proved her mother wrong. She earns a living. She pays her rent and her bills and gets supplies for the dolls. She buys things to put in her refrigerator—pickles, bread and grapes—things that she eats little bits of, never very hungry but afraid as others have always been for her, that she will waste away. And with what's left, she buys flowers from the men out on the street, one new bunch as soon as the old one starts to wilt—gladiolas to magnolias to roses to begonias—Lucy's way of marking the seasons.

Lucy found the first doll when she was about eight, over on 63rd Street on her way home from school. The garbage collectors were out on strike. The city was a mess and smelled bad, no longer seeming like a place to live unless you had to, which is the way it was often described. A woman tossed a doll out of the window and it did helpless flips until it landed on the sidewalk on top of a pile of newspapers, orange peels, frozen food boxes, used kleenex, and coffee grounds. Lucy waded into the heap, feeling the garbage squishing beneath her feet. As she reached for the doll, she heard a police siren wailing and she fled, stuffing the doll into her book bag. The doll had one gouged-out eye and knife slices in its belly. Lucy hid in the shadows of a stairway down to the subway until the police car passed by. She brushed the coffee grounds from the doll's one good eye, whispering, "It's just garbage." Over the years she has rescued some eighty or ninety such dolls from buses and benches and trash piles and gutters. When she gets them home, she bathes them and puts them on her doll table, where they lay for months at a time, awaiting new body parts or hair or a clean outfit, or at least a decent burial in a shoe box.

The doll table sits smack in the middle of Lucy's loft, separating the street-side kitchen from the bed and darkroom to the north. "Why do you live in a city if it's a barn you want?" her mother writes. The table is no more than two old doors resting on four sawhorses, and it's a mess. But, like the mess in Lucy's brain, it's orderly disorder. With one thrust of a hand, she can reach for the things she needs—felt or glue or bits of hair, string, wire, cloth, needles. Officer Marvin keeps asking her how she can live in this hole, swears at Jesus when he bumps his head on the exposed pipes. "If it's so bad," she asked him last week, "Then why do you come?"

"Take a look in the mirror, Lu," was what he said. "How can I stay away?"

As she waits for Officer Marvin now, Lucy looks in a thin, full-length mirror next to the refrigerator. She is supposed to be beautiful. People tell her this from time to time, strangers mostly, who whisper it as though it's not her right. But beauty is only confusing, and Lucy would gladly trade hers for even a few specks of Officer Marvin's calm. She is never sure what she sees behind the tainted mirror's spots. There is too much feature for the face; huge, murky eyes get in the way of everything else about her. She is so thin, she might snap like a twig in such a strong pair of hands as his. She is ghostlike, so pale the merest touch on her skin leaves a mark. After even the most gentle lovemaking, she is bruised and scratched and blotchy. In the end, Lucy judges prettiness by peacefulness. The painting of the mill in the gold frame is truly beautiful because it is serene. So is a doll which closes its eyes in a starched dress, finally mended. Lucy doesn't have a peaceful aura. People change in their small spaces when she comes near. They fuss or fidget or start breathing harder or giggle or get irritated or shuffle in their chairs. So in some way, she must be ugly.

This is why she likes Officer Marvin. He doesn't change when he's with her, gives her the same time of day as he does Aphonse, the drunk man on the stoop. Officer Marvin is always calm and careful, has glassy blue eyes, one that wanders left of its center, and the other which searches and searches, long past Lucy. He's a policeman and has seen many things. He walks a beat down near the waterfront. Today he arrives carrying his bottles of beer and water in one arm and a broken doll in the other.

"Found this down by the tankers," he says, taking off his cap as he steps inside. "Some kid musta chucked it."

"She's a Molly Make-Up Doll," Lucy tells him, taking the doll from him and straightening its twisted legs. "Her hair grows and retracts. She has eyelashes that pull out from her lids, and she comes with six different shades of lipstick." She appraises the doll's injuries—crushed forehead, painted body, chewed-up fingers on one hand, hacked off hair.

"My sister never had any dolls," Officer Marvin says, as he puts his six-pack and water into the refrigerator. He talks often to Lucy about his family, which is made up of people all either dead or gone. "She was a real tomboy."

"So was I," Lucy says.

"I don't believe it, sweetheart." Officer Marvin pulls his shirt out of his pants and comes over to stroke Lucy's cheek with the cross on the chain around his neck. Now that he has begun touching her, he won't stop. "There's not one ounce of boy in you, Lu. Jesus. It's almost a sin the way you look." He nearly hurts her in a squeeze.

Lucy loves the smell of Officer Marvin's hard, soapy body. "The only friend I ever had was a boy," she tells him, laying the gold cross back flat on his hairless chest. "He was older than I was. I never really did girl things."

"What did you do with this boy?" His face comes closer.

"We just played," Lucy says. "He never cared that I was a girl."

"Guy must have been blind," he says, lifting up her hair and kissing her on the neck. She pulls away from him. He turns his lips back to his beer and walks over to the doll table, picking up an armless, legless torso and dangling it by the hair. "This one's gotta be a lost cause."

"That's a Chatty Cathy," Lucy says, following him over to the table. "She could be forty years old." She takes the doll from him, rights it and smoothes its hair. "You might look this way too if you were that old and you'd had a hard life."

"Honey," he says, pulling her toward him. "I've had one hell of a life. And I am that old."

"You are?" Lucy strokes his head in sympathy and wonder. His hair has slices of silver in it. He encircles her waist with his huge hands, making the purring noise that means his drinking is done, and flings the torso doll onto the bed on the far side of the room before he leads Lucy there. She doesn't really understand the things they do in the bed, not in any complete kind of way. She knows that they undress and touch first cold lips and feet with calm consideration. She knows that there follow heat, movement, and a forgetfulness of who they are before a tightness inside her unravels and a stillness settles. She knows that the pleasure is ephemeral and not really hers to keep. But she knows that in the end, it is not an ugly thing at all.

Afterwards, Officer Marvin sits up and lights a cigarette, putting the hot match to wet lips before he sets it down on the bedside table. Naked, he really is handsome, with all of the muscle and vein and skin of him to see. But with the smoke all around him, he's not as gentle, and the pupil of the wandering eye goes to the very edge. Finding the torso doll tangled up in the sheets, Officer Marvin flings it back onto the doll table, sending some of the mess scattering to the floor.

"Really, Lu." He looks all around, gives a shudder. "This place looks like Hiroshima after the bomb. I'll take you somewhere."

"Where?" Lucy puts a hand on his warm chest.

"Away from here. Anywhere."

"Can we bring the dolls?"

He pulls the sheet away from her and rolls toward her. "No, baby," he says, bringing his head down to her breasts. "The dolls stay here."

"Who will fix them?" Lucy asks, holding his head at bay.

"Nobody," he says. "They've been dumped, forgotten. Even the kids don't want them anymore. Anyways, baby . . . ." He is sleepy now, kisses her belly. "You never really do fix them, do you? I mean good as new."

She would if she could. Fix them good as new. She looks over at the pile of carcasses on the doll table as Officer Marvin rolls over on his side.

"It's my job," she tells him.

"Your job is down at the station with your cameras." Officer Marvin's head rises for one last word. "This stuff with the dolls, Lu. It's just plain . . . crazy."

Later, in the afternoon, Lucy goes for a walk with Officer Marvin before he goes off to work. In spite of the heat, she puts a red satin scarf around her shoulders. Officer Marvin gave her the scarf one day in the spring for no reason at all. She is safe outside with Officer Marvin, crossing his shadow and wearing his scarf—safe from the cars and the muggers and the din and the dirt. When Officer Marvin wears his uniform, people change, just as they do around her. They stop talking or look sharply or the other way, or lose the rhythm in their steps. Outside, he doesn't turn his head. He doesn't smile or small-talk much, not the way he does in bed when he takes the barrettes out of her hair and lets it fall thick and reddish to her waist, where it hangs with a quiver until it settles. He doesn't speak softly as he does when he tells her, "That's some head of hair you got there, Lu."

Today they walk in Central Park. The air is wet and still. People aren't feeling well—thick and fuzzy, like the mold. Cars screech and birds squabble and the buses don't come on time. Lucy and Officer Marvin walk to the duck pond. Lucy has brought her camera and takes pictures of the stained and crumpled grass near the water's edge. The rim of a waxy paper cup fills the right hand corner of the frame, just at the place where the white identification card would sit on the white cloth at the station, upon which the blood-stained knife would lay.

Lucy kneels on the grass, which is damp with the seepage from the pond and throws pieces of old bread to the ducks, which glide over to snap them up. Officer Marvin sits on a newspaper, so he won't get a spot on the rear of his uniform, and stares at Lucy until she turns around, her eyes still at the viewfinder of her camera.

"Where would you take me?" Lucy asks him, framing his face and his chest, down to a hand reaching for a blade of grass.

"Oh, I don't know." He seems to have changed his mind. "You could stay a while at my place," he offers. Lucy snaps a picture of him as he brings the blade of grass up to his mouth. "A few days anyways." Near the duck pond, where the water matches his eyes and his uniform, Officer Marvin is harder to see. "You know, a little white paint would do wonders for your place, Lu."

A sound comes skimming across the water and swells up into

Lucy Madison's ears, an endless wailing scream, the kind of noise she imagines the dolls would make if they could when their arms or legs got ripped off. But this is a human sound, mournful and full of pain. It's a cry that's gone beyond "help me" and ends up demanding something more. Lucy drops the camera down from her eyes. She can see who made the noise, a woman who sat just a minute before talking to a man across the pond. Now the woman is lying on the ground, and the man is walking quickly away from her.

Officer Marvin jumps up from the newspaper and runs over to the woman, who has stopped making any noise at all. Lucy watches him run, with the grace and speed of some wildcat she's seen in a car ad on TV and can't name. That boy they talk about down at the station, the one who fell on his gun—he must have seen Officer Marvin running after him like this and known he had no chance. Maybe he just gave up and fell on purpose. Officer Marvin bends over the woman and talks into his police walkie-talkie as he tends her. Ripping off a piece of his shirt from under his jacket, he binds her leg, then gets up and starts to chase the man, who is stumbling away into the distance. Lucy walks to the other side of the pond and looks down into the woman's eyes.

"Are you all right?" she asks.

The woman doesn't answer. A circle of blood seeps through the white make-shift bandage on her leg. Lucy raises her camera to her eyes. A red light flashes to remind her that this is the last shot on the roll. Her fingers pause before clicking the shutter. Through the lens, she sees a coiled snake rise up from the woman's bloodstain, which then turns into a string of pearls, which straightens into a sheet of falling rain and then solidifies into one of the oak trees in the Ruisdael painting with the gold frame. She snaps a picture of the woman's wound, and when she takes her eye away from the viewfinder, the oak has quite logically turned into the maple tree hovering over them in the park.

"Hey," the woman says. "Why'd you take a picture of my leg?"

"I'm sorry," Lucy says. "It's an unusual color, an interesting design."

"I'm lying here bleeding," the woman says. "And you're taking snapshots."

"I don't have any more film," Lucy says. "Are you all right?"

"That cop seemed to think so," the woman says.

"Officer Marvin?" Lucy says.

"You know him?"

"Yes," Lucy says. "What happened?"

"I got shot."

"And Officer Marvin's trying to catch the man who shot you?"

"Yes, your Marvin will be a hero if he catches Jerry. It won't be hard. Jerry has bad legs."

"Why is he running away?"

"He robbed a bank," the woman says. "And I helped him." Water drips from her eyes—tears of pain, Lucy guesses, for the woman seems too angry to be sad.

"Don't worry." Lucy touches the woman's arm. "We'll get you to a hospital."

"Yeah, they'll fix me up. I'll be doing jumping jacks in jail." The woman's speech starts to slur; her eyes pinch together with her pain. "I married him." She is talking to herself now. "I did whatever he told me to." She tries to rise and winces as she flops back down on her back. "And he up and shoots me."

"Why did he shoot you?" Lucy asks.

"I said I'd had enough. I said I wouldn't do it again, that I'd tell. He's a maniac. He should be in jail."

"I've been in jail," Lucy tells her.

"You? What have you ever done?" the woman asks, with a scorn to which Lucy has become accustomed.

"I take pictures," Lucy tells her, wondering about the order of the answers she gives. "And I fix dolls."

"And you fix dolls," the woman repeats softly.

The ambulance men come bumpity-split across the grass with a stretcher. The sky smoulders and wind lashes the trees. Raindrops splatter bits of Lucy's hair to dark red and she ties it into a knot at the nape of her neck. At the first crack of thunder, the ducks retreat in a crisp line to the water's edge. The woman winces as the ambulance men lift her stiff onto the canvas. Lucy stuffs her camera under her shirt and starts to run. The lens of the camera bangs into her stomach and collides with her breasts. She tries to keep up with the white-coated men, who move in a smooth, gliding walk, like ice skaters.

They pass Officer Marvin on the way to the ambulance. He has handcuffed the bank robber, the man who could not run to save his life, and is pushing him up against a police car. The man pants and shakes his head. Lights flash and a radio pours out static and garbled voices. With no more than a few warning drops, the rain comes down in sheets. As the ambulance men slide the woman's stretcher into the white van with the backwards letters, Lucy stops and watches Officer Marvin. He is suddenly no more than a stranger who makes himself familiar by showing up in recurring dreams. Lucy can no longer remember his voice or his smell or the feel of him. With the huge hands that have reached for her so often, Officer Marvin frisks the man who shot the woman, his hat tilted low on his forehead, talking all the while. Something he says makes the man spit at Officer Marvin's feet. The rain pours down. The man is sick. His hands are trembling and he's breathing hard. Smiling a terrible smile, Officer Marvin yanks the man by the chain of the handcuffs, opens the door of the police car and flings him inside with the same motion he flings Lucy's dolls from the bed to the table and back. Then he wipes his wet face to clear his eyes, and slams the car door. Lucy wonders if what she has has felt all along for Officer Marvin has been no more than fear.

Lucy slips into the back of the ambulance and sits on the seat across from the wounded woman. One of the men is tending her—hooking her up to an IV, taking her blood pressure. "Friend or relative?" he asks Lucy, motioning to the woman with his sharp chin.

"Friend," Lucy says. The driver pulls away from the curb. The rear door, not properly closed, slides open, and Lucy's red scarf blows from around her neck and out onto the street near Officer Marvin's feet. He calls out. "Lucy! Where are you going?" Lucy thinks that she may not see Officer Marvin again, and so she takes a good look at the dripping boy doll in blue, waving his arms and shouting in the rain, getting smaller and smaller. The driver steps on the gas and puts on the siren. The wounded woman winces when the ambulance hits a pothole. She has tears in her eyes and scraggly hair and a hole in her leg. Shot and betrayed. Lucy feels solid and all of a piece. She dries the wet part of her camera with a dry corner of her shirt. She has some time and a little money to spare. She will push crazy back to the edge of sane. She will wrestle the driver to the floor and drive the ambulance down smoother streets, take the woman back to her loft. She will get some dynamite and blast all the guns from the hands that hold them. The woman groans as the ambulance lurches through a red light. Lucy reaches out to touch her arm. She will bring the creep to justice and mend the busted woman, steal the mill painting and sell it for a million dollars, then move to the other side of the world. Out of the rain spattered window, Lucy sees an object fly by, spinning in the wind, falling to the street, making a din, or no sound at all, rolling, bouncing, stilled in the gutter—ball, bullet, bone. The woman's eyes close. Lucy raises the camera to her eye, swings the lens from the woman's face back to the window and back to the woman's face. The shutter won't budge. The woman is still. Maybe Lucy will just go home and load up her camera again with film.

EMPIRE BEAUTY SALON

O n an August day in New York City, a woman's yearning comes full circle. The morning begins like any other. She opens her beauty parlor, tilts up the hairdryers, sweeps no more than night dust from the floor, smoothes the sand in the sand tray, and rearranges the shells on the shelf. As the eight o'clock news comes on the radio, the Waikiki poster on the wall catches her eye. The muscled surfer hovers on the crest of a giant wave while the coffee perks. Three people have been found murdered in the night, the announcer says, and the air is bad. The telephone operators are back on strike and there will be Shakespeare in the park that night. City pride, a street study reveals, has never been higher.

Out of the woman's yearning comes a wry laugh. She fills a bucket and goes out to splash water on the sidewalk, scrubbing it clean with a wire brush. She is forty-eight years old and not unhappy. She owns the Oceana Beauty Salon on West 112th Street and business is good. The mortgage is paid and she has health galore, more, perhaps, than she will ever be able to use. She hasn't been sick but that one day when she lost the baby, a baby she never really expected to make it anyway. Her police-man friend Brett walks her beat and her friend Tony owns the best Italian restaurant on the East Side. The woman is a New Yorker born and bred, but if affection and pride are the mea-sures, she has never really felt that she belongs here.

The woman has always loved the ocean from a distance, in books and photographs and TV shows, and the feel of it on her toes on trips to Coney Island or the spray from the Staten Island Ferry on a windy day. Over the years, she has amassed a large collection of travel books and posters and brochures on sea-bor-dered lands, having combed the city's bookstores and travel agencies to find them. All of the ocean paraphernalia—the shells, the anchor, the sand—has been bought in New York City, it being a place where one can buy anything, even the stuff, if not the essence, of dreams. Her beauty parlor is some-thing of a landmark, its front face covered with shells stuck on stucco, its twin potted palm trees standing guard out front, defying cold, smog and vandals alike. The ocean music she plays has lulled more than one customer to sleep under the hairdryers, and stops passersby on the warm days, when the sounds of waves roll out onto the street.

The woman's customers are regular and loyal. Many of them are elderly, although she will cut anyone's hair and considers this just to be chance. They all share with her a yen, if not for the sea, for something equally as compelling. In the woman's beauty parlor, they are free to dream. Even Mr. Hurlehee, one of the woman's few male customers, keeps coming back with his receding hairline, although she often suggests that he call the toll free number and speak to the hair specialist who jabbers with a lisp on late night TV. Mr. Hurlehee won't hear of it. He has searched the city far and wide for the feel of hands as soft as the woman's on what is left of his hair, for an ear as keen and a chair as soft. He comes more often than is necessary for a trim and some poofing, as he calls it, and is most often lost in a book which the woman picked up once at a church sale, a book called *The Magical Island of Fiji*, with full-page color photographs.

"A man could really hang his hat over there in Fiji, Roxanne," Mr. Hurlehee has been known to say.

And Roxanne—for that is the woman's name—has been known to reply as she snips off tiny bits of his hair and the traffic snarls outside, "Could hang it right on a cloud, Mr. Hurlehee. Watch it ride away." She and Mr. Hurlehee have chuckled to think of hat racks in hatless lands. They've even had lunch a few times, once with martinis.

Mrs. Agnes Pepperdine, who owns the dry cleaners a few doors down, has come to the Oceana Beauty Salon every Thursday for thirteen years after her palm reading session with Madame Angela, sure that Roxanne can somehow recreate the aqua color of the Mediterranean Sea in her limp grey curls, and make all of Madame Angela's predictions for her come true. Mrs. Pepperdine has spent many an hour in Roxanne's chair, studying the brown-skinned girls in hula skirts and bikini tops walking the beach on the Bora Bora poster on the wall. "No wonder they look so good," she has often speculated, blowing on wet, red fingernails while Roxanne does her up in curlers. "No winter. No carbon monoxide. No MSG. Now that, Roxanne, would be a good life."

And Roxanne has often replied in a solemn voice for the dream that they share. "No subway trains. No lines at the supermarket. No traffic jams. No wonder those girls look so good."

It is in fact, on the very day that Roxanne learns of of Mrs. Pepperdine's death, that she finally reckons with the yearning. "Agnes was found stone cold," Mrs. Bensonhurst—a customer and mutual acquaintance—tells Roxanne. "Three days after the fact and not by that millionaire son of hers."

"Who found her?" Roxanne asks, starting to comb out Mrs. Bensonhurst's wet, tangled hair.

"The Christian Science Monitors started to pile up on the doorstep," Mrs. Bensonhurst explains. "A neighbor went for the super."

"Is she gone?" Roxanne asks, thinking in a crazy moment that maybe it's not too late to stop Mrs. Pepperdine from going to the grave with dingy curls.

"You don't get much deader than dead, Roxanne." Mrs. Bensonhurst says.

"I meant has she been buried yet?" Roxanne says.

"Today," says Mrs. Bensonhurst, turning her face this way and that, to see herself at different angles in the mirror. "Over at the Soldiers' Field next to her husband, not that he was ever very good company."

"I never met him," Roxanne murmurs, reaching for a comb. Ms. Bensonhurst's hair has never really needed her. It is like steel wool, holds its curl at all costs and never seems to grow. Roxanne tugs away, upset that Mrs. Pepperdine will have to leave the world with sour milk in her refrigerator and so many dreams unfulfilled, with only an ungrateful son left to see to things. An unspeakable distress fills Roxanne, as the waves crash through the speaker on the wall—maybe an anger.

"Did you hear me, Roxanne?" Mrs. Bensonhurst is asking, suddenly aware that Roxanne's hands are still. Roxanne starts to comb again and Mrs. Bensonhurst goes on, "I was saying how even a million dollars can't bring back a dead mother."

At this moment, Roxanne bends to the yearning's will. She sees how there will be more ends now than beginnings, how all of them will be swallowed up by one horror or another, and taken away, one by one. She sees that she has no real obligations or ties, how alone she really is. She understands, be it a curse or a blessing, that she will be on the earth for a long, long time. She sees that she alone is the maker of her fate and how that makes fate easier to mold. All of this comes to her not with self-pity or sadness, but with relief. Roxanne decides that she has had enough of her city, any city, and that she will move to a seacoast town.

Roxanne chooses Maine because a trip to Camden with an old lover once made a dent in her heart somewhere, because it's not too far away, but far enough. In Maine, she will know the language and the hair and the TV stations and the cuts of meat at the supermarket. She would not be good in the places on the travel posters—Tahiti or the Riviera or Puerto Escondido. Her white skin would burn and her thick ankles would never learn to dance on the hot sand. Truth be known, she can't even swim. Nor would she know what to do with the dark, slippery hair of the brown beach girls, if they ever came to her with it. But surely in Maine, where there is fast food, hardship, and a cold, cold ocean, the hair is still in need of a Roxanne.

Out of an atlas, Roxanne settles on the town of Morocco, Maine, as her new home, satisfied to seek the exotic only in a name. It is the dot on the tip of a jagged spit of land north of Damariscotta, and only a bus can take her there. She takes the ten-hour bus ride, three of them spent winding down tiny roads from Augusta to the coast, and finds the perfect storefront for her beauty parlor, sandwiched on Morocco's Main Street between Ablow's Drug Store and a knick-knack shop which sells the kind of things which line the shelves of Roxanne's New York salon—sea glass and fishing net, seagull pins and sand dollar paperweights. Back stairs lead up to a two-room apartment overlooking the lobster pond and Morocco's harbor. The walls are freshly painted and the floors are of wide pine. She signs a lease that day.

Roxanne hires a local carpenter and discusses her plans for the beauty parlor. He is swarthy and silent, with the blackest of hair and a rumbling voice. He is neither lobster fisherman like his father nor carpenter, really, he explains, but an aspiring pharmacist. Having been rejected once from the Bangor College of Pharmacy, he is doing odd jobs while he studies and waits for the next application deadline to roll around. "Can you do this and that?" Roxanne asks him, needing a person of specific temperament and skills. The boy can do this and that. He can do most anything she wants, he assures her, understanding right away that Roxanne is a person who knows what she wants.

In late September, Roxanne returns to Morocco on the bus with the matching luggage set she picked up at Causeway's Bargain Basement on West 44th. The beauty supplies have come ahead of her in a cushioned truck and the shop is ready. Frederick, the young carpenter, has done more than a fine job. The Empire Beauty Salon is as much a sight on Main Street, Morocco, as the Oceana was on West 112th. The store sign is just how she pictured it—a plywood face of the Empire State Building rising above the door. Frederick has installed plate glass behind the cut-out windows and painted in the sills and moldings carefully. Inside, on the wall across from the hairdryers, hangs a blown-up photograph of Times Square at night, with blurry lights and street signs, the neon streamers of moving cars, the clock stuck forever at 11:59 on a forgotten New Year's Eve. On the opposite wall, stretching from one corner to the other, is a mural on canvas that one of Roxanne's New York customers painted for her. It is of the Hudson River, first as it might have been in days gone by, filled with clear water and fish and swimming children, its banks dotted with small houses and trees. Farther along, the skyline rises and the trees fall. The fish and the children disappear and the water fills with oil swirls and tin cans. As smoke and dirt obscure water and air, all life is removed.

Roxanne works alongside Frederick for hours, unpacking boxes of books, maps, and photographs of New York, which she has bartered for the sea stuff back in the city. Roxanne puts a model of the Statue of Liberty in the window, a garland of fresh flowers resting on its crown. Frederick hangs up posters of ice skaters at Rockefeller Center and the U.N. Building and the Staten Island Ferry. Together, they prop up the literature on a magazine rack that Roxanne got once from a man in the concession stand business.

"Where d'you ever find a thing like this?" Frederick asks her.

"I got that rack from a friend," she tells Frederick. "For a midnight song."

At the end of the day, Frederick and Roxanne spend a long time admiring the finished shop, which is redolent of fresh-cut pine, musty books, shampoo and satisfaction. Both have made note of the other's persistence and strong, unbending arms.

Roxanne settles easily in Morocco, Maine, mostly because she is a person without a need for importance or absoluteness, someone who doesn't necessarily have to be who she has always been before. When Carrie Eaton says flatly, "More off in the back, Roxanne. I won't be back until spring," Roxanne is glad to oblige. She never thinks to try and change a person's mind or look, having eschewed the alchemist tasks of beauticians. The whims and desires of her customers are nothing and everything to her. She simply applies her expertise to their desires, just as the shoemaker would fix her shoes the way she asked him to.

Roxanne is not a showboat or a gossip, as the town had feared when they watched the Empire State Building sign rise and her shop take shape in Frederick's hands. She is a good business woman and neighbor, competent and sensible. "Nothing extra about her," the smitten mailman reports, spreading the news on his rounds. "She won't be a half bad fit 'round here."

In early October, a small man with a crease of authority in his brow stops by Roxanne's shop. "Mr. Doug," he says, introducing himself with a twist of his bull neck. "Town manager. 'Fraid I have to close you down for a few days."

"Why?" Roxanne asks.

"Trouble in the sewer," he says. "Could be two, maybe three days."

Roxanne nods her head as a bad smell rises up from the street and creeps into her shop. She doesn't fuss about lost business or the stink, but instead studies Mr. Doug's strange pointed ears and ringless fingers, and invites him in for coffee, remarking, as she ushers him to a chair, "Broken sewer doesn't do anyone much good."

Roxanne is always on the lookout for a beau, as she likes to call that man that she may someday find, rather than a lover. In her mind, love has only a little to do with what she might finally do with such a man—raise a glass of milk, choose a brand of cleaning fluid, read chapters aloud from a book. She would keep this man at a distance; he would want it that way, too. At thirty-nine, when she met her husband Frank, Roxanne had just about given up on love. Frank played the banjo and sold subway tokens underground for the uptown trains. He died at the age of fifty-one, after seven years of their marriage, just when Roxanne was beginning to figure out what love was—something akin to letting go, comfort stung by resignation. Roxanne thinks Frank died from the darkness and the fumes which spewed from the trains, although it went down on the death certificate as a liver disease set to galloping by Frank's love of whiskey. Frank used to say that Roxanne was the best thing that ever happened to him, and though she'd pshawed him every time, it had made her feel good. Roxanne doesn't blame herself for Frank's death. She only thinks that another woman might have kicked him up the subway stairs and into the clean air, might have poured his whiskey down the drain and insisted on some conversation and a softer beverage. But Frank liked his life so well—his sports page and his slippers and his bottle and his wife. Roxanne had thought no more of changing him than she ever had a customer's hairstyle. And when they lost the baby, it had made even more sense to let one another and well enough alone.

Roxanne is a good-enough looking woman, with strong features which will survive when the rest of her starts to crumble. She is not tall, though there is a tallness about her. In middle age, she is solid. In old age, she will be regal. Her velvety, unlined skin is her best asset, and her stringy brown hair, ironically, her worst—unwilling to take a curl or a tint or a twist or a wave or a curve or a slant or any suggestion at all—refusing to do anything but hang lifelessly at her broad shoulders.

Sometimes, during those first fall days in Morocco, although she realizes it is crazy, Roxanne imagines that Frederick might be the beau. He is young, but he might just as well be old. He is self-contained and seemingly unattached, to any person or any age. Frederick spends a lot of time in the Empire Beauty Salon with Roxanne, becomes a fixture which comes to surprise no one. There is a peaceful, unspoken understanding between Frederick and Roxanne. When he's not studying or working on his application to pharmacy college, perfecting every word of his Personal-Statement-In-Four-Hundred-Words-Or-Less, he takes out his tools and putters around the shop, keeping things in good repair. He washes the windows and touches up the paint, rearranges the books and magazines on the rack. Idle in November, he collects 114 signatures of approval and puts a red flashing light on the top of the Empire State Building sign. Roxanne calls a halt as December sets in and Frederick appears one day with a bucket of yellow paint and the intention of painting highway divider lines on the floor. "The East Side Highway," he explains. "Right here in Morocco."

"Next you'll be setting up a toll booth at the door," she says, filling with a hopeless affection for him, as some snow melts on his bushy eyebrows, "palming quarters from the customers and giving directions to Shea Stadium."

"What happens there?" he asks.

"It's where the Mets play," Roxanne says. She could really love a boy who doesn't even know where the Mets play. "Baseball."

"Toll booth's not a bad idea," Frederick says.

"Why not make a model of the Brooklyn Bridge instead?" Roxanne asks him. It is on this cold day that she finally gives in to the urge to touch Frederick, laying a hand on the arm which swings the gallon bucket of paint. "There's room over in that corner." She has already sent for prints of the bridge's design from a New York librarian friend, and bought dowel and lathing and glue. She knows that the Brooklyn Bridge will keep Frederick busy and nearby for a while. Whether or not he is the beau, she likes his presence, and sometimes hopes, perhaps as a mother does in some back reach of her mind, that Frederick's application to pharmacy college will be turned down again, that she will be his champion and his consoler, and that he will stay with her forever in the Empire Beauty Salon.

By the end of the first spring, Roxanne wants to know whether or not she will spend the rest of her days in Morocco, Maine. At forty-eight, there may not be time for another epiphany or move. She closes down the shop on a Wednesday, stopping everything to consider. In the very early morning of an April day, Roxanne wakes to the darkness and can sleep no more. As the light rises from the dawn, she sits in her rocking chair and looks out over the harbor to the islands, searching the screech of the gulls for an answer. When she starts feeling sleepy from the rocking and the sunlight, she gets up to rummage in some unpacked boxes. She reads some old letters from Frank, not so much letters of love, she decides, but satisfaction. She finds a song he once wrote her on a napkin at an outdoor cafe. It went, "Roxanne/I'm your fan/Hope to be your man/ Someday." He'd already been her man by then, but left the words because they'd come out that way. Roxanne tosses out the letters but holds on to the song, for a song, no matter how bad, should always be saved.

Roxanne sits by the hour in the rocker, shaken from her trance by a rumble of thunder. The sky suddenly darkens and the wind shifts to the northeast, swinging the sterns of the lobster boats around. Roxanne gets up, stiff from the sitting, and puts the kettle on the stove. The doorbell rings and Roxanne answers it in her bathrobe and slippers. The town manager stands before her, looking like a Martian with his clean-shaven face and crew cut hair and pointed ears.

"Mr. Doug," Roxanne says, still not sure whether this is his first or last name. "More trouble in the sewer?"

"Shop's been closed three days now," he says. The Moroccans seem to prefer to call it a shop. "Everything all right, Roxanne?"

"Everything's fine," Roxanne tells him.

"You're not sick, are you?"

"No," she says. "I'm not the least bit sick."

"I thought we might take the air," Mr. Doug says authoritatively, as if she were sick and the air might cure her.

"The weather doesn't look so good," Roxanne says, pointing up to the nearly black sky.

"May take a while," Mr. Doug says, "for the sky to overflow."

"I can't leave just now," she says, gesturing without aim back to her living room. "I'm in the middle of something."

"Well, if you ever come to the end of it," Mr. Doug says, peering into the empty room, all business once more, "just let me know."

After Mr. Doug leaves, Roxanne goes back to her thinking with hot tea and a new sadness. There is an unfamiliar emptiness inside her now, always plugged up before, she guesses, by the old yearning. As a gull swoops down to dive for a fish, a new lump of feeling drops down into the hole, clanging as a bead would in an empty tin. With a pang, she remembers how Frank used to bang up the stairs with bread and whiskey in a bag, calling out, "I'm home Rox. The god damned world ain't licked me yet." Frank's swearing and bad grammar used to embarrass Roxanne. Now his ain't's seem like sweet, skewed poetry.

This, Roxanne guesses in her rocker, is loneliness come to call. And like Mr. Doug, who came at a bad moment, it must be shown the door. I am forty-eight years old, she goes fiercely back to her thinking. Widowed. Working. The 573rd inhabitant of Morocco, Maine, not counting the winter batch of babies. I did not come in search of an Eden. There is a chaos here, born of isolation, a hardness born of limitation, a hopelessness that laps up on shore from the impassable sea. But there is also a peacefulness, a great feeling of space and possibility. There is hard winter here, but also soft summer. There is good sense, and there is nonsense. There is kindness and there is greed. There are children. And dogs. And mothers. And men. The final balance would be the same in New York or the real Morocco or Timbuktu. There is no reason, Roxanne decides, not to stay here where she has plunked herself.

Later, as the thunder rumbles and lightning streaks the sky,

Roxanne dozes in the rocker. She returns to New York in a dream, wandering aimlessly through its streets in a blinding rain, calling out the names of her old customers, "Mrs. Muriel Throckmorton! Miss Bella Bernstein! Mrs. Agnes Pepperdine!" The women appear out of tenement house windows with wild and messy hair and flap their hands at her. "You deserted us, Roxanne," they hiss. "You flew the coop." When Roxanne wakes, the storm has passed. As the peach of twilight falls back into the harbor, she waits for the shadows of the women to disappear back into their windows. She has no regrets, only memories and dreams. The gulls retire to the shore with echoing squawks and Mr. Ablow closes up the pharmacy next door. Roxanne hears Frederick's voice. He has taken to spending time with Mr. Ablow, as he used to before Roxanne came. She opens the window and calls out, inviting them both for dinner. It is only logical that Frederick would seek out the town pharmacist as a mentor. And who is to say that Mr. Ablow, a widower and a kind man, is not the beau?

A year goes by. Roxanne's beauty salon fills with regular customers. She gains a few pounds, which, people say, do her well. Frederick gets turned down from the pharmacy college again but loses neither face nor heart. The Personal Statement, now raised to 500-words-or-less, takes new leaps toward perfection. The salon has never looked more ship or shape, now a monument to her old city. More space has been found on the crowded walls for pictures of Central Park and Chinatown and the Macy's Day Parade. The magazine rack is lined with brochures and books detailing historic monuments and city walks and tourist attractions. One corner of the ceiling has been made into a planetarium and Frederick's model of the Brooklyn Bridge stands tall on a corner table. The people of Morocco give these things a glance with polite, but not feigned interest, because they speak of Roxanne. Roxanne doesn't often talk about her past. She doesn't reminisce or compare or glorify or tell her customers how she got to here and from where, or how it used to be, when Morocco meant no more to her than a hot, faraway land of veiled women and camels, bordered by a cool sea.

But comes the day when Frannie Haskell sits down in the chair and asks Roxanne, "What's it like, that city you came from?"

"It's just a place," Roxanne says, lifting up Frannie's blond hair and tying the cape around her shoulders.

"Oh, come on, Roxanne." Frannie has a beautiful retarded baby and runs the movie house up on the hill. "You don't expect me to believe that."

"Well. . . ." Roxanne considers. "You should see the Manhattan Yellow Pages. It's the thickest book you'll ever come across. A kid came into my parlor once. Jimmy Crane. He was fifteen, tiny and quick as a cat. He did flips on skateboards in the park near my house and passed the hat. He told me he wanted a mohawk. All the kids had them, he said. It was true. I sat him down on the Yellow Pages and talked him into a crew cut. Next day his mother came in to thank me, said as long as she was there, was there anything I could do with her hair. She'd just come through chemo and had some patches. It was a tough job."

"Patches?" The light in Frannie's eyes gets Roxanne going for a while. She layers and snips Frannie's bangs and gets out the blowdryer. "I did some teasing and stretching," Roxanne tells Frannie. "That woman fought that cancer like a demon and her hair came back in beautifully. She ran one of the elevators over at the Empire State Building."

"Ever been there?" Frannie asks.

Roxanne shakes her head. "No," she says. "I kept meaning to. But there was this building near my old shop, thirty stories high and only one room on each of them. Looks two-dimensional, just like the sign out front." She dusts the hair from Frannie's neck, gives her a hand mirror, and swivels her around in the chair to have a look. Nodding approval, Frannie gets up and wanders over to the magazine rack, picking up a pamphlet on "Architectural Wonders in the Big Apple."

"Wha'd'you say that building was called?" she asks Roxanne.

"The Flat Iron Building," Roxanne says, bending to sweep Frannie's hair into the dustpan. "It was some architect's idea of how to keep something ordinary from getting lost in a big, crowded place."

"I'd like to meet that person," says Frannie.

"I looked him up in the phone book once," Roxanne says. "Thought about giving him a call, just to tell him I liked his building. But in the end, I didn't. I'd built him up so much, I figured it wasn't really fair to hold a wonder up to its maker."

Frannie nodded. "Best just to leave a good thing be," she said.

The next winter, after a few bitter nights in January, the harbor freezes over for the first time in twenty-seven years. Roxanne is forty-nine and wears long underwear, top and bottom, under her dime-store print dresses. Her added weight has settled becomingly. Touched by the sea air, her hair has grown mysteriously thick and reddish, and taken on a slight curl. Mr. Doug asks Mr. Fister, who runs the lumber yard, if he's noticed that Roxanne's no strain on the eyes these days. The long-smitten mailman lingers at the salon, stopping for a cup of Roxanne's coffee and cream, when invited. In her pile of mail one morning, sandwiched between the electric bill and a Museum of Modern Art Catalog, Roxanne finds a postcard from an old customer. It shows a woman with ruby lips and hands on shapely hips, standing on a sandy beach wearing an old-fashioned polka-dotted bathing suit. Underneath her, in letters meant to look like waves, reads the message, "GREETINGS FROM THE JERSEY SHORE!" Seeing Mr. Hurlehee's cramped, neat handwriting embarrasses Roxanne, as if she has come upon him shaving in his underwear.

"Dear Roxanne," the postcard reads. "Finally made it to the ocean myself. Joined my brother in the dry cleaning business. I haven't had my hair cut since you left. Hope you are well. Love, Morris Hurlehee."

Mr. Hurlehee's distant, curlequed, love makes Roxanne cry on this cold, cold day, and she doesn't cry often. The mailman sneaks away, leaving his coffee half finished by the door. Mrs. Betty Link comes in for her appointment and notices Roxanne's red eyes. Roxanne slips the postcard into her work apron pocket and blows her nose. Mrs. Link announces that this kind of weather breeds nothing but drunkards and colds, and recommends a hot rum potion. As Roxanne is getting Mrs. Link ready for her perm, Frederick comes rushing into the shop. Jumping up as if to dunk a basketball, he crashes into his model of the Brooklyn Bridge, sending hunks of it flying into the air. He bends down to pick up the pieces lovingly, but without the sorrow he would have felt the day before.

"What is it?" Roxanne asks. "What happened, Frederick?"

"I got in," he whoops with a Cheshire cat grin. "Third time around. They just couldn't say no."

Frederick is the warmest, most joyous thing in Morocco that day, and later Roxanne invites him up to her room for a celebration, pulling out from under her bed the gift she has been saving for this day, an old book, bound in leather and lettered in gold leaf, "A Carpenter's Guide," written in 1869, an almost useless thing of great beauty, which only Frederick could love. He studies the book for a long time while Roxanne sips at a vodka gimlet and makes a sort-of souffle for dinner.

"Never had eggs for dinner," Frederick says, finally closing the book. He pulls the card table over to the bay window and lights the candles. They spear peas with their forks and watch the water lap the boats as the lights of distant houses flicker. After dinner, Frederick comes around to Roxanne's side of the table and reaches out a square hand.

"How'd this happen," Roxanne says, taking his hand and smoothing the blackened thumbnail with her finger.

"Never been much of a hammerer," he says.

Roxanne pulls him forward and he sinks down on his knees. She runs her fingers through his thick hair and murmurs into it, "A hammerer you'll always be to me."

Later in the night, Frederick slips out of bed and starts to get dressed. Eyes open a crack, Roxanne watches him, his body solid and smooth from years of hauling lobster traps from the sea at his father's side. When he's done, he stands at the foot of the bed, with his shoes in his hands. Thinking her to be asleep, he whispers, "Thanks, Roxanne."

"Don't thank me, Frederick," Roxanne says sleepily, propping herself up on a pillow, "for such a small thing."

"I'm not talking about the book," he says.

All lingering sleep leaves Roxanne then. She feels suddenly lost and shriveled, an old crone who has lured a boy into her bed in a strange land, a boy who will take the last bits of her dignity and her youth away with him, soon tossing both aside, because he has more than enough of his own. The pleasure Roxanne has felt in Frederick's uncertain arms turns to shame, a feeling that is strange to her, like a new taste in a baby's mouth. She tries to picture Frederick a baby in his father's arms. And for the first time, Roxanne thinks of the baby she lost as one that might have filled her arms, or a hard and empty moment such as this.

"My old man isn't going to be too thrilled," Frederick says with a wry smile.

"About what?" Confused, she thinks Frederick is still talking about her.

"About my good news," Frederick says.

"Does he expect you to stay and help with the lobstering?" Roxanne asks. She wonders why she has never asked this question before, realizes that she has never even met Frederick's parents, though she has often mistaken herself for his mother.

"No," Frederick says. "He's gotten over that. He just doesn't think much of a career in a drug store."

"Why do you want to go to pharmacy college, Frederick?" Curiosity comes to Roxanne late, as it has so often before.

"It's a good profession," Frederick says. "I get to use my head. To help people. And it's way out of this town."

"You don't like this town?" Roxanne is truly surprised.

"I like this town all right," he says cautiously. "I just don't like this kind of town." He struggles with the zipper on his jacket and shakes his head. "I'll never understand how you ended up in a place like this, Roxanne." Frederick's question is fearful of an answer.

"Luck mostly," she tells him, leaving it at that. "I like it here."

"Grass is always greener, I guess," Frederick says. His hand twitches on the doorknob. He is eager to be off and spread his news. "I'll never forget you, Roxanne," he says, slipping sideways out of the half-opened door. His eyes plead with her not to try and stop him. "Thanks again."

Roxanne can only pull the sheet up tight around her and say to Frederick that he is more than welcome.

When Roxanne turns fifty that summer, the people of Morocco give her a surprise party. They rent the town hall on a Friday night and Mrs. Weed, Roxanne's last appointment of the day, lures her there with a story of a pot-luck dinner. Roxanne has taken to attending such gatherings, finding them practical for a person of her situation. No one hides or jumps out at her, but Roxanne has truly never been more surprised. The hall is decorated with streamers and a big sign on a sheet reading, "HAPPY BIRTHDAY ROXANNE. HAIR'S TO YOU!" A band plays old-folk music and Roxanne dances on the parquet floor with every man in town, but not one jealous wife's eye upon her. Frederick's mother, soon to be a customer of Roxanne's, introduces herself. She has just had a letter from Frederick, with news of an aced exam and a pharmaceutical girl-friend.

"He said he'd enclosed a photo of her," she says. "But I couldn't find it. Frederick wanted me to be sure and give you his best."

Roxanne searches her eyes for suspicion or disgust but finds only Frederick's cool kindness. "Frederick's a good boy," she tells his mother. "Really, one of a kind."

Dinner is roast beef, rarish, corn on the cob, a bean casserole and a jello mold, not so much for the eating as the looking, with miniature imbedded marshmallows that spell out Roxanne's name. Mr. Doug, with skin so grazed by sun and sea it's almost purple, sits at the head of the banquet table and tries to think up a toast while Edna Creel, the postmistress, brings out a huge Betty Crocker cake, made in the shape of a skyscraper. Mr. Doug remembers the feel of Roxanne's hands on his back and the sweet smell to her wispy hair from one night the autumn before. All of his calls have gone politely unanswered since then. When it comes time to speak, he can only say wistfully, raising his glass of champagne. "Here's to you, Roxanne. Here's to fifty more."

On this starless night, near midnight, Roxanne is the only sober one to leave the hall, and not because she hasn't been drinking. She feels light headed and ageless, both touched and justified. In her hands, she carries a party hat, some cake wrapped in a napkin, and a gold locket with a scrolling *R*, her gift from the townspeople. Roxanne thanks the friends who mill about her outside on the grass. Declining all offers of a ride, wanting to stretch her legs and the good feeling of the night, she starts to walk home.

It's a soft night and the air is thick with the smells of road dust and bay leaves. From time to time as Roxanne walks on the unlit road, she senses something following her. But each time she turns around, there is only her disappearing shadow and the swallowed curve of the road. She is spooked in a way that she has never been before, even in the city, where she was mugged once, shaken and bruised and taken for a few dollars. She screamed till she was hoarse at those punks, sent them running at least. At home she treated her scrapes with iodine and set her bruised self to soak in a hot epsom salt bath. Here, with no danger to touch, and no one to hear her cry, she can only breathe deeply and push the wind behind her. Roxanne breaks into as much of a run as she can remember from the old days of roaming the streets of Brooklyn as a child, thinking with anguish that if she can no longer run, she's lost everything. A bird's hoot makes her stumble and she skins her knees. Sweat covers her temples and her palms, as she pushes her aching legs on to Main Street. There, she falls back breathless into a walk on the familiar, cracked sidewalk, smoothing her hair and her checkered work apron, which she never bothered to take off during the party. Finishing off the cake in the napkin, Roxanne ambles up past the shops to the Empire Beauty Salon, the flashing red light on the sign her beacon. She peers with satisfaction into her dark, spotless parlor, then cuts down the side path, stopping abruptly before she reaches her stairs. Sitting on the bottom step, in the loose crouch of a city stoop sitter, is Mr. Hurlehee, of Yonkers, and more recently of the Jersey Shore. He tips off his Yankees cap to her and they laugh together as they used to, for he has grown completely bald.

"So why did you come?" Roxanne asks, clutching her party hat and crumpled napkin in one hand and the gold locket in another.

"Dry cleaning's not for me," Mr. Hurlehee says. "It's too . . . well, it's just too. . . ."

"Clean?" Roxanne says.

He laughs. "I thought you might understand," he says.

"Well," she says, sitting down beside him on the step. "Maybe it's not such a bad thing."

They look out over the harbor, watching the lobster boats bob gently in the blue-grey night.

"I've just come from the city," he says. "They tore down your beauty parlor," he says.

Roxanne nods. It would pain her more if they'd left it tomb-like, untouched, or if someone else had come in and tried to make it another kind of place. She pictures the bulldozers crushing the shells and levelling the palms. "What else could they do?" she says.

"Pretty place you found here," Mr. Hurlehee says, pulling up weeds from the ground in a hunch. "But it's no more Fiji than the Jersey Shore, is it?"

"It's the same water," Roxanne says, rising to her feet in some small, unexplained anger. "It's all part of the part of the earth that's not the land."

Mr. Hurlehee's knees crack as he rises to soothe her. "It's nice," he says. "It's really nice, Roxanne."

"You must be tired," Roxanne says. "Come on up. I'll make you coffee."

Mr. Hurlehee hasn't brought a suitcase or a warm coat, Roxanne notices. Fletcher's Upstreet has a good man's jacket on sale. As they climb the steps, the locket falls from Roxanne's hand. She stops and stoops to peer through the cracks in the stairs to the ground below. The champagne catches up with her as she bends over and lights dazzle the sides of her eyes. Blinking, she tries to clear away its fog. Mr. Hurlehee waits for her at the top of the stairs.

"What is it, Roxanne?" He speaks with a soft frog in his throat, as he used to after he'd settled his big feet on the silver footrest at the Oceana. "Have you lost your key?"

The glitter of the locket on the ground catches Roxanne's eye and she starts back down the stairs to fetch it, as relieved as if she'd come upon some of the dignity she lost with Frederick on that cold winter night, or a bittersweet memory of Frank, or one shell she wishes she had kept from the old salon, with a curved mother-of-pearl lining, soft as a baby's skin. Having retrieved her gift, Roxanne has only one task left for what is left of the night—to convince Mr. Hurlehee that the sea is the sea is forever the sea. Holding the locket in her hand, she looks up past Mr. Hurlehee to the black sky, where one faint star has been let loose to wander. The harbor lies like glass. The town is empty and only the street lights hum. Even the gulls have given up the ghost. Roxanne is startled by the shrillness of a voice meant to be soft. "We don't use keys, Mr. Hurlehee," she hears herself say, "here in Morocco, Maine."

THE GUMBALL MAN

February has a way of pushing people to their limits, and I
don't remember a worse one than this—the cold so bitter, the ground so cracked and dry, the grey sky so grey.
My Volkswagen starts, but just barely. Molly sits in the back in
her car seat, singing a made-up song. The heat is no better than
a joke, for the hole at my feet is now the size of a melon. We
drive down Mass. Ave. to Molly's school in Porter Square. We
call it school, although it is really only Alice's house, because at
almost four years old, Molly has her own ideas about what to
call what.

"It's six-count-'em-six degrees in Downtown Boston," says
the weatherman on the car radio. "And tonight it may creep
down to zero." This will make for good, week-long conversation, more if you throw in the wind chill factor. "Why, on the
top of Mount Washington this morning. . . ." I turn off the
radio, in no mood for obscenities.

I get Molly out of the car and prop her, stiff with the trap-
pings of winter, on Alice's porch while I ring the bell. We blow
kisses backwards into our mittens and then say that we love
each other, as if we may never have the chance again. When
Alice comes to the door, Molly says, "Go home now, Sylvia."

I turn away obediently, and get back into the car. Every day
that I leave her here, heading up Alice's stairs, I fear that I will
never see her again—that the shingled house will swallow her,
that she will fall off of the jungle gym in the back yard, or that
Derek will come back to steal her, taking her into the black
hole that holds captive the children on the waxy sides of milk
cartons.

But Alice has children of her own and eyes in the back of her
head. And Derek has neither the heart nor the cunning of a
kidnapper. I am full of new, unfounded fears, because I am pregnant again, with another man, in another world, after such a
long time. And though this, unlike Molly, is a "wanted" baby,
one who won't have to settle for slipshod parenting, or sleep on
a mattress on the floor of her grandmother's house, or wear

goodwill clothes with stains under the chin, I don't know if any of us—Molly, Abbott, or I—is ready yet for this intruder.

After dropping Molly off, I head for the xerox store at the end of Upland Road, across from the T station, to make a few copies of my latest short story, "Trapeze Tangle." It's about a doomed love affair between two circus performers—a bareback rider and a trapeze artist, who find out from the lion tamer at a bad and breathless moment that he is both of their fathers. At the end, I threw in a crime of passion, feeling that someone had to die, but not sure who, first having the trapeze artist stab the lion tamer, then having the bareback rider poison the trapeze artist, finally letting the lions out of their cage to maul their master.

I can see nothing these days but a great, empty space between good and evil. Like Molly, who stops people in the supermarket with a scowl, hands poised on hips like a cowboy waiting to draw, demanding, "Are you a good guy or a bad guy?" I need to know. In the end, it had to be the lion tamer who died, the one who with callousness and cruelty, by the reckless handling of his own life, ruined so many others.

Four months yet to go, although I am huge already as if with twins. Molly was a still and tiny baby in the womb. This one grows big brazenly and with constant motion. "Trapeze Tangle" has been in the works now for almost as long as the baby has, until yesterday when I called it done and typed feverishly into the night so that I could freeze it in xerox black and white for a while, until I can't stand it any longer and get out my red pen once again. The story is out of control—crazy, sentimental, literal, uncouth—wilder than I have ever dared to be. I can only hope that it is so bad or so different or so desperate, that because of the strange way I'm feeling these days, full of tearful contradiction, some unlikely gemlike quality has crept into it, and somebody will decree it a masterpiece of something.

Ralph comes over to wait on me from his post at one of the xerox machines. Today I wish it were anyone but Ralph. Because Ralph adores me in some way, paints me an angel resting in some lofty palm of God where I have never lain, and the high altitude of this perch leaves me breathless.

"Morning, Mrs. A," Ralph says. He is maybe 19, still filled with enough hope to be doggedly cheerful. His blue eyes cross slightly beneath light-framed glasses. Lanky, pale-skinned and lathered with freckles, he keeps his reddish hair short. "Cold enough for you?"

"Plenty," I say. This business about pregnant women never getting cold is a myth.

"The latest Abbott opus?" Ralph tugs the manuscript out of my hand. It doesn't deserve his gentleness or his reverent gaze as he scans the first page. If only the title weren't so silly. A simple "Circus Day" would have done just fine. I nod, barely.

"And I've got some other stuff, too, Ralph." I hand him an untidy pile of papers. "A parking ticket I don't aim to pay—I wasn't anywhere near that bus stop, a poem Molly and I wrote, about—" I pull out one of my scribbles.

> "Little girls who don't wear shoes
> Will their toes quickly lose."

Ralph laughs. "Some other stuff, too, Ralph. Letters, bills, the usual Abbott mess. One of each please."

"Mind if I make a copy of the story for myself?" Ralph asks.

"Sure," I say. "I'm flattered. But don't expect too much from this one, Ralph. The baby . . . seems to be steering me in different directions, making me a little . . . crazy."

"Oh, yeah. The baby." Ralph's face falls a little. "How are you feeling?"

"Bigger than life size," I say, "but not too bad."

"Just don't have the baby here, OK?" Ralph says. A lot of people think this is a funny joke. It is no reflection on Ralph.

Ralph goes back to work, starting to read my story as he walks. I unbutton my coat and lean against the counter. I could wait happily here all day. It's a large airy place, the best of its kind, with clean floors and shelves of neat piles, the mingling smells of ink and paper, the whirring of well-oiled machines. I don't want to go back out into the cold, or into the car where my belly must do battle with a rusty seatbelt and the trickle of heat only teases, or home to our empty house, where there is no

Molly or Abbott and now no circus tent. Even Abbott's surly cat is gone, banished to a home in the country for fear it might claw the new baby.

The woman standing beside me at the xerox counter lives still in a girl's body, so painfully thin, one bowl of soup must fill the column of her corpus to the brim. Her black hair is coiled tightly in a bun at the nape of her long neck; one leg crosses the other gracefully at the knee. The antithesis of me at this bulky moment, she is like some fragile old bird, who once, long ago, in a flight of confusion, landed on the wrong side of the equator. Peering over her shoulder, I see a flyer for a dance performance by the Atlantic Ballet. It must be a new company; I used to keep up with such things. Maybe after the baby is born, I'll go to watch this bird dance with her flock. I'll take Molly, who, ever since seeing *The Nutcracker* this year, thuds around on tiptoes being what she calls a baskerina.

The sort-of elegant man on my other side has one wandering eye and long, veiny hands, with nervous fingers that shoo flecks from a stack of papers, still fluttering from their journey through the xerox machine.

"Could you make it a bit darker?" he asks Ralph. "This 'best of luck' line is a little spotty. "I watch his bony finger brush over the logo of a small literary magazine to which I've often sent my work. "Dear Contributor," I can just make out the letters over his shoulder. "It is with regret. . . ."

"The new rejection letter?" I ask him. Maybe this man will ask me what I do and one thing will lead to another. "I discovered her in a xerox store in Porter Square," he will someday tell the tale. "Belly out to here, and wearing red cowboy boots."

But the roving eye only pours out annoyance until a kinder light dawns. "Oh," he says. "You must be a writer."

"Yes," I confess. "I've papered the walls with such letters."

"Our submissions have doubled this past year," he says, as if to apologize for all those times that he thought too little of my work. Ralph brings back the darkened papers. "Yes, thank you," the man says. "That's much clearer."

As I bend to rub the soft, aching space behind my knee, a

man comes into the shop, carrying a large cardboard box marked in big black letters, JUMBO. Wearing a Red Sox cap, he is short and stocky, of unguessable age, with hands like my husband Abbott's, square and soft. He heads over to the corner, where, for the first time, I notice a gumball machine.

"Here to fill up the machine," he calls out.

"How 'ya doing, Ed?" Ralph calls back.

"Not bad," Ed says. "Considering it's cold as bejeezus out there."

The man lifts the lid of the machine off easily. I guess if I wanted to be a gumball thief, no one could stop me. Recently, I bought smoke detectors for the closets and bolt locks for all the doors in our house. God, I feel huge and helpless and scared about things these days—the new baby and Molly's nightmares and driving around rotaries and looking for the murderer in my circus. To make matters worse, my stalwart Abbott is having some kind of crisis, too. He is buried in his work and distant with me, "getting ready," he calls it, for what I'm not sure. Still, he finds time for Molly. They get along famously. She's been easy for him; she's not his. Abbott is 40, ten years older than me, "too old for this business of babies," he scoffs, "shitty diapers and sleepless nights." But it is Abbott who has readied the baby's room—refurbishing an old bureau, painting the floor a speckled grey, and picking out the bumper pads for the crib.

"What color do you want to paint the walls?" he asked me a few weeks ago, never waiting for my answer. "Light blue? No, there's that thing about pink and blue. A pale green, maybe. No, that's the color they paint the inside of schools. A nice, unbiased ivory, I think. You'd like that, wouldn't you, Sylvia?"

"That would be lovely, Abbott," I answered from the doorway, grateful that these things were getting done. I cannot even step into this empty, echoing room yet, without feeling that I am somehow betraying Molly and me—our past, our beginnings.

Molly was so still in the womb, I used to worry about her. My morning sickness left me at about the same time that her father did, one hot week in summer. I patched things up with my mother, whose only real quarrel with me had ever been Derek. "Useless," she called him, with the kind of venomous spittle she used to describe child molesters and spies. "You can say I-told-you-so all you want," I promised her, "if you'll take me and the baby in for a while." She took Lamaze classes with me and told me so plenty, then came to the hospital to help get Molly born. During those first months, she took care of Molly while I worked part-time at the Peabody Museum gift shop, selling fossils and plastic mummies and postcards that did no justice to the glass flowers. In the afternoons, I piled Molly into the backpack and we sold encyclopediae and seed packets door to door. After a year, I'd saved enough to take a class at Harvard Night School. I wrote a few stories and fell in love with my professor. Abbott does not like my description. "I do not profess," he grumbles. "I just try to teach. And we did not *fall* in love, Sylvia. There was no loss of altitude, as I recall."

"How would you put it, then?" I once asked him. "You came to my attention," he said, with a flicker of his mouth that he lets pass for a smile. "And then I brought myself to yours."

Whatever. I was so glad to be admired and courted by this sturdy, mustached man, so relieved to see the glower leave my mother's eyes when Abbott came for dinner, to let her know that he was the opposite of useless, so glad to see Molly's eyes light up when Abbott rapped "Twinkle, Twinkle" on the door, so glad to see the tiredness and uncertainty leave my eyes.

"It makes no sense for you to be alone this way." Abbott wasted no time in wooing us. "Raising Molly alone, struggling so." It was his way of saying that he loved me, by making sense of my non-sense.

"No," I agreed. "I guess it doesn't." It was an odd proposal, made over coffee at the Cafe Pamplona, very Abbott-like. I married him with gratitude and odd, burgeoning love. Molly wore a blue sailor dress of mine from childhood, one I'd worn to my Uncle Bill's wedding in Seattle, just before my father died. Abbott wore his usual tweeds, put to shame by some new Italian shoes. My mother dressed like a bride, a vision of lace and flowers, and I dressed like a mother, in a color I can't even remember, something practical, though. Molly threw rice at us on the steps of City Hall and led us, skipping, back to Abbott's house on Fulton Street, where we have now lived for two years—as one patched-together family.

Once the lid of the gumball machine is off, the man opens his box on the counter and takes a small trowel wrapped in plastic from his coat pocket. He eases it out of its sheath and takes it by the black handle with the firm, caring grip of a gardener. By now everyone is watching him—the ballerina, the magazine editor, and a fat man with many complaints. The box of gumballs, finally revealed, is more beautiful than anything I have ever seen. I move closer to get a better look, thinking how Molly would love it—this shiny, tumbling world of sweetness and color.

"I want this many," she'd hold up ten wriggling fingers, never enough to express that overflowing next-to-infinity amount that intrigues small children and scientists alike. "One for now, one for all the kids at Alice's, the rest for after dinner."

"Just one, honey," I would try to reason with her. "Sugar makes holes in your teeth."

"I'm getting all new teeth soon, Sylvia," she told me the last time we came to blows about candy. "The tooth fairy is going to bring me lots of money."

Damn. I've been meaning to talk to her about that tooth fairy thing. I don't begrudge Molly her magic or a few quarters. But I just don't like the fairy part.

The man shovels the gumballs carefully into the machine, smoothing each trowelful with one square hand. I once tried to win a stuffed Easter bunny for Molly at the Star Market, pink and purple and bigger than her, by guessing the number of jellybeans in a jar. But 638 was much too far away from 352, and she cried and cried before she could forgive me. How could I know such a thing? I have no feeling for numbers and amounts. Is it two cups of water per one cup of rice? Or the other way around? Is a football field fifty feet long, or fifty yards? Is four a good number of people to have in a family? The machine probably holds no more than a hundred or so gumballs, though it seems like the man adds them endlessly, smoothing and layering, smoothing and layering, until every square inch of the see-through case is filled and he puts the lid back on.

"What will you do with your baby brother?" Abbott keeps asking Molly, prodding her for ideas. I find it too large and unfair a question, however innocently asked. How can one know what to do with a brother, before that brother is even born? My mother had a Down's Syndrome baby once, before me, my brother, William, who only lived for two and a half days. Because of this, I have had amniocentesis—a test in which a long needle is inserted into the womb and fluid extracted—fluid that tells many of the body's secrets, good and bad. And though all of our news was good, I don't like knowing so much about this baby, that he is a boy and to be called Peter, that he is well-formed and sure to be big like Abbott.

Abbott couldn't hide his joy. "A boy," he beamed when we found out. "I never thought I'd have anything close. . . ."

"Not even a pet monkey or a goldfish?" I tried to turn the melting moment into a cold joke.

"No, really," Abbott said. "I always thought I'd just dry up into a stodgy old coot who shooed children from his front lawn." This was as close to mushy as I'd ever seen Abbott get, and it scared me into feeling mean. "But a little boy," he went on. "A son. Thank you, Sylvia. Thank you."

The meanness filled me and splashed out onto Abbott, though I knew it was a well of happiness and not chauvinism, from which his words had spilled. "It's your sperm that determines the sex," I said. "Thank yourself."

"I meant thank you for the baby, Sylvia," Already, Abbott knows me well. "Not for a son."

"I know," I said, giving him a clumsy hug. "I'm sorry." Abbott put his arms around me and whispered into my ear, trying his hand at a bad joke. "It's been two years now, Sylvia," he said. "I don't mind if you call me by my first name."

"I'm sorry," was all I could say once more. For just as Molly cannot call me Mom right now, nor can I call Abbott—Henry.

We made love that night for the first time in months, the lumbering love that I imagine elephants must make, love that gave neither of us much physical pleasure, but made us both feel better, a difficult task done.

"What's wrong?" Abbott asked afterwards, as we lay side by side, my belly rising upward and a trickle of Abbott's boy-making sperm drying on my thigh.

"Nothing," I said. "I mean, I don't know." The fears are not rational, or explicable. I am oddly intimidated by the maleness that swells my body, the occupation of my body by a greedy someone I don't yet know, the sapping of my food and soul and strength. Molly was all mine; this baby I will have to share. Sometimes I think I will just give him outright to Abbott, and call myself the babysitter. I feel an early, useless sadness, too, because Abbott and I are practical, conscientious people, who will not litter the world with more than one child. This baby will be the last, and I worry that he will not be enough, or that he will be too much.

"Why are you crying?" Good Abbott tried one more time. "What is it that's making you sad?"

"Hormones," I told him, turning my face to the wall. What will I do when I no longer have hormones to cover for my confusion?

"So, what will you do with baby Peter?" Abbott asked Molly again last night.

"Well—" Molly is happy always to talk to Abbott, who treats her like a grown-up person the way I can't, because she will always be my baby.

"I will feed him grapes cut in half so that he will not choke, and I will not put bubbles in his bath just in case so he will not drown, and. . . ." Like Abbott, Molly is a careful planner, and disdainful of contractions. "And I will take him to the park and push him on the swing," she said.

"Yes, "Abbott said happily. "We will take him to the park. And play ball."

"Will Sylvia come too?" asked my faithful Molly.

"Yes," I said quickly from my desk, where the lions had just licked their chops. "I will come, too."

Like a coward, I passed in a typed copy of my only published story for Abbott's first class, a morose tale of a pregnant teenager's abortion. It had appeared two years before in some now since defunct magazine in California, when I was heavy with Molly and steeling up for life as a single mother, just in time to justify my life choices.

Abbott asked me to stay after the second class. "This story's quite good," he said, twirling one end of his mustache. "Quite powerful, quite poignant." The way he said poignant, I thought it had to do with my being a woman.

"I'm so glad you liked it," I said, though that wasn't what he'd said at all. "Call me Sylvia, please."

"With a little work, Sylvia, I think someone might publish it."

"Someone already did," I confessed.

"Aha," Abbott said, and asked me out for coffee. Within four nights, I lay in his arms, sweeping the past under his bed and planning the future, knowing that he would never hold any of that past against me—Molly, Derek, or poignancy.

Molly's father, Derek, is a musician, a fine and lazy one, whom I met when I was eighteen. He played the trumpet in a band on the beer-glazed floor of a Cambridge bar where I'd already spent too much of my time. For eight years, he flopped in and out of my life with such irregularity and nonchalance, that my old and tired love for him began to feel like the love I might have felt for a brother. Our sentences became half-finished, our sex like the refrain of an old, scratchy song. And like a brother grown, he flew finally out of my life when I told him about Molly-who-was-to-be, scared about fatherhood and husbandry and rooting, to the Bahamas to play his trumpet on a cruise ship that sailed round and round the islands.

"We're pregnant," was the way I put it to him all those nights ago when we sort of shared an apartment down near the car barns. I wanted to inculpate him, to scare him, to dig into his thick conscience with one sharp word, both because I knew he would not stay and because I wanted to make sure he wouldn't.

"We're what?" Derek had just taken off his shirt, was getting ready for bed.

"Pregnant," I said.

Derek stood there, in the middle of our dark room, naked to the waist, silent for some time. "Shit. Shit. Shit," I heard him sing in a whisper. He came over to me then and took my face in his hands, starting to make love to me as he always did when some trouble brewed between us. "I'd do anything for you, Syl," he said. "But a baby . . . that just can't be."

"It already is," I said, breaking away from his warm body. What had he been thinking about all those times when we weren't careful, when we allowed ourselves to paint sleepy portraits of our imaginary children in the dark—androgynous nymphs with Derek's fine ear and curls, my slim waist and full mouth? His lips found their way to the nape of my neck and he coaxed me into bed as he always could, where, for the first time, there was no kindness in the screw. We tried again and again throughout that sleepless night, neither of us wanting to end on so angry a note, but Derek just grew more soft, as I grew more hard.

"Well, Syl," he mumbled near dawn, "I guess that's all she wrote."

"Yeah," I said, "I guess so." I stroked his hair the way I do Molly's. As always, in the end, it was me who comforted him, rubbing his back until he fell asleep. Then I gathered my clothes and my courage and walked out into the still dawn, taking the best of Derek with me and leaving the worst behind. The only thing that was clear to me, as I rode the empty subway train to my mother's house, was that I wanted Molly, more wholly than I'd ever wanted anything before.

Derek still calls sometimes, from a port or just from nearby Somerville, where he comes back to roost with his friend, Benny. I've been to see him play his trumpet in nearby bars, melted in his music once again and kissed him near the lips without fear. There is no point in trying to hurt Derek. Like the aliens of sci-fi movies, he is unwoundable, his tan flesh growing back instantaneously over even the deepest gashes. He deludes himself, about Molly and me, thinks we still wait for him on a widow's walk while he toots to the sea. It would never occur to him to feel guilty or remorseful in any way, to think that he is a bad father, or a non-father. He writes Molly sloppy letters from a tiny sun-drenched island in the Caribbean, where he helps to run an excursion boat business in the winter. "I'll take you to dinner in May," he writes. "We'll have truffles and chocolate milkshakes." He keeps all of his promises to Molly; they are few and small, and she has great faith in him. "Be good to your mother." He often adds some instruction about my care at the end of his letters. "She likes mint in her tea," or "February is hard on her." All this with never a mention of Abbott, who will straighten Molly's teeth and watch her be a cabbage in the school play, who will count the hairs going grey on my head and help me pick out the shade of my false teeth. Professor Henry Abbott. Our savior of sorts.

Abbott met Derek once, at his request. They shook hands and chatted between sets over a beer, then two, at the Bear Rock Cafe, where Derek was doing a gig, and ended up not hating one another, even though each had vowed he would on my behalf.

"He's OK," Derek said of Abbott in a smoke-filled puff of approval, wiggling his fingers over his trumpet as he got ready to play again, as if he himself had chosen Abbott to succeed him. "Not a half-bad Joe."

And on the way home, Abbott said of Derek, "He's very talented, Sylvia," as if that were reason for forgiveness. "With luck, Molly's inherited his ear."

"I know," I told both of them. I know. They are both right. I have been right. We are all all right. Abbott is a good, good man. And Derek, though he must remain the bad guy in this story, is not detestable. From a safe enough distance, through a smoky haze of sweet sound, he is maddeningly loveable.

Oh, Derek, some days I miss you so. You would like to watch the sweet gumball man with me, would understand why his simple ritual of care warms me on this cold day. We would go for breakfast at Andy's diner and say the hell with the things we were supposed to do before the morning was through. In her spiffy waitress uniform, Edna would take our order and we'd eat soggy eggs and drink bitter coffee with endless thimblefuls of half-and-half. We'd marvel that in 1988, thirteen unlucky years away from 2001, there were still gumball machines and people whose job it was to fill them up. "All this," Derek might recite from a song he once wrote, about living in a world where,

> People no longer stoop for coins
> Of less value than a quarter.
> Greed might bend for the dime,
> But the dime's too small.
> Nickels heavy for the strain,
> Pennies just a pain.

Already, as I wait in the xerox store for Ralph to bring me my papers, I am preparing answers for my family, who will not understand this man's magic, though, while accounting for myself at the dinner table, I will feel compelled to describe it. Abbott will ask me what the hell a gumball machine is doing in a xerox store, and Molly will want to know why I haven't brought her any.

The gumball man comes toward me at that moment, his wide palm filled with colorful balls.

"Take one," he says. "For the baby."

"It'll be a year," I say, "before the baby even has any teeth. But I'll take one for my older daughter. Thank you."

"Have another," he urges, as my hand reaches out to his palm. The echoes of his soft voice send me back twenty-five years, when sugar was a treat and not a sin, when a dime bought ten of these, and when it was safe to talk to strangers. I pluck three gumballs from his hand. Red for Molly. Green for baby Peter. Purple for Abbott, who does not eat candy. He will give his to Molly with the grin of a giver and be kissed for his kindness. I put mine in my mouth; my teeth crunch the sugary globe. The gumball man makes the rounds, offering his candy to the ballerina, to the editor, to Ralph and the complainer. All hands rise to protest, but no one finally declines.

Ralph comes over then with my papers.

"I read the first five pages of your story," he says, handing me the pile. "It's different, more. . . ."

I wave away the thoughts that follow. "What do I owe you,

Ralph?"

"It's almost like a fairy tale," Ralph says, while figuring quickly on a note pad. "Two times 27 plus nine plus tax. . . . Call it $3.50." I get out my wallet as Ralph goes on. "The bareback rider . . . she's the angel with the golden hair, the one whose touch can tame beasts and men alike. But what does she see in that muscle-bound egomaniac?"

"He flies through the air," I try to explain. "He doesn't smell like horses."

"The circus," Ralph shakes his head. I can't read the strangled tone in his voice. "How did you ever come up with the material?"

"I spent time at the Barnum and Bailey in November," I say. "They let me in to see the animals. I talked to a few clowns."

After the last writing class and the fourth night in Abbott's bed, I asked him to talk to me again about my work—honestly, I stressed, though we both knew this was no longer possible.

"Well," he said flatly, "you are a writer."

"What kind of writer?" I asked.

"A good one," he said. "I only ever take good writers to bed."

"Abbott!"

"Ok, ok. Your work is solid, quite lovely at times."

"But?"

"You want me to say something terrible, Sylvia."

"No, just something that doesn't sound like solace for a lost child."

Abbott slapped his big knees. "OK," he said. The answer sprang so quickly to his lips, it took me by surprise. "You create fine worlds in your stories, Sylvia, full of love and humor and real pain, but sometimes they are stagnant, inexitable."

"How do you unstagnate a whole world?" I asked him.

"Be braver," he suggested. "Open Pandora's boxes, leap fences, change faces, make people fly, start wars, chop off people's heads if need be."

"Whose?"

Abbott shrugged. "Those who need them the least, I guess," he said, turning over to go to sleep.

That's when the circus first came to mind.

After this, I read some of Abbott's work, made brave by the sting of his truths. He writes long, sharp-tongued stories about middle-aged men in foreign countries, who leave women on the steps of national monuments, to feed birds or watch iguanas slither up adobe walls. He is embarrassed by these men and is dedicated to trying to be different from them. Abbott's writing is so sharp and smooth, it takes my breath away, makes me wonder why I even bother. All of his work gets published, for a substantial fee. But I cannot like his stories, just as he cannot like mine. Still, we will eat chicken tacos for dinner tonight. Still, we will take Molly sledding at Fresh Pond tomorrow, if it's not too cold, and then come home to patch the hole in the Volkswagen. Still, we will have a son come June.

I asked my mother for a gumball machine once, for Christmas, when I was about eight or nine. I saw one in Irwin's Toy Store, its clear charm ball round and full to the brim, the silver base and coin slot gleaming.

"We'll see," my mother said, in a hopeful way.

I saved my money, readied a shelf in my room, even told a few friends. But I got a chemistry set instead, to study amoebae in drops of pond water. My mother always wanted me to be a scientist or a doctor. But science and medicine only reminded me of the one time she had talked to me about my brother William, about the chromosomes that had gone haywire and collided in such a disastrous way. I could only be sick and wonder endlessly why I had been spared this awful fate. I used the chemistry set a few times, to mix up magic potions that puffed smoke and could make people disappear. Sometime later, my mother gave the set away to Goodwill. She must have forgotten about the gumball machine.

The gumball man opens the money drawer under the machine with a small key. The bottom is strewn with coins—mostly nickels and dimes. There cannot be more than a few dollars in that drawer, not nearly enough money to pay him for his time, for the gas in his car, for his runny nose and the kindness of a morning. He collects the coins and places them carefully into a drawstring bag. Replacing the trowel in its plastic sheath, he adjusts his cap, buttons up his coat, and closes up the cardboard box. Just as I gather my things and button my coat, I feel a blast of cold air at my ankles. A man enters the store, slowly closing the door behind him. He is balding and thin. I would say that he has lived on the street, though not for long. His eyes are bleary, maybe from drink, though he does not tip or shake like a drinker. His clothes are worn and mismatched, but his shoes fit him and they are in better shape than my boots. Something in the way he lingers by the door pulls our eyes his way, tells us that this man comes here for some reason that is not ours, and that he will be the one to shape the next moment. Silence slowly descends as the machines stop whirring, the papers stop shuffling, and voices trickle to a halt. I feel a pain in my stomach; the baby kicks me up near the ribcage. And then the man pulls out a gun.

"Don't anybody move," he says, walking into the heart of the store. "Stay as still as you can." The barrel of his gun comes our way in slow motion, as the world speeds by outside the plate glass window. "You behind the counter," the man says.

"Ralph," Ralph says.

"Empty the register, Ralph. Put all the money in this bag." He hands Ralph a cloth sack. Ralph fills it with bills and the man turns back to us.

"The rest of you take out your valuables and put them on the floor." Obediently, we empty our pockets and slide off our ornaments. I feel a grim satisfaction that I have no jewels to my name, that I am always low on cash, that my watch has said 4:13 for three days now. I rescue a snapshot of Molly and my mother taken in a Woolworth's photo booth and place my wallet and watch down on the tile. The editor bends down with a ring and some loose bills. The fat man, who cannot bend, tosses down a gold money clip, a calculator, and his watch. Suddenly, his loud voice pierces the air.

"You've got a hell of a nerve, mister," he tells the robber. "Robbing innocent people."

"Quiet," the robber says. "Your wallet, please."

"All of a sudden he's Mr. Emily Post," the fat man says. "I hope they give you life, buddy."

"Quiet!" Anger rises in the robber's eyes. With his gun aimed and steady, he moves over to the ballerina, who is frozen in the fifth position. As he comes closer, her hands begin to tremble.

"What about you?" he asks. "Why are you just standing there?"

"I just came from the ballet school across the street," she says, opening her coat to reveal a tiny body sheathed in tights and a leotard. "All I brought was money for the xeroxing." She digs in her pocket, comes out with a five dollar bill in her bony hand.

He grabs the bill, then inches closer to her, his face almost touching hers. "Nothing else?" he says. "You've got nothing else for me?

She shakes her head, thin lips blue with cold. The baby kicks me again, down low this time.

"Leave her alone," I hear myself say, my voice echoing off the walls. "Take what you want and leave all of us alone!"

The robber whirls around, more in disbelief than anger.

"What?" he says, staring at my Gargantuan stomach. "What did you say?"

"I said . . . 'leave us alone'!" My voice is more shaky this time around; still, words do not fail me. They are flung from my throat by some anger that's been roiling inside of me for some time and that now lifts me high above reason or danger. I can't remember what I have to lose, only that it must be protected. I must be gone from here, in time to pick Molly up from Alice's, to make Abbott his dinner, before the baby is born. For some reason, I have been given a chance to change the course of the moment started by the robber, and to squander it would be another kind of crime.

"I have a baby in here who'd like to be born," I tell him. "Before some lunatic like you takes a pot shot at him."

"Some lunatic like me?" The robber comes closer, as near as baby Peter's bulk will allow him. My heart races as I look into his wild, bleary eyes, trying to gauge the depths of his desperation. I remember how my mother once scolded me for making faces at a man out a car window, a man who then pulled his car up beside hers, gave her the finger, and then edged her into the far lane.

"Don't ever do that again, Sylvia," she said. "A nut like that might get out of his car and take a hatchet to you."

"But I'm only a kid," I remember saying.

"Kid, schmid," my mother said. "Crazy people could care less. They see no farther than their craziness."

But this robber is neither blind nor deaf. Something I have said has shaken him, enough so that he will risk a precious moment to answer me, to tell me something that he knows.

"Listen," the robber says. "The kid would be lucky never to come out." He waves his gun in the direction of the street. "It's brutal out there," he says. "A complete mess. I've just come from Dunkin' Donuts, and no one there was smiling, just trying to keep warm around their coffee cups. There's not enough to go around, no money, no food, no heat. Believe me, lady," he says, touching my belly with the tip of his gun. "That baby's better off in there." At the touch of that cold metal, I feel sick and wretched, finally knowing the end of the sick feeling that I always start to have when I think about my brother William, who fell so soon into that great dark hole of waste and lost chances and death. As my legs begin to tremble, I reach deep into my mind for the right thing to say, the thing that will keep me alive.

"Take that thing off me," I say in a hoarse whisper. "Please, take it off me."

The robber lifts the gun slowly, with something like hurt brushing his pained face. "You got it all wrong, lady," he says in a strangled voice. "I'm not a lunatic."

"Then put the gun down," I say. "Put it down before some-body gets hurt."

The robber looks at the gun, turns it over in his palm, then looks out at the street and around at all of us, finally shaking his small head. "No," he says in a dull voice. "I can't do that, now." He bends down, gathers his loot, and stuffs it into the bag. It is only as he's rising to his feet again that he notices the gumball man, who has been standing stone-still by his machine through the whole ordeal, one hand holding his bag of coins, the other resting on his carton.

"Hey, what about you, Candy Man?" the robber says. "What do you have for me?"

The gumball man holds out the change purse, his face untouched by fear. The robber takes it, fingers it, weighs its worth, then looks inside and back at the gumball man with disbelief. For a long time, they stare at one another, in the kind of contest I used to have with Molly when she was a wise, unblinking baby, and always lost.

"This is it?" the robber asks.

"That's it," the gumball man says.

"Keep it," the robber says. "You need it more than I do."

"Nope," the gumball man says, "I don't think so."

But the robber won't take the bag, thrusting it back as if it held the seeds of a curse. We stand waxy statues as he hurries to the door, his sack filled with our pocketfuls, things that for a long time to come will be meaningless. A subway train rumbles by underneath us and rattles the store windows. Speaking loudly to be heard above the noise of the train, the robber turns to us just as he heads out the door.

"That's one thing I won't have on my conscience," he says. "Ripping off the gumball man."

REMARKABLE

My brother Andrew was never more to me than a round face in a baseball cap smiling out of a photograph on our living room wall. It was the last picture ever taken of him; a month later he drowned. The wall was papered with faded flowers, but the roses behind the frame stayed fresh, and I used to think they kept Andrew partly alive. I would stand in front of the photograph and talk to him, ask him the questions no one would answer for me, about what he had been like and why he had died before I had a chance to meet him, what his favorite color was and whether he thought our mother Lydia was crazy like some people said.

We were different somehow, and not just because of Andrew. Neither of my parents worked, though both were forever busy. I was told that we "managed" on stocks left to us by my grandfather, which the family lawyer kept turning into money. My father was an inventor of gadgets that never quite worked, and Lydia was an opera singer who'd once had the voice of a nightingale, until Andrew died and she left the stage. She was the most beautiful mother I knew, but she never drove the carpool or went to PTA, hardly ever left the house at all, living in a silent, far-away world which neither my father nor I could enter.

"Is Lydia mad at us?" I once asked him, when I was no more than seven and Lydia had not come out of her room for two days.

"No," he said. "Your mother's not mad, or crazy. She's just sad."

"Because of Andrew?"

"Yes," he said. "Because of Andrew. She hasn't been the same since he died."

"Was she the same before?" I asked him.

"The same as what?"

"The same as other people," I said.

"No," he said, a look of love darkening his handsome face. "Lydia was never like anyone else I've ever known. She used to be proud of that. Now it just frightens her."

Andrew was six years old when Lydia got pregnant with me, a late in life surprise. My father started to build an addition onto our house by the sea in Kingston, Rhode Island. Lydia set out to knit me a long, shapeless something, which I kept long into my childhood. She sang opera day and night in the sweet soprano that I have never heard, until she drove Andrew and my father crazy, but a good kind of crazy.

And then, when I was no more than a tadpole in the womb, Andrew died. People said that Lydia went over the deep end with him, that she never grieved the way she should have. She left Andrew's room untouched, wandered in and out to fluff his pillows and rearrange his toys. The lawn grew into a jungle; the paint on the house began to peel. The wood frame of the addition grew grey with weather, salt and sadness, before my father tore it down with a sledgehammer one night and left the beams in a heap to rot. The neighbors began to whisper, sent Mrs. Bradwart to tell Lydia that the house was a blister on an otherwise fine hand. And when my father finally did get around to painting it again, Lydia insisted on black.

"Give them something else to talk about," she said. All this I have learned in bits and pieces through the tangled grapevine of our small town.

And so I was born to this bruised and troubled family—a bittersweet bundle of only half-felt joy. I began my life in the darkness and silence of my dead brother's shadow, feeling guilty as pictures of me crept up around his on the rose-covered wall, sorry that I was not pretty and blond, mad that I could not throw a softball far enough or put back together a train. Lydia bought me frilly clothes out of the Talbots Catalog, the kind that made her look elegant and me just plain stupid. I got them dirty, ripped them on purpose if they were just too terrible to wear. And then Lydia would call me a careless, ungrateful child and I'd wish I'd been born Andrew, or at least a boy.

"Andrew was remarkable," Lydia once told me, soon after my eighth birthday. Lovely in a velvet skirt and white blouse, she was dusting the baseball picture, her warm breath fogging the glass. I was helping her, but she went over everything with her rag that I had already wiped with mine. I was used to that, still believing it took two people, one of them my mother, to do anything properly.

"And what am I?" I asked her, hoping to be summed up by an equally good and comforting word. "You, Elizabeth," my mother said, drifting toward the dining room chairs and shaking the dust back into the air, "are more of an enigma." I ran to the dictionary to look up that word, that sounded like a sickness and meant me, and when I found out that it did describe me—a mixed-up puzzle of a kid—I had to believe that Lydia had been right about Andrew too, though I had hoped for so long that he had just been an ordinary boy.

There was a terrible sadness in our dark house by the sea, a terrible silence that roared in my ears when I lay in bed waiting for the waves to lull me to sleep. I used to wonder where they would take me if I slid a raft into the ocean, where they might have taken Andrew if he hadn't been washed up on the shore that day. Morpheus steered clear of our black house. None of us slept very much or very well. My father's ideas kept him awake most of the time. For days and nights at a stretch he would sit at his desk under a bald light bulb making diagrams and twisting wires and monkeying with batteries and wood. When he was finished, he'd call me in and we'd sip champagne and test out whatever it was that he had just invented—The Perfect Grapefruit Peeler, or The Automatic Page Turner. And I was always so impressed and proud of this father who could make things that almost worked.

Lydia wandered around in the dark cleaning things that never got clean, sweeping floors but forgetting to pick up the piles of dirt with the dustpan, rinsing dishes but not bothering to wash them. During the day she wore dark glasses and shooed the sunlight out of the house, shutting doors and blinds and windows obsessively. When my third grade teacher told us to write an essay about our mothers, I wrote, "She cleans and chases out the light," and Mrs. Farwell put circles and question marks around the last part.

Lydia used to cringe at the slightest noise, startled out of far-away places where she traveled in her mind, with Andrew, I was sure. "Hush, Elizabeth, hush," she told me a zillion times. I practiced walking on my toes and mapped out a blind man's maze around our old house, which steered me past all the creaky boards and stairs.

My fourth grade teacher told my father that I was too quiet and withdrawn, that I should be encouraged to crawl out of my shell. Thus began the era of our "expeditions"—to the hardware store to look at tools, or down to the pier to watch the lobster-men bait their traps or over to Odie's Pond to skip rocks. I slowly learned that everywhere except in Lydia's house, you had to be noisy to get by. And the day I came home from school with the penmanship award, I forgot about Lydia's fragile ears and slammed both doors.

"Elizabeth, please!" Lydia said. She was sprinkling Ajax on the stove top, but most of it was falling onto the floor. "How many times do I have to tell you about those doors?"

"Sorry," I said, stepping over a mop in a pail. "I won a prize in school today."

"A prize?" she said. "What kind of prize?"

"I have the best writing in the fifth grade," I told her.

"Isn't that nice," she said, and started to slop water on the floor. "Your brother had beautiful handwriting, too."

"You can't clean a dirty floor with a dirty mop," I told her. "This whole house is a pig sty." Lydia's white face turned even whiter, and my father appeared from out of nowhere like he sometimes did and sent me to my room.

I barricaded the door shut with the bureau, but I needn't have bothered. No one came to get me for dinner. Later, when even Lydia was in bed, I snuck downstairs for a snack. After licking the peanut butter off the knife, I made a scratch in the glass of Andrew's picture frame and taped my penmanship certificate over his face. It hung there for two days. On the third day, I took it down and tore it into pieces.

"Sorry," I told Andrew in tears, trying to rub out the scratch with my finger. "It's not your fault."

It was nobody's fault, I knew—the sad mess of our lives. No

one had been to blame for Andrew's death, least of all the unborn me. But I couldn't help thinking that my brother was the high price paid for my life, and that nobody thought much of the trade.

But time slowly righted our tilted house. Every year that I grew older and stronger, Andrew grew further away. Soon after I made the scratch, his picture disappeared from the wall and my father put up a mirror in its place. I still stood often in the same spot as I grew older, studying my changing face and body. I was not beautiful or delicate like Lydia, but I was pretty in my own way—round and dark and mysterious, a boy once told me. My father sold his idea for The Musical Toothbrush: "Your child won't ever forget to brush again," the advertisement read. Lydia started pansy boxes out on the porch and I asked my father if we would always have to live in a black house. He said he didn't see why and we painted it white together. But the white paint didn't cover the black very well and when it chipped, you could see dark spots underneath. Some things would never change, could never change: Lydia's fear of the world; my father's hopeless love for her and his knack for failure; my painful shyness. By the time I left home, I thought I had done all my growing, all my changing. I went to college, found an apartment, chose a career, considering all of these milestones to be end notes instead of beginning trills. I was lonely, but I had always been lonely. Taking care of sick people was important work, good work. I was grateful that being Elizabeth was so much easier than it had used to be. Had not my early years seemed so long, had I not felt so old and irrevocable at the age of 21 when I entered nursing school, it might not have taken me so long to believe that there might be someone out there in the world— some man, some child, to whom I might one day be remarkable.

Four years later, I was working the night shift in a Providence hospital. I went to Danny's Deli every day at dawn, for a grilled cheese sandwich and a glass of milk. I loved that time when I met the sleepy world in passing as it woke and I went home to bed. One day I noticed a man sitting on the stool next to mine.

He was drawing on a napkin.

"Are you an artist?" I asked him, peering over his shoulder. I didn't often talk to strangers, didn't often talk to men. But I was my boldest at that in-between time, knowing that nothing would come of it, because the lives of passing strangers never really met.

The man looked up at me, startled. "I wanted to be," he said. "But my parents thought art was frivolous." He had the same kind of neglected elegance that Lydia had, fine features and fair hair. And there was another familiar look about him, one of sadness. I saw it in his light eyes and cast mine downwards, noticing that the hem of his pants had come unsewn. He started to draw again and I watched his slender fingers dance back and forth, making bleeding streaks on the paper napkin. He finished and held the drawing out to me.

"Keep it," he said, "if you really like it."

I looked at the sketch, a good likeness of the short order cook behind the counter. "Thank you," I said. "I do like it."

He got up to pay his check, and I felt an unfamilar ache of longing, an overwhelming desire to stop him from leaving. If I'd been anyone else, I would have said something sensible, like, "So what do you do?", but being Elizabeth, I said the first crazy thing that came to mind, mortified to find that I'd offered to sew up the hem of his pants. I'd brought a needle and thread to work the night before to mend my uniform on the bus.

The man looked up at me curiously and then down at his pant leg. I started to tell him that I had only been joking, but he had already slung his leg up onto a stool.

"Please do," he said, still looking puzzled. "Tell me. Do you often sew up the pants of strangers?"

"No," I said, knowing as I took out my needle and thread that what happened next was out of my control and feeling strangely calm. "I never do."

The grill man brought over my sandwich and shook his head. I sat there on the stool and sewed up the blond man's pants, brushing the bone and the hair of his ankle from time to time. The warmth of his leg shot up to my neck and into my cheeks. I pricked him with the needle, fumbled my apologies.

"That's OK," he said, and rubbed the drop of blood away. "Would you marry me?" he asked, then added as an afterthought, "My name is Michael Woods."

I laughed but he didn't laugh back, and I just kept on sewing, too scared even to breathe, to blow away whatever it was in the air that was keeping me and the blond man together. Because by the time I had tied the knot and broken off the thread with my teeth, I had decided that if, for some crazy reason, he had meant it, I would marry him.

We had a small wedding that summer at City Hall. Michael had no family to speak of, just uncles and cousins who didn't know him from Adam, he said. Lydia came out of the house-for the occasion, lovely and ageless in pale blue silk, blinking and baring the whitest skin in Kingston. My father wore his only suit—a double-breasted pinstripe from another era but still like new—and a red carnation in his lapel. We slipped into the judge's chambers and I turned instantly from a child into a wife. Five minutes later, when we parted on the sidewalk, my father kissed my cheek and slipped an envelope into my hand.

"From your mother and me," he said. "And The Musical Toothbrush."

Neither Michael nor I liked Rhode Island very well, but neither of us had the courage to move somewhere we might like better. We used our wedding money as a down payment on a small house just outside of the city. Michael ran an accounting office downtown and I kept on with my work at the hospital. I did everything I could to make our house warm and light and airy, the kind of house I had dreamed of as a child. I tried to fashion our rooms after pictures in magazines and store window displays, but I had no knack for comfort or coziness. More Lydia's daughter than I knew, I could not live without spareness and disorder, and so I created both. And Michael was a gentle but brooding man, not satisfied with himself or his work, one who marched methodically on the black squares of the checkerboard, but who would have liked to dance off on the red. Though a different house, it was a familiar home.

"Are you happy, Lizzy?" my father asked me a year later over one of the lunches we tried to arrange from time to time. I mashed my baked potato with my fork, found no answer right away, for him or for me.

"Michael's a wonderful man," I told him. "He reminds me of you."

"But are you happy?" he asked. He was bright-eyed, I noticed, breathless.

"What is it, Dad?" I asked him. "What are you about to tell me?"

"Lydia and I are moving to California," he said.

"You're kidding," I said. My fork clattered onto my plate. "How did you ever convince her to leave?"

"She's suddenly taken it into her head that she'll last longer in the sun. I want to go soon, Lizzy. She may change her mind. I've got a great idea for a Sand-proof Beach Towel."

I was touched that he wanted my blessing, sad to know that I was going to lose him.

"I hate to leave you," he said.

"Go to California and make The Sand-proof Beach Towel," I told him and leaned over to kiss him. "I'm happy."

If we'd had that conversation two years later, I could have said it with more conviction. Because when Michael and I had a son, I didn't think any one person had ever been happier. The baby arrived five weeks early and without a fuss. The doctors examined him worriedly, so tiny and flushed with yellow. But there was nothing wrong with Andrew; he was just impatient to get on with his life.

My parents came back East to see the baby, who was still dark and wrinkled and sleepy—pretty only to me. I put my son into my father's arms. He held him awkwardly, studied him painfully, finally smiled.

"Sturdy little fellow," he said, opening and closing his arm at the elbow. "Good pitching arm."

Lydia's arms stayed folded tight against her chest. She touched the baby's clenched fist fearfully, as a child reaches out to pat a strange dog. "What an odd little prune," she said. "I'd forgotten." We ate hospital food around the bed—tired sandwiches and soft, warm fruit. Andrew slept in his crib and cried out from time to time. We talked of each other's weather and houses and how it was always good to get home. None of us called the baby by his name.

It just never took. Though he remained Andrew on his birth certificate, we took to calling our son John, which was his middle name and the name of Michael's father. But as fate would have it and years passed, he grew to look like his uncle in the baseball photograph, the same sunny round face and blond curls. My smiling brother had finally come walking out of the picture frame, come all the way to life as my son. I wanted to tell John about his uncle, thought he should know, but a wind of panic took my breath away each time I tried.

Lydia wrote once and asked for a picture of her grandson. I sent her a letter instead, full of apologies for a broken camera and vague descriptions. I told myself that I was doing it to save her pain, to save us pain, and not to spite her. She didn't ask again and so she never knew how much my son resembled hers. Soon we did nothing more than exchange Christmas cards and occasional phone calls. And we might have gone on forever that way.

* * *

The telegram came one summer day when John was nine. I'd always thought that I'd have bad news about Lydia first, but it was her message and it read: YOUR FATHER HAD STROKE. CAN YOU COME. It was late afternoon and I cried as I started to make dinner. Lost in sad thought, I peeled all of the carrots in the house to the core, two bags full. Michael came home from work, looked at my bleary eyes and the pile of carrot shavings.

"What's going on?" he asked. I handed him the telegram.

"Oh, Lizbeth, Lizbeth," he said, taking me in his arms as if to dance. "I'm so sorry. Go as soon as you like. Take John. I can manage for a while on my own."

"I can't just up and leave," I told him. "What about work? What about the garden?"

"The garden!" he said. "These are your parents, your father. You mean you actually might not go?"

"Of course I'm going," I said softly. "It just isn't easy." I couldn't explain to him about Lydia and me and my father and Andrew, how we were different and how I was scared.

I went to the travel agency in town, feeling all over again like Lydia's daughter, a straggler left behind from the last century, with my long straggly hair and one of my father's old sweaters and my tie-up shoes. The young travel agent had a streak of green hair and wore a black dress, tight and carefully ripped on one shoulder.

"I like your outfit," she told me, as she wrote up the tickets.

"You do?" I asked.

"It's wild," she said. Each of her pointed fingernails was painted a different color. "L.A.'s wild too. I've been there three times. You going on vacation?"

"What?" I looked at her, confused. "Oh, no, not really." I wondered if she could tell that taking a vacation was something I didn't know how to do. "My father," I explained. "He's ill."

"Oh, the family factor," she said.

"Yes," I said. "The family factor."

Lydia met us at the airport. In nine years, I'd aged more than she had. She stood small and pale in a crowd of bouncing, tan people, wearing dark glasses on her forehead and a shawl around her shoulders. John ran ahead down the ramp. I saw the shock on Lydia's face when she saw him, and felt a prick of guilty happiness, washed by shame.

"My God," I read her lips, which still trembled as I reached her side. She stared at John as we all fumbled hello. Then she smoothed her dress and pretended he was like any other boy.

"You've grown," she said.

"Maybe you got smaller," he said.

"John!" I said sharply, mad that he had shown Lydia his wise-guy colors before any others.

But she only laughed and the tinny sound rang strangely in my ears.

"You're right," she said. "I'm shrinking in this sun."

Lydia drove us home in a white convertible. Two gleaming headlights and fins gave it the look of a hulking shark.

"I didn't know you knew how to drive," I said, sliding onto the seat.

"I've had to learn," she said. "This was your father's idea of heaven, driving around in this car."

She adjusted the rear view mirror, her head barely reaching above the leather-covered steering wheel. She revved up the engine and I laughed.

"What's so funny, Elizabeth?" she asked.

"The car," I said. "It's wild."

We drove down Ocean Boulevard and I looked out at the clean, uncracked sidewalks and the spying palms. I saw why my father had believed that California might save him, felt a sadness because he had come too late. But I was happy to be in this blessed spot, where everyone except Lydia seemed to be having fun, where movie stars cavorted and splunched their hands in cement, where even the most ordinary people drank sweet drinks from coconuts and lived inside glistening brown skins—people so different from me. It was a miracle that I had ever sprouted John. He was the kind of boy everyone calls a good kid at first glance—happy-go-lucky, all of a piece. California was filled with them, I saw—white-haired urchins with brown skins and popsicle stains around their mouths. I turned around to watch him. He was bouncing back and forth in his seat, whispering "wow," his angel hair blowing in the wind.

Lydia began to talk about my father. "I think he wants to die," she said. "Two months now he's been home from the hospital and he won't eat or drink."

"Two months?" I whipped back around to face Lydia. "Why did you wait so long to tell me?"

"I didn't want to burden you," she said.

"You should have told me, Lydia," I told her. "He's my father and I would have wanted to know."

"I thought I could manage alone," she went on. "But it seems

I can't." She blurted out her zigzag thoughts, tripping over the words as if she hadn't spoken to another human being for years. "Just like that it happened. He was just sitting in his chair, reading. But the way he looks at me, you'd think it was me who had reached in and stopped his heart. He's so changed."

"Bad hearts never give much warning," I told her, but her next words drowned out most of mine. The odd feeling came over me again. This wasn't the Lydia I knew, this Lydia who drove a convertible and talked incessantly. "It's so much work taking care of a sick person," she went on. "Cooking, cleaning, bathing, shopping. He needs a nurse is what he needs."

"I am a nurse," I told her. She turned to look at me curiously. The white shark swerved toward the sidewalk.

"I'd forgotten," she said, and patted the silver bun of her hair.

We turned onto a quiet street lined with bougainvillaea and pulled up in front of a small stucco house.

"It's pink!" John whispered to me with disgust, as we followed Lydia inside.

"That's nothing," I whispered back. "The house I grew up in was black."

"It was?" he asked.

"Didn't I ever tell you that?" I asked him.

"Nope," he said. "You never tell me stuff about when you were a kid."

We set our luggage down in the hall. John ran off to explore. My father sat in a wheelchair away from the window, looking out into space. I went over and kissed his cool, grey cheek.

"I've come to take care of you, Dad," I whispered, my eyes filling with tears to see him so twisted and sallow and furious. "I've brought John with me. Your grandson, John."

John came over and shook the limp, spotted hand.

"Nice to meet you," he said, just the way strangers do, just the way I'd taught him. A sad and wasted introduction. It was too late for a friendship between my father and my son.

In the days that followed, John spent most of his time with Lydia. He liked her because she demanded nothing of him, did not insist on his being a child.

117

"Why don't you go out and play, honey?" I urged him. "We don't get to California too often."

"There's no law says you got to spend all day outdoors," Lydia said. "Stay inside if you like."

"Too much sun gives you cancer," John reported.

"Wrinkles, too," Lydia said and John nodded his head in agreement.

"Yes, I've noticed you've aged quite a bit lately," I told him with a smile.

They understood one another, Lydia and John, without ever having met but that once, when John was a baby. While I took care of my father, they sat inside at a card table playing Crazy Eights, exchanging no more than a handful of words as the hours passed, all of them about rules and points. They went out on expeditions—to buy medicines and rubbing alcohol and cotton, and came back with chocolate sauce on their faces.

Sometimes I caught them at the door as they came in, eyes shining with the secret of some adventure they would not share.

"Did you have a good time?" I'd ask one or the other.

"Just errands," one or the other would say.

I spent most of my time with my father, but there was such pain and bewilderment in his one good eye that I could not often bear to meet it. The stroke had left him partially paralyzed and one side of his face sagged down in folds, like the creases of a dried apricot. I nursed him as I would any other patient. I did not chatter to him the way Lydia did, feeling sure that just as silence had been her choice for all those years in the black house, now it was his in the pink house. I felt an overwhelming love for my sick father, who had taken such good care of me. I mixed him a martini each evening, the way he used to, and held it up to his mouth. He sipped at it with a straw, and though most of it dribbled down his chin, he seemed to enjoy it. I read to him, too, the newspaper, the back of the cereal box, a mystery novel I had brought or one of John's comic books. I sat beside him and held his hand and wiped his brow and the drool from his chin, desperate to perform small acts of love, as I had been when John was small, to change a dirty diaper, to kiss a scrape and make it better.

One evening, I sat in the plaid armchair while my father dozed, listening for the screen door to slam. Lydia and John sauntered in an hour late for dinner without apology. I put the food on the table. They sat down giggling, then became glum.

Lydia always ate like a bird, but it was not like John to play with his food.

"Why aren't you eating, honey?" I asked him. "You love macaroni and cheese."

"Lydia says you shouldn't eat bright-colored foods," he said. "Besides, it's all cold and rubbery." He picked up a pile of orange noodles and goo with his fork and let it fall back onto his plate.

"You've never had a problem with bright-colored food before," I said. "And it was warm an hour ago, when you were supposed to be home."

"We were out shopping," Lydia leapt to John's defense. "We had to get lotion."

"You just bought some the other day," I said. "How much lotion does Dad need?"

"He needs an ocean
Of lotion
To keep in motion," John sang out of tune.

"I take it you're finished," I said. "Go get ready for bed."

"What did I do?" he asked.

"Nothing," I snapped, and put another spoonful of macaroni on my plate.

John stomped off to his room and I looked up at Lydia. "You're spoiling him, you know."

"He's my only grandchild," she said. There was a clearness in her eyes, a ferocity I had never seen there before. "Why shouldn't I?"

"He hasn't been himself since we got here. He's secretive. He's . . . moody. I want him to get out, meet some other kids," I told her.

"He likes me," she said.

"I'm glad you two hit it off so well," I said, "but that crack at dinner wasn't like him."

"That wasn't a crack," she said. "They put dyes in the food,

Elizabeth, poisonous, cancer-causing dyes. And your father *did* need more lotion. I rub him down every night before bed. It's the only thing that makes him feel good anymore."

I ate the last bite of my macaroni and Lydia played with hers. We both had our secrets, she with her backrubs and me with my martinis.

"California's a good place for children," she said suddenly. "Your father tried to tell me that years ago. Have you and Michael ever thought of moving out here?"

"No," I told her. "We're very settled in Rhode Island."

"It would be nice, wouldn't it, to keep the family together?"

"I didn't know the family meant so much to you," I said, before I could stop myself.

"I didn't either," she said. It wasn't an apology, just a new-found fact. She got up from the table and went to check on my father.

I put the dishes in a sinkful of water to soak and went down the hall to make peace with John, to read him a story as I had almost every night since he was old enough to listen.

"What'll it be?" I asked, plunking down on the bed. " 'Wrinkle in Time' or 'Spiderman'?"

"Nothing," John said. He was beautiful in paisley pajamas that he hated. I smoothed the hair off his forehead. He pushed my hand away. "I want to read by myself tonight."

"OK," I said. "Then I'll just say goodnight." I got up off the bed. "I'm sorry I snapped at you at dinner," I told him.

"Why did you?"

"You were being rude," I said.

"It was just a joke," he said.

"Well, your timing was lousy," I told him. "That's part of being a good comedian."

"How come you're acting so weird, Mom?"

"I'm not acting weird."

"Yes, you are. You're always in a bad mood. You're different out here."

"That's funny," I said. "I was just thinking the same thing about you." I sighed, pulled my feet in and out of my slippers.

"It's kind of hard for me to be here, Johnny. A lot has happened between me and Lydia, things that have nothing to do with you. And with your grandfather being so sick. . . ."

"I like Lydia," he said.

"I know you do," I said. "I'm glad."

"She told me about Uncle Andrew," he said. "How come you never did?"

I sat down again on the edge of the bed. "I never knew him, John. He died before I was born."

"You could have at least told me that I had an uncle once," he said.

"Well, technically, you didn't."

"Well, almost," John said.

"Yeah," I said. "I almost had a brother, too."

"How did he die?" John asked, pulling his legs up under him, lotus style.

"He drowned, back in Rhode Island," I said. "I never really knew what happened. Your grandparents didn't like to talk about it."

"Lydia says he had a sprained ankle from baseball practice and got stuck in the undertow."

Stunned, I bit the inside of my cheek. In three weeks, John had learned more about Andrew than I had in thirty-seven years. I sat on the edge of the bed, staring at John's caterpillar eyebrows, listening to my heart race.

"How come you don't call me Andrew?" John asked. "That's my real name."

"We decided you were more of a John."

"Then why did you call me Andrew in the first place?" he asked.

"I wanted to honor your uncle in some way," I told him. "But then I decided that it wasn't fair. I wanted you to have a name that was all your own."

"That's dumb, Mom," John said, but he smiled. "You know how many guys are named John?"

"Lots?" I guessed.

"Tons," he said, and wiped his nose on his sleeve. "What was he like, Uncle Andrew?"

"Lydia says he was remarkable." I told him all I knew.

"What does that mean?" he asked. "I mean, I know what it means, but. . . ."

"Oh, I don't know. Talented, unusual, special in some way."

"Am I remarkable?" I reached over to pull down the leg of his pajamas, grateful for the chance to be friends again. "You're better than remarkable," I said.

"Why?"

"Why? Because you're artistic like your father and musical like Lydia and you're a great putterer like your grandfather and you're handsome like your Uncle Andrew was. And because you're my son."

John smiled again. I thought I was forgiven.

"I want to be called Andrew," he said.

"You can't," I told him.

"Why not?"

"It's too late," I said.

John stood up on the bed and started to jump up and down, chanting, "Andrew Turner! Andrew Turner! That's! My! Name!" and plugging his ears to block out my voice. The door opened slowly and Lydia came a few feet into the room.

"You see?" I gestured to John. "He's having a tantrum. His first."

"He has every right," Lydia said. "You gave him that name. Then you took it away."

Why didn't you ever stick up for me, I wanted to ask her, like you do for my son. Why has your strength and caring come back too late for me?

John jumped off the bed, still chanting "Andrew Turner!" and ran for the door.

"Where are you going?" I yelled.

"To the bathroom!" he shouted back.

Lydia brushed his arm as he reached for the door. "Don't run," she whispered to his deaf ears. "You'll slip on your pajamas."

When he was gone, I turned back to Lydia. "I only named him that for you," I told her.

"For me?" she said. "Whatever for?"

"An apology, I guess."

"An apology?" Lydia looked puzzled. "What do you mean?"

"Or maybe it was a gift," I said. "I was always looking for just the right thing, something that would make you happy."

Lydia slumped down in an armchair by the door, piled high with dirty clothes. "I didn't want to be happy," she said.

"You didn't want anyone to be happy," I told her. "That wasn't fair."

"How could I be fair?" Lydia put her hand to her cheek. "It was all I could do to get you safely born after Andrew died. People thought I was crazy, you know."

"I know," I told her. She looked up at me. "And what did you think?"

"I wasn't sure," I told her. "I was confused. You were my mother, but I thought I was supposed to take care of you."

"Don't be silly," Lydia said. "You were only a child." The old look of vacancy and sadness came over her face. Strands of long grey hair dangled from her bun. "But you didn't ever really need a mother, did you, Elizabeth? You were always so grown-up."

"Not always," I told her, slipping into the whisper of my youth. "Not always, Lydia." I stood still before her, listening for the sounds of water moving in the bathroom. All was quiet except for the ticking of a clock. I was saddened by the years gone by, by our distance and our misunderstandings, touched by Lydia's frazzled hair and the slump of her slight body on the heap of clothes. She closed her eyes and I went out into the hall to look for John.

The bathroom was dark and empty and I ran downstairs. The front door was open wide. As I stood in the doorway, a warm breeze brushed my face. Shadows passed by on the street. Soft Latin music blew over a backyard fence and I smelled meat cooking on a barbecue. Someone walking by said, "hi," and I waved back. I was not afraid for my son; I knew he hadn't gone far. I stepped out in my bare feet onto the night-dewed grass and looked up to find no stars. Cupping my hands to my mouth, and drawing a deep breath, I called out his name with a kind of wild, hopeful abandon, hoping that of all the Andrews who could hear me, the right one would answer.

J*E*W*E*L

I need answers I never get. That's why I'm going to Madame Rose's House of Fortune tonight. Five dollars, that's what she charges. It's not a lot of money, even for me. I've been saving my tips all week. Maxine and I have to do chores around the motel—making beds and emptying wastebaskets and cleaning bathrooms. We leave a note under the ashtray which says, "Please remember your chambermaid." There's a picture of a maid in a uniform and a line to fill in your name. I make the letters fancy—J*E*W*E*L—with stars in between.

My name is Jewel Rose Martin. I'm eleven and I'm a girl. My sister Maxine is fifteen. We live in a trailer park and my Dad runs the Hester Green Motel out front on the highway. Maxine's been to Madame Rose's twice. The first time was a couple of years ago. She stole the money from Mom's purse and got caught, then had to come straight home after school for two weeks straight. Maxine didn't care. She sat down on the trailer steps with some nail polish after Dad got done yelling at her and said it was worth it.

"What's worth it?" I hate to always have to ask Maxine these questions. She's so smug.

"Being in prison is worth it," Maxine said. She put jubilee red on one fingernail, then black on the next. Maxine's brave about her looks. Whatever she does, she knows it's going to look good. And if it won't look good, she doesn't do it.

"What's being in prison worth?" I asked.

"It's worth knowing just what's what and what's going to be."

"You mean like how many children you'll have and if you'll get cancer?" You see how I have to play dumb and kiss up to Maxine.

"Madame Rose . . . isn't a . . . mind reader . . . Jewel." Maxine blew her nails dry in between the words. "She's not God, you know."

"So what does she tell you, stupid Maxine?"

"She tells you what the future could hold, like a catastrophe coming or something going on with your heart or your soul. You

124

gotta read between the lines."

"What'd she tell you, Maxine?"

"No way I'd say. You'd probably ruin my future if I told you."

"Can she tell you who you're going to marry?" I have to believe what everyone tells me, that sooner or later I'm going to like boys.

"Nope." Maxine stood up and put her head between her legs and started shaking her hair back and forth like a whip. I watched the tips of it trailing in the dirt. Maxine washes her hair every day. "She could tell you who you *might* marry, though."

"Big deal," I told that Maxine, and went off to throw rocks into the creek out back of the trailer park. "I can tell myself that."

I was nine then. Fourth grade. A lot happens in two years.

Right now, at peak foliage time and near Halloween, the motel is packed. We make a big to-do, dragging out the papier-mâché witch onto the lawn, putting jack-o'-lanterns in the rooms and wearing costumes while we work. This year we're doing *Alice in Wonderland*. I'm the Mad Hatter, Mom's the Queen of Hearts, Dad's the Cheshire Cat, and Maxine's Alice. People come from all around to see our haunted house, which we set up in a rusty old trailer out back near the woods. We put spaghetti in a bowl for intestines, and peeled grapes for eyeballs, apricots for cut-off ears, raw eggs for guts. After a while, the bees swarm all over the guts and it starts to smell, and we sling the glop over the fence for Dondi, the pig next door. After that, fall gets sad.

I figure Maxine just didn't ask Madame Rose the right questions. I aim to go up there and have her get right to the point. I got the money in my pocket and I have a plan. *Zombies' Revenge* is playing at the drive-in tonight. I'm going to pretend to go and then run into town to Madame Rose's. Around dusk, I switch on the motel sign and go sit out on the trailer steps with Maxine. She's reading an Archie comic and I just sit there and do nothing. I've been scrubbing toilets all afternoon since I got home from school and I'm tired. Mom comes out and glows in the light which is the color of the inside of peaches. She puts her hands on her hips and looks up at Bar Mountain, which is covered with beautiful trees, a big heap of red and orange and yellow. She swats me and Maxine's heads with the dish towel and says supper's ready, cheeseburgers and crinkle-cut french fries, your favorite, Maxine. I like this dinner best too, but Maxine was born first, so it gets to be her favorite. Inside the trailer, Dad says, "wash up, girls," and folds down the table out of the wall. We don't talk much at the table, except to tell Mom how good it is. I eat my fries biggest to smallest; Maxine the other way around. The crickets start up early and the moon sits waiting over by the mountain.

"Can we go to the drive-in tonight?" I wait until Dad tips back in his chair to ask.

"It's the last show of the year," Maxine says.

Mom and Dad give each other a look. "Guess it's all right, if your homework's done," is what they always say, never really asking for an answer, so we don't have to tell no lies. We finish up supper just before showtime. Dad says to Mom let's retire to the sofa and they do. Maxine and I hurry up and clear the table. Being across the highway from the drive-in is one of the best things about living in Winot, New Hampshire. It's pronounced *why-not*, but the French Canadians come down and say *we-know*, and whenever Dad hears that, he mutters, "the-hell-you-do." Our trailer is the biggest and the best one in the trailer park, built into the ground with a skirt all around it to make it look as much like a house as a trailer can, and a flower garden in back, which Mom keeps looking pretty. The Hester Green Motel is out on the edge of Route 7, about fifty yards away. Hester Green was an old dead witch who still gets blamed for things around here—droughts and crimes and hard winters, because of all the spells she cast. Even a whole town can't ever shake all the evil she left lurking behind her. When I get mad at Maxine, I call her Hester. The drawing of Hester Green on the motel sign makes her out ugly, with warts on her face and a big, crooked nose. Maxine has no warts, just a few zits now and then, and her nose isn't big exactly, but it *is* crooked. Still, she's pretty and lots of boys are after her. She's got big breasts, and she's counting on them taking her a long way, but no boy's going to take her any way she's not willing to go, she tells me as we stack up the dishes. She's always yakking to me about boys. Like I could care less.

"What way's that, Maxine?" I ask her. I scrape all the dinner scraps except the meat onto a plate for Dondi. Doesn't seem right to feed a pig part of a cow.

Maxine doesn't even answer me. She's got on a tight shirt and is tucking in her breasts, getting them even.

"Which way might a boy take you, Maxine!" I have to yell to get her to answer and Dad tells me to pipe down.

"Down the road to temptation." She says it low under her breath and wiggles her fingers in front of my face. "Some day a boy will put his hands all over you, Jewel, and he'll want you to do the same thing back to him." She doesn't make it sound so terrible, though.

"No way, Maxine," I say. "Your turn to wash."

Maxine's dips her hands into the soapy water, dainty, like it would melt off her nail polish. I eat the last burnt french fry and slide the cookie sheet into the sink. Then I check the front of me, where there's nothing but flatness, day after day. Two girls in the sixth grade have breasts and the curse, which seem to go hand in hand, but I don't have either. Mom's built like a B-52 bomber, but all the women in Dad's family are flat as boards. Could be my fate. I look at the good sides. I'll always be able to run fast and if nothing *ever* happens, maybe no one will want to marry me and I can go shirtless in the summer forever. Maxine has to wear a halter and her bra straps fall down and make ridges in her shoulders. She plans to be married and pregnant by the time she's eighteen, and she can't run for shit.

What really worries me is Dad, how he might feel about me if I stay this way forever. Right now, I'm eleven and he doesn't expect much. But everyone knows about Mom, how she was the first runner-up in the Miss New Hampshire Pageant in 1963. Dad says she should've won except for what she said when they asked her what was the world's worst problem. She said just one word—unhappiness. Guess it wasn't enough of an answer. Mom just doesn't talk much. It's like living with a statue sometimes. She's smelled like lemon for a long time now, ever since she saw a movie where somebody squeezed lemons all over herself and it made her sexy. Mom doesn't believe she's beautiful. I think if they'd understood all of this about Mom, she could've been Miss America.

Dad sneaks out of the motel about a million times a day, trailing that lemon smell like a hound dog back to the trailer, just to find Mom and touch her. Sometimes she'll push him away with the tips of her fingers and sometimes she'll let him kiss her on the neck. Sometimes she says not in front of the kids and sometimes they go at it like we're not even there. Maxine and Mom sure are built. I'm going to ask Madame Rose what my chances are. Don't seem like any reason to live or die. I just want to know.

Dad keeps telling Mom that we don't have to live here in Winot, that he'll get her out of this podunk town some day, that we'll move across the river, if she likes, to Pomford, where mostly rich and sometimes famous people live. There's a writer whose book is on the best-seller rack in the drugstore. On the back page it says she resides with her three dalmations in the sleepy hamlet of Pomford, New Hampshire. Then there's a man who used to be the governor. He jogs on the side of the road with a walkman and has very skinny legs. Maxine and I used to ride over the bridge on our bikes to Pomford to look for the rich people's houses. But it's been a while since Maxine and I did that kind of thing together. All of the houses in Pomford have to be painted white with Pomford-green trim. It's the law; they even got their own color. One guy raised a stink about his rights once, and he must've won, because that house is still there, purple as all get-out, right on the town green. I'd like to meet that man. I doubt anyone from Pomford ever comes over to see Madame Rose. Over there, they probably figure whatever they don't like about the future they'll be able to change. I figure I'm stuck with my future.

But it doesn't look so bad, my future. I'll help Dad run the motel and take care of Maxine's children until I figure out what else to do. Until then, I don't think we'll ever leave here, seeing how Mom doesn't even want to and how Dad's never done anything else except run the Hester Green. Besides which. . . . This is kind of a joke in our family. Anything with the word witch in it. Besides which . . . I like it here. Some people call where we live God's Drawer, but others get all upset when you mention God and the country in one breath. Right now, it's hard to believe there's anywhere more beautiful on the earth. The colors on the trees make all other colors seem fake. Try holding a red leaf up to a fireball or a yellow one up to Mom's Chevy Camaro. I don't see how I could ever leave here, even though I think about it plenty, traveling up to Canada or west to California or across the oceans to sit in a jungle or walk along the equator or see that statue of the mermaid. I couldn't see not having the seasons, like the movie stars in California who have plastic Christmas trees and never wear boots, or the Eskimos who sleep in snow beds and call it summer when the ice is only one foot deep. How can anything ever really change?

Here in winter, we hole up and play cards and go skating down where the creek floods over the reeds. In the summer, you get flavored ices at the drugstore and suck them dry until you shiver, and the sweat feels good running down your face just before you let go of the tire and hit the water down at the deep part of the creek. But I love the spring best, when the creek cracks open, sounding like someone blasted the sky open with a shotgun. The water rushes down to the flatlands and the ground begins to soften under your feet, just a touch by a touch. The leaves creep, slink and pop, and the fiddleheads start to furl up out of the ground.

Sometime around when school lets out, the men come with brooms and trash bags to clear up the cement lot across the highway at the drive-in theater. They take the padlocks off the concession stand, which is just a pile of concrete blocks, and then a truck comes and unloads candy bars and popcorn and hot dogs and all of the condiments in little plastic containers and a rack of uniforms. Dad says my kids won't ever believe I used to watch movies in a car out under the stars.

Most of all I love it when the screen lights up for the first time, when those movie stars hop up into the sky with the moon and the planets, on a motorcycle or a horse or just walking down a train track whistling.

I've got idols, but they change. I cut out pictures from the teen magazines and plaster them all over my part of the wall in the trailer. Maxine's side is all filled up with a big poster of Marlon Brando on a motorcycle looking as smug as she does. I read how they have a bus tour of the stars' homes. I'd like to go on that, but maybe I'll never be pretty enough to show my face in Hollywood. Mom says pretty is as pretty does, and she should know, I guess. Dad says I can't help it, I'm only eleven and look at Maxine, she's even worse. Maxine doesn't mind when he says something against her. She'll stick out her tongue at me or slip Dad the finger when his back's turned. She's proud of all the things she gets in trouble for. I don't think I'll ever be as pretty as Maxine or Mom, but I got nice eyes and Dad says I'll have more than my share of the pie, long as I watch my mouth. Everything that can't be talked about straight out around here gets called the pie. *This* pie means boys. Maxine's got a big mouth, too. I don't know why mine gets all the attention.

Maxine would never tell me about the second time she went to Madame Rose's House of Fortune. It was just last April after that kid in her class jumped off the bridge, and the whole town was acting weird, blaming each other and thinking how it could've been them. Maxine went out one night and Mom and Dad got a call that she'd gotten into some trouble downtown at Madame Rose's. Dad said, "Christ, almighty, not again," and stomped out to the truck. Half hour later, he hauled Maxine home drunk and crying. She refused to come inside and stood out in the trailer park yelling, "Everything sucks!" over and over again. People in the other trailers started pulling back their curtains and peeking out. Finally Maxine puked and Dad went out with a bucket of sawdust and dragged her back inside. It was a long night of hollering after that. Can't keep a fight a secret in a trailer. Someone stamps their foot and the whole place shakes. Yelling doesn't crack a mirror, but it can rattle a few dishes on the shelves. Maxine kept saying how she hadn't done anything wrong and Mom asked how could she ever trust her again, and my father just kept shaking his head and saying, "The woman is low life, Maxine. Don't you have any sense at all?"

"She's just a fortune teller, Mike." It wasn't often that Mom spoke up against Dad.

"I wouldn't be surprised if she did more than tell fortunes, Deb. She's had the law up there."

"She's a whore," Maxine said.

Snakes started coming out of Dad's eyes and he said that was enough and Maxine didn't argue.

I just kept on asking questions. Sometimes I feel like it's a job I don't get paid for. "What else does Madame Rose do up there?" I said. "Why'd the cops come? And what did Maxine *do?*" But like I said, I don't get answers around here.

After we'd all flopped into bed, I asked Maxine what it was all about. None of my damn beeswax was all she would say. I pulled her favorite necklace out from under the covers and dangled it in her face. But Maxine never was one to take a bribe. She just took the necklace back in the middle of the night and cut off a patch of my hair up near the part for revenge. Mom noticed it the next day when she was braiding my hair before school.

"Who did this, Jewel?" She combed the bald place hard. I reached up and felt the bristles and I was as mad as she was because my hair was the thing Mom and I both liked best about me and the braiding was the one thing we ever did together, me kneeling on the floor in between Mom's legs each morning, my elbows on her knees.

"I don't know," I said.

"Well, it's a real shame." Mom threw down the comb and started to cry. "Now we'll have to cut it all off," she said.

"No!" I grabbed Dad's red hunting cap and stuffed all my hair into it while Mom went to get the scissors. "Leave my hair alone!" I told her. Mom stared at me, holding the scissors up high in her hand like she was about to stab me. I'd never seen her cry and she'd never heard me yell at her. After a while, I said "please," and she put the scissors away.

You see how the reasons I got for going to see Madame Rose

keep piling up—to see what Maxine could have done to make
Mom and Dad so upset that night, to know what the future
holds and what low life is like, and to ask how to grow back one
patch of hair. Maxine must've put hair remover on my head,
because that spot has stayed nearly bald all this time. The things
my father said about Madame Rose that night don't surprise me.
He can see the worst in everyone, except for Mom. It's a game
for him. He sits in the motel office, reading race car magazines
when it's slow. But when the registrees pull up on the gravel
turnaround, he's all eyes. He watches them get out of their cars
and stretch. They usually pull down their underwear or tuck in
their shirts or check in the car mirror to see if they've got messy
hair or stuff in their teeth. And in the little while it takes for
the people to walk from their cars to the office, Dad sizes them
up. Like today, when I was with him in the office, taking a break
from cleaning the motel rooms, a man pulled up in a blue Ford
Falcon and got out of his car.

"Here he comes, Jewel," my father said. "Mr. Milk Q. Toast."
He did a drum roll with two pencils and started talking like the
guy in "Dragnet," which is his favorite show. "It's three-fifteen
Eastern Standard Time . . . in the bustling metropolis of Winot.
The wife's been nagging this guy for the past hour to stop. He
wanted to keep driving, but he figured he might murder her if
he did. 3:30. After they check in, he'll go for a long walk. 3:40.
She'll ask for extra pillows and use up all the hot water before
the afternoon's over." I was laughing so hard my sides hurt.

The man opened the door and stepped over the office
threshold, setting off the witch's cackle we rig up every
Halloween and said, "Oh, heavens."

"That's just Hester," Dad said. "Don't mind her." He stood up
and started pouring on the charm. He asked how was the man's
trip and had he been to these parts before and then he picked
out a key, the best room we got available, he always says. He
told the man where to buy maple syrup and see the foliage and
to try the Alpine Slide and Santa's Village if they had kids. "No,
no children," the man said, and then Dad gave him a firm hand-
shake. Dad puts on a real show, but he isn't a fake. He really
likes all the people who come and go, likes making them com-

fortable and showing them around. He always tries to figure out why these people of all people stop at our motel just when they do. He's always saying how if they'd left their houses a second later or stopped for a burger, everything would have been different. It's no more than fate, I guess, but it keeps him wondering forever.

Dad just has a bit of a mean streak, which seems to rub off on me a lot. He'll yell at me for squeezing the toothpaste tube in the middle, and let Maxine off the hook for the same thing. Last year when I broke the ship in the bottle that he made for Mom, he called me a clumsy ox and wouldn't talk to me for a day. Most of the time, though, he treats me like an angel. Sometimes I think Dad likes me better than Maxine and that makes him ashamed. I know I feel ashamed even thinking it. Funny thing is how often Dad is right about the registrees. That man, Mr. Milk Q. Toast? Sure enough, after he took the key, he said his legs were stiff and was there a nice place to walk around here. Then his wife came into the office, saying how tired she was and how they should have stopped in Keene at the Holiday Inn, and how she hoped at least we had a decent shower.

Maxine and I finish up the dishes. Dad gets a beer out of the fridge and hikes up his pants, then zaps on the TV with the remote control. Mom folds her legs under her on the sofa and starts staring at nothing, the way I do. Maxine and I go to change and when we come out from behind the curtain that makes our room, Dad whistles and says, "Watch out Loni Anderson!" Mom says we look nice and maybe it's time to pass that shirt along to Jewel, Maxine.

"Need a few bucks?" asks Dad.

"Nah," I say. But Maxine says, "sure," at the same time and takes the money. That pisses me off. We never even pay to get into the drive-in. We sneak in from the woods in back of the screen and lie on our bellies on a little hill until the movie's started. Then we're in like Flynn. Sometimes the ticket man chases us and yells, "pay your money like everyone else you god damned park rats," which is what they call us kids from the trailer park. But we feel like it's our right, getting into the drive-in for free. We hang out there on the lot all winter, freezing our butts off and playing with the cracks in the cement, kind of looking out for the place.

Maxine and I walk outside. It's a clear and starry night. I toss the garbage to Dondi the pig and oink at him a few times. Maxine calls me an idiot and Dondi doesn't oink back. When we get close to the road, I tell Maxine, "I gotta go back. I forgot something."

Maxine scowls the famous Maxine scowl. "What?" she says.

"Just something," I say. "I don't have to tell you everything, Maxine. You're not my boss." Doesn't take much to get Maxine to blow a fuse tonight. There's a new boy in school she's got her eyes on, and she wants to get over to the drive-in before anyone else. That's what the tight shirt's all about. Troy Buckner. All's fair in love and war, Maxine says. She's ready for both tonight. "Go on ahead," I say. "I'll meet you over there."

"Don't tell Mom and Dad you crossed the road alone, Jewel," Maxine says. "Or I'll kick your butt."

"You wish you could," I say, but Maxine's already halfway across the road.

Back at the trailer, Mom and Dad are watching "Mannix." Dad's head is on Mom's lap and two beer cans are empty and crushed on the floor. One of Mom's hands is going through what's left of Dad's hair. Mom never really watches TV, just listens. They barely notice me, except when I sneak out again, Dad lifts up his head and says, "Everything all right, Jewel?" When I get back to the road, the drive-in screen lights up, with the popcorn box and the candy bars dancing across the stage. I start running the other way down the road; it's no more than a mile to town. The moon's so bright, it might as well be day. I run along the river path, just where the bank dips down to the water. The water shimmers way down below. Shimmer. Shimmer. Shimmer. Ono-mota-peea. It's a word that sounds like what it does. Don't know what good knowing something like that will ever do me, but still, I like knowing it. Hiss. Sizzle. Thud. Kathunk. Mumble. Shimmer. The river is wide and twisty and in olden days, it ran the mills and made the town prosper. But now the town is poor and whenever I see the river, all I can ever think about are the two people I know who died in it. One was a little girl who lived in the trailer park. She and her mother went over the bank in a car on their way to the 7-11 to buy a brownie mix one night. I've done that with Dad a thousand times. The other person who the river took was Danny Price, the guy Maxine knew at high school. He jumped off the bridge on his birthday last April, maybe on purpose or maybe not, maybe thinking he'd pop right up again and swim to shore. Turns out he was too drunk to do anything but sink. I haven't been near the river much since then. Me and my friends used to go boating sometimes. We'd rent a canoe for fifty cents an hour and paddle up to Pirates' Island and eat M&M's and bury ourselves in the sand. Now Maxine goes out in the canoes with boys to smoke pot. The river's filled with smooching teenagers and other things you'd rather not know what they are. In the day time, the river's brown and it doesn't shimmer, it just sits there and waits.

Still, while I'm running, I can see why they call it God's Drawer around here, with the church steeples and the mountains climbing up to the sky and the good smells and the quiet and the winding roads. The wind blows my hair back stiff and my legs feel strong. When I pass close by a tree, I jump up and grab the leaves, swiping them off their stems. Then I open up my hand and let the pieces blow in the wind. I love fall. But it's just too sad. And wintertime. Well, wintertime's the price you have to pay for spring.

The 7-11's the first store you come to at the start of town. Further down Main Street, where the street lights begin, you come to the firehouse and then the library and then the IGA and the diner and then the drugstore and that's where I start to walk. Madame Rose's sign is all lit up, on the second floor above the barber shop. It says: "Madame Rose's House of Fortune. Advisor. Consultations." There's a hand flashing on and off. Maxine says that stands for the palm reading part of the half hour, the life line and all that. Circles go round and round the edge of the sign like drops of water. They disappear around a corner and then turn back into themselves again.

I can make out the ghost of myself in the barber shop window. I'm wearing my cowboy shirt with the fringe and new jeans, sneakers so I could run fast. Maxine and I always doll up when we go to the drive-in, so I didn't raise any suspicions looking so good. My hair is windblown from the running, and the bald patch is covered up. Maybe if the reflection showed color, I'd have pink in my cheeks, too. Maybe I look as pretty as I feel. I reach in my pocket to feel my money. The five dollars are folded up in a little square and the sharp corners dig into my leg. I pray to the almighty god if there is one that Madame Rose hasn't upped her prices.

I stand at the door for a long time getting my breaths even and waiting for my heart to slow down. I've never seen Madame Rose before, and this is pretty strange in a place like Winot. One thousand and some-odd is a big number, but it's not a lot of people to make up a town. Almost all of them you know to look at, and most to speak to, though no one feels obliged. You know who belongs to who and sometimes where they went on their vacation or what outfit they wore to a christening even before they wore it, because you might've bumped into them buying it at Erma's Boutique. Sometimes you even hear who went to bed with who, and every once in a while, it's family, which is a sin upon a sin. I wouldn't be caught dead sleeping with anyone in my family, or maybe that's the only way I'd be caught doing it. Dead. It's bad enough sleeping kitty corner with Maxine in the trailer. Either way, next to her big mouth or smelly feet, it's something I'll only do long as I have to.

I open the door next to the barber shop and climb up the stairs. It's gotta be Madame Rose who answers the door. She has black, curly hair in a red kerchief and jewelry on her arms and neck. She's got on layers and layers of stuff—shirts and shawls and skirts—all brights colors and spangles and sparkles. On her cheek, there's a beauty mark, which looks like it's about to fall off.

"Who have we here?" she says, opening the door part way.

"Jewel," I tell her. "Jewel Rose Martin."

"You here to see Madame Rose?"

"Yeah."

"Where you from, Jewel?" She doesn't ask me in and I start to worry that preteens aren't allowed and that she's going to send me home.

"My dad runs the Hester Green Motel," I slip sideways through the door. "Up on Route 7."

Usually people say they've heard of it, or they had friends who stayed there once, but Madame Rose just says, "Well, come on into the House of Fortune." I follow her through a doorway made of hanging beads into a small, dark room. On the table is a lit-up crystal ball and two wooden chairs. I smell a chicken on to boil and an old voice calls out, "Who's there, Rose?" All of a sudden, my bald spot starts to itch.

"Customer, Ma." Madame Rose has a low, rumbly voice, kind of like thunder. "Did you bring any money?" she asks me. I hand her my money, which is damp from my sweaty hand. She unfolds the bills and faces all the George Washingtons the same way, then rolls them up and slips them into her blouse. "So, Jewel," she says, pulling one chair out for me and sitting down on the other "What brings you to Madame Rose's?"

"I want a consultation," I say. "I want you to tell me the stuff you tell other people."

Madame Rose spreads her hands over the crystal ball and shadows jump up onto the walls. Her hands are wrinkled and they shake a little. When she talks, a sharp sweet smell slides out of her mouth and lands on top of the crystal ball where my nose picks it up. My nose is real close, trying to see what's in there. "You want me to tell you what's in store for you, is that it, Jewel?"

"That's it, I guess." I try to remember my questions, all of the piled up reasons why I'm here. I make myself mad and I must have on the famous Maxine scowl, because Madame Rose says, "You look like a skeptic, Jewel. First I'll tell you what I know about you, just from sitting here at this table with you." She lifts her hands up and down and the finger shadows slam up and down the walls like baseball bats. "Then maybe you'll have faith," Madame Rose says.

"I got faith," I say. The chicken smell starts to make me feel sick.

"Sshhhh!" she says. Her eyes close for a minute and she puts

137

one hand on my forehead and the other on the crystal ball. "There's a reason you have that name," she says. "To someone, you are most precious. . . . Your mother. . . ."

"No way," I say.

She lifts up her pointy fingers. "Sssssshhhhhhh!" she says again. "You didn't let me finish. Your mother . . . is very beautiful, isn't she, and sometimes very sad. You and she have your differences. That is inevitable." She lifts her hand off my forehead and opens her eyes wide. We both look into the crystal ball. I see black shapes, but she sees Dad. "It's plain to see," she says, "that you are your father's pride and joy."

"Shouldn't a father like both his kids the same?"

"You have a. . . ."

"Sister," I say.

"A family is a complicated thing," Madame Rose says. "Love has no rules. People change. Feelings change. In the end, these things balance themselves out. As long as everyone's getting something from someone." A slice of the pie. *This* pie means love. I go over it in my head. Dad loves Mom best and then me. Mom loves Dad best and then Maxine. Maxine loves boys and maybe then herself. And I love Dad and . . . everyone else about the same. "Long as no one gets hurt," Madame Rose says, "there's no harm done."

"No one else even knows," I say.

Madame Rose presses her beauty mark with her finger and takes my hand. "Let's read your palm, Jewel," she says. The old voice calls out, "Soup, Rose. Come and get it!"

"Coming!" Madame Rose calls back and then rubs my palm with her finger. "I see a long life here. Many new roads. And a man, one who will cherish you."

"When?" I know better than to ask who.

"As soon as you're ready," she says. "He's waiting for you."

"I know him already?"

She nods.

"From school?"

"That I can't say."

"What's he like?" I ask.

"He's very gentle and a little afraid. You must be careful not to scare him away."

"What do you mean?" I just don't understand how I could ever scare anyone.

"Rose!" The old voice starts to sound mad.

"Just a minute!" Madame Rose yells back. "You are brave, Jewel," she tells me. "But you are also stubborn. Stubbornness is blind, and it may bring you trouble, but in the end, your courage will see you through many hard times."

"I got hard times coming?"

"Every road has a few bumps," Madame Rose says. Her wrinkled finger traces the deepest line in my hand. "But at the end of the road. . . ." She looks back into the crystal ball. "I see a pool. A deep, clear pool."

"What's in it?" I ask. I still don't see anything.

"Happiness," she says.

"With the man?"

"Yes, he's there," she says.

The beads jangle and an arm reaches through to pull them aside. The arm is attached to Earlene Turnbridge, a girl in Maxine's class at school. "Hey, Jewel," she says. "Out pretty late, aren't you?"

"Earlene!" I pull my hand away from Madame Rose's. "What are you doing here?"

"I live here, Jewel," she says. "What's your excuse? You come to finish what Maxine started?"

"Maxine?" Madame Rose twirls around and nearly falls out of her chair. "Isn't that the name of the girl who came up here and raised hell that night?"

"Not too many people in this town by the name of Maxine, Ma," Earlene says.

"Ma?" I say.

"She's my mother," Earlene says. "Don't tell me you didn't know that, Jewel."

"I knew it," I say, and in a way, just at the last minute, it's true. I remember bumping into Earlene and her mother once at the IGA, Earlene and a dumpy lady with her hair in curlers and stretch pants and a few missing teeth, choosing out Pop Tarts.

"So why *did* you come?" Earlene asks me. "To find out who's going to take you to the junior high prom?"

"I'm not going to the junior high prom," I say. "I just wanted to see what a fortune teller is like."

"She's a witch day and night," Earlene says. I think how Dad would slap me if I ever talked to Mom that way. I know that Earlene's daddy died of a disease that ate him up quickly when she was little, and her grandmother came over from Echo Falls to live with them. That must be the old voice.

"What did Maxine do anyway?" I ask Earlene, but it's Madame Rose who answers.

"She came up here drunk as a skunk, calling me a liar and much worse. She went on and on about some boy and then she started busting up the place. She even broke my crystal ball." Madame Rose turns on the lights and I see that the paint on the walls is peeling and the tiles on the floor are starting to curl up. The card table has folded-up gum wrappers jammed underneath the legs to keep it from tipping and part of the ceiling is coming down. I bend over and see a crack in the crystal ball reaching from one side to the other, with dry glue caked all along it. "Business hasn't been the same since," Madame Rose says.

"That ball's been cracked ever since I can remember," Earlene says. "Maxine bumped into the table and it fell. That's not why people don't come here anymore, Ma. They just don't want a lush. . . ."

"Shut up, Earlene." Madame Rose points her finger at me and for one second she looks like Hester Green on the motel sign and I'm scared she might hurt me. "From what I hear," she says, "your sister is a little whore."

I want to know who called who that first and who really is the whore, Maxine or Madame Rose. Right now, I have to believe it's not my sister. "She is not," I say.

"You ain't no saint, Ma," Earlene says.

"I want my money back," I say.

Madame Rose laughs. "There's an old saying in this business," she says, "a dollar palmed is a dollar gone."

"How 'bout some of it?" I ask.

"You're a brazen little thing, aren't you?" she says.

"Oh, give the kid her money back, Ma," Earlene says.

"What's it to you?"

"It's the chicken in the pot, Earlene!" Madame Rose says. "It's all that crap you buy to put in your hair!" Still, she yanks the dollars out of her blouse and throws them on the table. I fold them up into a square again and run out the door and down the stairs. Madame Rose comes out onto the landing and yells after me, "Don't let me catch you or your sister around here again!"

"No way," I say, but not very loud. When I get outside, I bend over to tie up my shoelace. Earlene sticks her head out of the window and laughs. I don't feel so pretty anymore, kind of like a rat with a long tail in between my legs. Dirty now and with legs too short for running.

I walk most of the way home. The wind's picked up and the river's moving in little ripples, like it's got something to say. Every single star is shining bright. On a night like this, there's nowhere to hide. I feel like I keep walking past the same tree, over and over again, never getting anywhere. Must be more than a mile. I stop to sit on a bench, but the seat boards are busted, so I keep walking. Finally the drive-in screen comes into sight. I see a head come rolling down some stairs, just a head with the eyes bulging and blood spurting out of it. I've never seen anything so stupid. I walk right past the ticket taker who's sleeping in his chair. Maxine's hanging out on the grass with her friends near the concession stand, smoking a cigarette.

"Hey, Maxine," I say, real casual.

She jumps up and hisses at me. "Where you been, Jewel?"

"Nowhere."

"Bullshit." She grabs me by the arm so it hurts. "You been gone almost the whole movie."

"I thought you'd be so busy sucking up to Troy, you wouldn't even notice," I say. I don't know why I always have to talk so mean to Maxine, even now, when all I want to do is just stay with her and watch the end of the movie and the sky.

"One thing I always notice," Maxine says, "is when smart-ass Jewel's not around."

"Did you kiss him?"

"Whisper!" she says.

"Did you?"

"No, I didn't kiss him, Jewel."

"Where is he?"

Maxine jerks her head over to where a bunch of boys are sitting on the grass, smoking cigarettes. "Don't stare!" she says and jerks me around again by the arm. But it's too late. I've seen Troy and he's seen me see him. I make a face and he looks over at Maxine and she gives me the famous Maxine scowl. "I thought you got run over by a truck or something, Jewel."

"So what," I say. "You wouldn't even come to my funeral."

The boys snuff out their cigarettes with their feet, first Troy and then the rest. They start strolling over towards us, like the zombies are doing up on the screen, humming one note with their eyes crossed and their arms held out straight. Maxine keeps talking, louder and louder, supposedly to me but so Troy can hear. "I thought I'd have to be the one to tell Dad," she kind of sings it into her fist, like it was a microphone, "that his little Jewel got flattened under eighteen wheels." Troy unzombies and smiles at Maxine. He's not exactly handsome, but he's close.

"I went to Madame Rose's," I tell Maxine.

"You jerk," she says. "What for?"

"Same reason you went the first time," I say. "Why'd you go back and go nuts on her, Maxine?"

"She's a liar," she says.

"What'd she say?" I ask.

"She told me the next one to love me would love me forever."

"Who was the next one?" Maxine's had so many boyfriends. I can't keep track.

"Danny Price," she says.

"Danny Price who jumped off the bridge?"

"How many other Danny Prices do you know?"

"You liked him?" I ask.

"We were engaged," she said.

"Engaged?" I said. "How come you didn't tell anybody?"

"It was a secret," she said.

"Well maybe he did love you to the end," I say.

"Well his end wasn't my end," Maxine says. "So big effin deal."

It's the first time I've ever felt bad for Maxine and it's not a good feeling. I want to tell her that I'm sorry, but I don't know what for. I want to tell her that I understand the way she is, the way we both have to be, being who we are. I want to tell her I know Madame Rose is a fake, and that I'm probably wrong, about Dad liking me better. But Maxine's back to being Maxine, shoving her elbow into me and saying, "Give me money for popcorn, Miss Gotrocks. You must be loaded, doing all that extra work."

I no sooner unfold the money than Maxine grabs one of the dollar bills and starts over to the concession stand.

"That's three million dollars you owe me, Maxine!" I call after her. She turns around and starts dancing backwards. I see the boys' eyes turn and their arms fall to their sides. Up on the screen, the zombies attack the zoo keeper and let all the animals out of their cages. Maxine's shirt rides up and you can see her belly button. Her hips move and her dark hair bounces up and down on her shoulders. The zookeeper moans and groans in a bloody heap. A lion comes over and starts licking him. Maxine could hold her own in Hollywood if she lost a little weight. I watch Maxine and I want all of what she's got—that hair, those breasts, that smile Troy gave her, the kisses and the looks of those boys and the way she can dance her way anywhere. I want to have been drunk and I want to have been engaged. It isn't enough to be Maxine's sister, but I'm not sorry I am.

"Anyway, just desserts!" Maxine calls out to me. This is what Mom says when we get what we deserve. "You scared me half to death, Jewel," she says. "That's worth at least a dollar. Besides which . . . you missed all the sex scenes!"

I follow Maxine to the concession stand, where a boy in a uniform asks her what she wants like he would give her the moon. I got money to burn and I'm starving, so I order three candy bars: Mounds, Snickers, and Charlestown Chew. "Don't matter to me," I tell Maxine, unwrapping the Mounds Bar. "I've seen this movie before."

I look around for kids my age, but it being late and the end of

143

the season, it doesn't surprise me they're all at home. I sit a little bit away from Maxine and her friends, getting a neckache trying to see what's happening up on the screen. Maxine keeps changing places, talking to different girls, until she makes her way over to Troy. Next thing I know, she's sitting in between his legs and he's got his hands on her shoulders. One of the zombies tries to kiss the zoo keeper's beautiful daughter, who's washing the elephants. She struggles, but then she gives in and they go at it hot and heavy. I try to watch it all—the movie stars and the real stars and Maxine and Troy. But for some strange reason, as I finish up the candy bars, I keep thinking about my grandmother, and I hardly ever think about her.

My grandmother came to visit us last winter after my grandfather died, from Missouri, which is where Dad found Mom, eating at a diner where Mom was a waitress and when she asked him what he'd have, he said, I'll take you. My grandmother spent three whole days in our trailer wondering out loud how come my mother had come so far to this cold, god-forsaken place just to live in a trailer and clean all the world's ashtrays and all for the love of a. . . . The word she used for my father, I don't remember. She never even tried to like him and so he didn't bother back. She smoked and stunk up the trailer, but she didn't approve of drinking. When Dad caught her pouring his beers down the sink one day, he blew his stack. He said it was hard to believe someone like her had ever made someone like Mom and she said wasn't it a waste and if it weren't for the kids, and he said fine grandmother, why'd she waited all these years even to meet us. She left in a huff and Mom told Dad he should've left her alone, she was still grieving. Mom didn't talk to Dad for three days, which is how people in my family get back at one another—dead silence. Dad couldn't stand it, and he told Mom he'd do anything to make it up to her, except have her mother back again in his house. Trailer, Mom said, like it was no better than Dondi's pig sty. I guess the yellow Chevy Camaro finally did the trick.

I still remember most of the things that my grandmother said at our kitchen table, yakking with Mom by the hour, though Mom didn't do much yakking back, just nodded her head and said yeah, or, is that right? A lot of coffee got drunk and a lot of napkins got doodled on. I could kind of picture then how Mom used to be the little girl and my grandmother was the mother, with the dishtowel slung over her shoulder. My grandmother didn't care who was listening to her. The things she had on her mind got said, no matter what. I paid special attention when my name or Maxine's came up. She told Mom to keep a close eye on Maxine's behind, and she said that I, Jewel, was a little too smart for my own good and that I was headed for a comeuppance. Or upcommance. It was one of those two words. I keep looking for it in the dictionary at school. First under the c's, then under the u's. I could ask my teacher, but I don't want to have to explain, or have anyone nearby when I find out what it means, what I got coming. Maybe I don't really want to know. Could be that my grandmother made that word up, but she didn't seem like the type. That's Maxine's department, pretending to know everything. It's too bad, what happened at Madame Rose's. I wanted to believe what she said about me and Dad and the family pie. I wouldn't have minded ending up with that quiet man who drowned in my pool of happiness. Maybe it's a comeuppance, what I got downtown tonight at the House of Fortune, not what I expected, but, like Mom says, just desserts. I meant to ask Madame Rose about that word. I thought it might be easier to find in a crystal ball than a dictionary.

STAR BOX

I never did much like the sound of that Mr. Primavera, and so when he invites me for tea after the fact—the fact of Esther's being dead and buried, that is—I can only be offended. I remember Esther saying, with quicksilver wistfulness in her voice, that he was a bit of a Don Juan. She'd heard them on the stairs, seen them in glimpses through her door—women of all ages and sizes, coming and going at all hours of the day and night with the smell of tea. She'd heard them thumping above her in Mr. Primavera's apartment doing heaven knows what, as the music went round and round on his Victrola, though she didn't seem old enough to use the word.

Esther's husband, Avery Brubaker, was the dart champion at the Medford Pub and won a tropical vacation once on a quiz show which he traded in for cash. "Long as the man pays his rent," he said of Mr. Primavera, "whose business is it how many broads he's slamming?" Avery spoke his mind, Esther said, and never mind what was in it.

They seemed an unlikely couple, Avery and Esther. I suppose there are no other kinds. Avery worked for a chemical plant out on Route 128, taking often to the road for long stretches in an enormous cylindrical truck with danger signs posted all over it. He was a slight, arched man, thin shoulders dropping into a long waist and bowed legs. A coarse orange fuzz sprang out of the tops of his v-neck shirts, matting his arms from shoulder to wrist. Avery looked like a great, grisly caterpillar, gone upright and given a small bit of wit and language to abuse.

And Esther—soft, worried Esther, with the curly hair. She'd been pretty once, but had never known it. She buttoned her shirts high and religiously; I'd never once seen her bare collar-bone. She worried about the little things—someone had to, she said—the color of hothouse tomatoes and finding the right length shoelaces, the life of a lightbulb, books out of place on a shelf. She'd worked in a nursery before she married Avery, tending the plants and flowers in a warm damp greenhouse she loved. But Avery hadn't wanted a wife that worked, and why take a husband, Esther said, who was unhappy from the start?

I met Esther on a hot day last June, in a park up on Powderhouse Hill, surrounding the old fort. We used to take our dogs for an evening stroll and land on our favorite benches, which happened to rest side by side. Esther was a big woman, and her legs were bad, but in those days, they still got her around. We'd sit and chat and watch the children play and the clouds pass overhead. Our dogs, both since dead, would lay low on their paws and growl at one another. Esther wore a brown cardigan sweater. Mine was a dull green, almost identical in style, with braiding and a beaded collar. Sometimes, when I looked at Esther, I saw myself in thirty years—maybe even twenty—and the glimpse into time and spirit alarmed me as much as it gave me comfort. The park was filled with pale, dying light and children and echoing noise, full of everything Esther had lost, and I was still waiting to have.

Esther had children—a son and a daughter—both grown and childless and far away. "I'm afraid you wouldn't like them all that well," she once told me. They'd turned out to be rather cold, selfish people, she wasn't sure why, though she blamed herself for all of their distances and their shortcomings.

"'Course Avery and I were too young to start a family," Esther said. We exchanged bits and pieces of our lives in the park, passing them back and forth like neighborly cups of sugar. "Too young and too poor. Still, the children got their baths. They got their teeth fixed and they got a good education. It seemed like a miracle sometimes."

"Children don't raise themselves," I told her. "Children are helpless."

"Mine never were," she said. "What was your home like, Elaine?"

"Home?" Esther would toss the conversation over to me, intent on her knitting needles, always busy making things for other's people's grandchildren. Catching the ball with shaky hands, I began to tell Esther things I'd never told anyone else. "My house was very . . . hot," I remembered, digging deep into a dark, cluttered closet of memory. "I had to wear a woolen night-gown, even in the summer. The itching drove me crazy. I vowed that when I grew up, I would sleep naked every night."

"And do you dear?"

"Not often," I said, thinking of Rufus.

"That's always the way, isn't it? Witch hazel's good for the itch." Esther's fingers spun rectangles of lavender and blue. "You had brothers and sisters?"

"Two older brothers. They were in league." A popsicle melted into an orange puddle at my feet.

"Not against you, I hope."

"No." I drank fizzy water from a bottle and bit the corners of my nails. "Just against the world. They got away with murder, my brothers."

"Your mother must have been so pleased to finally have a little girl to dress up."

"She would have liked such a little girl," I said. "But I wasn't her. I didn't like dolls or dresses. I liked to dig for bones."

"Of course you did," Esther said soothingly, no judgment passed, no statement made.

"Do you know what my mother said when I told her I wanted to be a geologist?" I asked Esther. "She said, 'Fine, Elaine. You can start by digging out the rocks in your head.'"

"Sounds like your mother had quite a sense of humor," Esther said.

"No," I told her. "She didn't have any at all."

It was just six months ago, as the December winds blew into our collars in the park that Esther told me, "Well, Avery's gone."

"Where's he off to this time?" I asked her.

"Heaven, I hope," Esther said. "I wouldn't call Avery a bad man."

"Heaven?"

Avery died the way people can in his profession, in an accident where the chemicals exploded on impact and set his truck on fire, killing him somewhere on an interstate in Pennsylvania—instantly, painlessly, Esther was assured by another widow at a coffee-and-sympathy party down at the chemical plant. Esther made finger foods and a jello mold and spared everyone her sorrow by not bringing any along. Esther didn't see Avery's death as tragedy. She had no religion, but she did have faith. Avery had his spot reserved in heaven, in the corral where brave men go to lasso the wild horses that have bucked them on earth, to tell slightly tall tales of their wild rides on earth, to smoke cigars and down frothy beers forever after.

Soon after Avery died, Esther asked me for dinner one night. She liked to try out the "Recipes of the Stars" on the back page of the *TV Guide*. She watched soap operas in the afternoon, making love chains on a neat chart. Angela loved Brad who pretended to love Kelly who seduced Amber who jilted Antoine, who two-timed with the twins, Francesca and Nicole, one of whose baby was born blind, the other kidnapped from the maternity ward by Angela, who loved Brad, who pretended to love Kelly. . . .

Sandwiches cut in diamond shapes with walnuts and cream cheese were a Sammy Davis offering. Mary Tyler Moore's weight watcher special was cut-up pineapple served on its skin with cottage cheese and cinnamon sprinkled on top. Johnny Carson made a chicken with lemon sauce, though I found it hard to believe that Johnny Carson had, in recent years, touched the naked, bumpy skin of a raw chicken.

"Isn't it nice that the stars find the time to cook?" Esther's thoughts were as generous as mine were jaded. "Such wholesome foods, too. I would have thought they all lived on caviar and champagne. How's the Joan Rivers Meatloaf, dear?"

In those dark winter days, I'd come for dinner after work, once, sometimes twice a week. Esther would shake out my coat of cold and snow and drape it over Avery's armchair. She'd light a candle for Avery and set it on the table. I didn't know that she was counting time. I think she planned to be gone by April, not because Avery had been a good excuse for living, but because she suspected that she'd been left with no other. Avery's memory grew dim in the flickering candlelight, as we dipped potato chips into Bob Hope's Cheddar Cheese Spread and watched the city moon rise.

A month or so after Avery died, the talk turned to Mr.

Primavera, the tenant. He wasn't entirely well, Esther thought. He'd gotten a haircut; he'd had a cold. He'd been cooking something that smelled Chinesey. One of his women visitors had thrown something down the stairs and Mr. Primavera had rushed down after it. The women still came and went. Esther didn't want to be nosy; it was no concern of hers. After all, Mr. Primavera had very kindly been bringing up her mail, Avery's old task, knowing how her legs were bad on the stairs. Mr. Primavera had a receding hairline; however, he was not going bald. He'd brought her a photograph of himself as a child as proof. He had a full mustache, and wasn't as young as one might think at first glance. He was very polite, very pleasant. All in all, Esther thought, he was a fine man. But whatever could he be doing with all those women?

I'm sure this Mr. Primavera is neither Casanova nor sinner. If I have tea with him, I will make quick reference to Rufus, lest he misunderstand why I am what I look like—a thin, bookish woman who likes to live alone. "When Rufus and I went to the Roxy," I will say. No, that would be a lie. Movies were out, even slapstick or subtitles. "When Rufus and I were on our way back from the grocery store." Yes. Only lovers buy morning milk and eggs together.

Mr. Primavera doesn't have to know that I have pried myself away from Rufus. I have loved Rufus in some more than ordinary way. But maybe that is only because Rufus is not ordinary, because Rufus is deaf. He has never heard anything—water dripping or a children's wail or the hiss and rumble before the tea kettle roars, or anything at all except what I imagine to be a ceaseless, screeching hum in his head. After a while, this great gap of sound and rhythm was simply too colossal and frightening to cross. There were too many things that Rufus and I couldn't do—take naps or go on vacations or to the symphony, not so much because he was deaf, but because life for Rufus was just too serious to include such frivolities. When I was with Rufus, I found myself in constant self-reproach for not being grateful or hardworking or happy enough, although I'd always before felt enough of all three. It was too hard and too exhausting to find replacements for the most ordinary of human events, too late to rearrange my own self, so long and hard in the making.

A deaf silence is not golden, but a watery grey. Rufus and I tried to flop and jibe, to ebb and flow and swoop and pout and fly as other people who think they might love each other for a good long while will do. I took a sign class at the Adult Ed Center; he studied geology. I once dragged him outside in a summer shower and broke into an off-tune Billy Holiday song. Rufus stared. I unbuttoned my shirt, caught raindrops with my tongue, fell out of a graceless pirouette onto the sidewalk, saw smoke swirl out of my laughter. I tugged at his arm, pleaded. He would only move the top half of his body, eyes on the lookout for witnesses to my folly, fingers wiggling his innocence, his disavowal, his embarrassment.

"Lighten up, will you, Rufus?" I was mad and tried to say so in sign, drawing a lightbulb in the air, but of course Rufus did not understand. "Just . . . have . . . some fun!" I slapped two fingers end to end and played the clown—making faces, making fun, making eyes. Rufus just kept staring—disdainful, incredulous, uncomprehending—in the end they were all the same. My dance grew stiff, the dance of a sci-fi creature on a leaden planet with gravity to spare, and the song became no more than a mournful plaint, making light of the rain, without which we would all perish. I quieted myself, buttoned up my shirt, led the way inside. We dried ourselves, blew our noses, rubbed our wrinkled feet, got ready to make penance love. "You win, Rufus," I signed, draped in a towel, shivering, reaching out to touch his blue lips. "You win, Rufus. You're deaf."

"I'm deaf," Rufus said, finger to ear and then to mouth. He pulled the towel from me and stared at my body with the steady, impassive gaze of a bird of prey. He shook his head and swung his hands together, heavy in a cradle of dead air. "But nobody wins."

Sex for Rufus had nothing to do with passion or lust, conquest or fun. It was mission. Catharsis. For both of us, it was need. Sex with Rufus was like floating down a cool river. I don't know how much of my pleasure he shared. In bed, our thin bodies slid and turned. The silence was vast and limp, the sweat hot and cleansing. Our bodies crunched; we felt each other's bony fingers, reveled in our spare selves, our plainness, our indentations. We knew no inhibitions, none of our usual fears. We found the pools in our collarbones and the arches in our feet, the Vs in our ribcages. We were both left-handed and knew the periodic table by heart. We were generally clumsy and fond of figs. We fit. I used to wake Rufus from twitching, deaf sleep with a finger down the line of hair to his navel. He'd turn to me and fuck me with solemnity, approaching the task before him like all others, with a fierce commitment to succeed.

"How was it?" Rufus asked this with his eyes alone.

"G-O-O-D!" I'd sign the letters on his boy-smooth chest with that same finger, as we lay barely damp, untangled, in the sheets, dotting the exclamation point low. "You're so good." I'd bring my hand from mouth to palm and try to explain all the meanings of the word. But Rufus took all of them as insults.

By the autumn after the raw spring we'd met, I began to feel both selfish and neglected. I could not go on taking so much from Rufus and giving him back so little. I could not go on giving so much and getting so little back. I'd go to work at the museum and make myself forget Rufus for days at a time, until I found myself back in my car, on my way to the school for the deaf, wondering if men cruising for a whore felt the same driven, toe-tapping, devil-be-damned way. "It's over," I finally tried out the words one night in clumsy sign just around the time when Avery died, flinging my clumsy fingers to the wind. "I'm no good for you, Rufus."

Rufus misunderstood again, signing back, swaggering, proud. "I can be better."

"No," I said out loud, collapsing. "You *are* better. I'm the crumb."

I couldn't make him understand the word, over and over crumbling imaginary bread in my hands and letting the pieces fall, then dropping down on all fours to play the mouse who nibbled away at them, because this was the word that had come to me, the one I wanted to use. Rufus got down on his knees beside me with a grudging smile. "All right, Elaine," he was telling me. "We'll play."

"No," I said. "This is not a game." I lifted my fingers and made them speak—flopping, waving, tapping my palms. "Get up. Goodbye." I pushed my thumbs forward into time. "Forever."

I left us both feeling foolish, and angry, no longer man and woman, mice that we'd become.

"Please come to tea on Thursday at five fifteen." Mr. Primavera's invitation comes in a plain white envelope, typed on an old typewriter with a faint ribbon and clogged up O's. I take the note out again at the museum, putting aside the pieces of an early primate vertebra recently found by a Dutch tourist in Indonesia. I feel the note, sniffing it, studying it under my light box, trying to put it into some context, to get some sense of something from it, some smell, some feel, some aura, as I would a relic from the earth. But the note is timeless, unexceptional, odorless. It is no more than a summons, really. And I am not a sucker for pleases, having been raised by a mother who gave pennies to reward them.

I decide to go. For Esther's sake. In memory of Esther, who caught me in my slow tumble from the planet Rufus, who asked for nothing but my so-so company, who made me Carol Burnett's Veal Verdiccio and recommended a good shampoo for wispy hair, who up and died out of the blue. She would have urged me to go for tea with Mr. Primavera, to get out a bit more, not to end up like that boy Jack, all work and no play. Afterwards, were she alive, she would smile and pluck the details from me one by one as she fed me fluorescent orange macaroni and pale green celery stalks—the color of his bed-spread, the feel of his sofa, the fruit in his fruitbowl—don't leave anything out, dear—were his socks matching? How strong did he take his tea? Did you see any of the women? What were they wearing, or not wearing? Esther would not flinch. She really would want to know.

"Don't mind the cats," Mr. Primavera tells me at the door. Three appear at his ankles and start to rub against his legs.

"They get more uppity every day. You must be Elaine."

"I am Elaine." I step inside, bolstered by that fact. The rays of gleaming yellow eyes fall upon me. Slowly, one by one, the cats come to life, eyelids lifting, tails twitching, backs arching, pink tongue revealed in a yawn. One licks its paw on the couch; one eats from a bowl; one stretches on the windowsill. "Esther never mentioned that you had cats," I say.

"I'm not sure she knew," Mr. Primavera says. He is small, big-eared, clean—an urban elf in a "Beethoven Was One of the Boyz" T-shirt. "Please sit down." I sit down in one of two mismatched armchairs, placed side by side in what is virtually an empty room, save the cats and one large, worn, Oriental rug. "Salada okay?" he asks.

"What?" A bust of Beethoven stares down at me with knit plaster brows from its perch on a shelf next to the record player.

"I like having my fortune told by a tea bag," he says.

"Fine, anything," I say. "As long as its caffeinated. I've got to go back to work later tonight."

"Esther said you were a nervous person."

"She did?" I swing my head around to catch Mr. Primavera's eye near the purple of the lit stove-top, feeling instantly betrayed. It is one thing for Esther to have told me about Mr. Primavera's hairline. For we are both women, and she spoke of it with nothing but reverence. "I work long hours at the museum," I said, "I'm . . . busy."

"What did Esther have to say about me?" Mr. Primavera asks, rolling his head my way as the tea kettle whistles.

"She said you were . . . very . . . neat." I tug at my hair with a dark look and try to make it sound like an accusation.

"Neat?" he says, looking around the room, as he hands me my tea. "Not much to it. Avery called it the feline flop house."

"Did you know Avery well?" I take my tea bag out of my cup and wind the string around the spoon. My fortune on the tag reads "*Life is what happens while you're making other plans.*" A stream of sunlight catches one of my fingers and warps it.

"I worked with him down at the plant for a while," Mr. Primavera says.

"You drove those trucks?"

"Me?" Mr. Primavera laughed. "Good god, no. I worked in the shipping office. It takes a certain kind of person to do road work."

"Dead, you mean?" Mr. Primavera has brought out the sarcastic in me, and the macabre, two sides I don't know well.

Mr. Primavera shakes his head. "Not dead," he says.

"Brave?" I say, although I know this is not what he means.

"No," he says. "Brave people swallow their fear. Avery had none."

"Why did he call this the feline flop house?"

"I take them in," Mr. Primavera says. "Strays, sick, maimed, blind. I had an epileptic cat once. She had her last seizure right there on the couch. I buried her down by the river."

"Very generous," I said. "Esther was the same way."

"She made that man a pie every night," he says. "Can you imagine?"

"You make her sound like Betty Crocker," I say. The hot tea fills the pit of my stomach. I have lost all of the weight Esther gained for me.

"Betty Crocker is my idol," Mr. Primavera says, raising his eyebrows and one palm. "Seriously."

"Look," I say. I lean forward and plant my elbows on my knees. "Esther wasn't stupid. She was very independent. I think she saw Avery for exactly what he was." I am strangely comfortable here, free to uncross my legs and speak my mind.

"What was he?" Mr. Primavera asks me.

"I only met him once or twice," I say. "But I would have said he was something of a boor."

"Bore?"

"Boor."

Mr. Primavera shrugs. "Esther seemed happy enough."

"If she were happy," I say. "I don't think she would have died that way."

"What way?"

"Of nothing in particular. No one dies of old age anymore."

"No one ever really did," Mr. Primavera says. "They only told us that." We sip our tea. The doorbell rings and Mr. Primavera looks at his watch. "That must be Marjorie," he says.

"Marjorie?" I slip my shoes back on and straighten up in the sagging chair. "I've stayed too long," I say, though it hasn't been long at all. "Thanks for the tea." I get my coat and open the door. Behind it stands Marjorie, wrapped up too warmly for late spring in bright, striped clothes—scarf and turtleneck and thick makeup. A big dog sits on a leash beside her, all eyes and not enough hair for its bulk, panting from its run up the stairs. The three cats appear at the door and start to hiss. Mr. Primavera hisses back at them and they retreat. He smiles and ushers Marjorie and the dog inside as I leave. The smells of damp dogs and humans mingle. The dog turns around and barks at me. She looks a little bit like me, I think, a little bit like Esther. Marjorie, that is.

From Mr. Primavera's I go to visit Rufus at the school for the deaf, where he teaches gym and is an assistant teacher in math. In the dusk, the school looks like a pleasant enough place—a rambling, shingled old house in good repair, with a modern addition tastefully placed behind. The woman at the front desk smiles at me. "Haven't seen you in a while," she says. It's 6:15. I consult the chalkboard at the main door. Pink letters tell me that the leisure hour has just begun. The movie of the evening is the "Pink Panther." Rufus often stays late on Fridays to work out in the gym. I sign my name in the visitor book and head down the corridor. The gym is empty. I find Rufus in the math room, sitting at a desk, a pile of papers before him, looking out into space, his mouth dropped open. He is wearing his teacher clothes—rumpled corduroy and flannel, the knot of his tie yanked free. It pains me to find Rufus this way at an unappointed moment—unoccupied, unengaged, a dull look in his eyes that cannot define itself. Rufus has never had the luxury of knowing what it means to be bored, and rest is laborious, a void. He is resting because the chalk board says it is time, and he obeys the chalkboard not because he is ruled by it, but because it brings order to his life.

When Rufus sees me, he jumps up with startling strength, bringing that tightening to my stomach that for so long I mistook for fear and then learned to be sex. Rufus is a mismatch of flesh and age, just as is Mr. Primavera. The face is far too old for its twenty-six years, a face that might have kissed the brows of a thousand dead children for all its pain. His body is strong, unscathed, a body you'd expect to be hurling a discus or raising high the roof beams. I robbed the cradle; I am thirty-two. But Rufus has long been older than I will ever be.

"Elaine!" A soft croaking noise I've come to recognize as my name slips from his lips. His mind races to consider why I've come, how he'll treat me, as leper or long lost lover. How unwise of me to appear at this moment, how unfair, after all this time, after tea with Mr. Primavera, elusive and unsure. Rufus has the edge and knows it. He starts up from his chair with a twisted smile, but when he remembers that we no longer touch, he sits back down, slowly tipping his chair back and forth against the blackboard, letting me watch him as he knows I've come to do, as a movie star does of habit for a camera, the thrill of adoration paled, resigned to a performance, instead of a real show. He twirls a pencil in his fingers and gestures to a child's desk. I sit down, bumping my knees. Rufus gets up and writes slowly, in sprawling letters on the blackboard, "What do you want?"

I give Rufus the shrug I've been practicing for so long, the shrug of a lifetime, the one that will explain that I am only out of sorts, not out of reach, out of touch, but not necessarily out of love—that most of all I am just scared.

I first met Rufus a little over a year ago, in April, when I took a group from the school for the deaf on a fossil dig at Pilgrim's Hill. I stood in the damp forest watching the deaf people dig, feeling the world slipping away, the senses leaving me one by one—first hearing, then smell, then touch, and finally vision as the new greens and browns fell into a cool black void. Rufus was the most possessed of them all to unearth something, the most reverent of the things the earth reluctantly coughed up to him. He pawed at the ground with his blunt, chess-player hands, scooping out handfuls of dirt and caressing each thing he found, bringing it to me for inspection and identification, never disappointed by just a twig or a stone or a dead bug or a clump of moss. Nothing in that forest, in that small highway bound, trash-littered clump of the newly-thawed 20th century earth, was going to disappoint him. It was the way Rufus touched those things of the earth that made it impossible, when he asked me later on the bus ride home, if I would take him on another dig, to say no. Impossible, when his hand first touched me across the cracked green leather seat of the bus, not to want to tell it to wander, to explore. To dig.

There is a knock at the classroom door. A tall boy enters. He reads the writing on the board and nods to me with a quick jerk of his head. This is greeting. This is Billy. Billy is young, maybe nineteen. His hands move constantly. He lost his hearing in a construction accident working alongside his father, two years ago, two nights before the prom. The echoes of the things he's heard keep him mad, keep him moving, ever stalking the sounds he knows he's missing, that may be trailing him, taunting him, lurking in dark corners—his mother's nagging, race cars revving, fights brewing, prom music playing, sweet groans from a parked car on a midsummer's night.

Billy shoots an invisible basketball into a hoop with a silent pop of his lips, gesturing towards the gym.

"Later," Rufus signs, lifting his arms. "Fly away, Billy."

Billy gives me the evil eye on his way out, dribbling an invisible basketball all the way. "There is no later," he signs, before the catch.

Rufus and I sit desk to desk and sign a simple conversation about the weather and work, the snippets of talk that have always before been but a slight prelude to lovemaking, but now must constitute the whole of our connection. A light rain is falling. We can't stroll the grounds. "Come on," Rufus signs. We take a walk around the building. The common room is filled with people, playing cards, some just sitting, some watching "Jeopardy," jumping up to sign the questions, "What is Athens?" "What is rutabaga?" "What is an aphid?" The only other sounds are the rhythmic, hollow bouncing of the ping-pong ball on a long, green table and the rain hitting the skylights. Rufus and I buy Snickers bars at the canteen, and walk down the halls, our sneakers squeaking on a floor that would have made even my mother's look dingy.

"How is your friend?" Rufus signs.

"Which friend?" I ask.

"The knitter." His hands wriggle busily; he purses his lips.

"She died." I close my eyes and lay my head on prayer-ready hands, more dramatic than the deaf would ever have it.

"Dead?" His palms meet, one up, one down, and flip quickly as his eyebrows rise. "When?" He circles one index finger around the other in time.

"March." I spell it, letter by letter, shocked to discover how long it's been since I've been to visit Rufus. But he is not surprised, that I come and go and say things I don't mean, that summer is almost here, and that someone has died.

"I'm sorry." Rufus's fist rubs his chest in sympathy, but not sorrow. He comes near me. Like the push of the Squiggle Z button on my computer which negates the command last given, his touch on my arm erases my goodbye. I feel his breath on my face. His palm rolls us toward the door.

Once off the grounds, Rufus slides into the driver's seat of my car and takes the wheel with a nearly wicked smile. Like Esther, he is strangely pure, excited by the tiniest of demons inside him. Rufus drives fast along the river drive, grinding the fragile gears. I want to touch him as he drives, his leg or his arm, but instead I count the strokes of the windshield wipers, and the blotchy sycamore trees by the side of the river.

Back at my apartment, we ride up in the rickety elevator, backs pressed against opposite sides, eyes locked. We undress and go to bed and stay there into the night, rolling in and out of love and sleep, relieved to have each other back as foils, receptacles for our spillings. After we make love, once, twice, and then again, we hold on to one another uncharacteristically, draped in the dark, dozing on and off. Sometime in the night, Rufus makes omelettes with scallions and cream cheese, which our bellies can't hold. We drown what we've eaten with black coffee and sleep soundly at last. In the morning, I mend Rufus's shirt while he does sit-ups on the floor. And then I drive him back to the school for the deaf.

A few days later, I go back to re-push the Squiggle Z button, to undo the mistake, to unlapse the lapse. It is still raining. Rufus is playing basketball in the gym with five or six boys. He's been expecting me. There is only readiness in his eyes. He slings a towel around his neck and signs to Billy to take over, barrelling the ball into the boy's belly, stealing his wind. We walk the barren halls again, fast, and I strain to keep up with him. Rufus pulls me into a supply closet and closes the door, pulling me to him, half of a demon's smile rising on his face. I push him away and tell him that the other night was just a dip in a pool, that I hope we are still friends, that I just came to talk. Sure, he says, a sneer lifting his sagging face. He couples his first fingers, switches them back and forth. "Friends." His hands line up edge to edge, thumbs in, moving back and forth like a saw. His mouth moves blah, blah, blah; his legs cross in anger. "Go ahead, Elaine. Talk."

I tell Rufus about Mr. Primavera in clumsy, makeshift sign. The light in Rufus's eyes dies. I tell him about the cats and the bust of Beethoven and the women on the stairs, thinking it will make a good story, but Rufus is not interested in anything that even faintly resembles fantasy.

"How much do you like him?" Rufus asks.

"I don't even think I do like him," I try to explain, bumping up against the locks of a mop.

"Do you love him?" His fists cross across his chest and one thumb points to a shapeless, noosed him, dangling in space.

"No."

"Do you love me?" Rufus reins the thumb back in and jabs it against his chest, the fists still crossed, still pressing.

I can only nod my head yes. And shake my head no. And nod and shake and nod. "What do we do with the silence, Rufus?" I ask out loud, slowly, deliberately, so that he can read my lips.

Rufus sticks up his middle finger and is gone. He leaves me in the supply closet with stacks of brown paper towels and toilet paper and cleaning fluids. I am shocked, not by Rufus's anger. I've been expecting that, waiting for its relief, as I used to when I finally found the spiders my brothers had let loose in my bed and squished them dead with my shoe. I am shocked because Rufus's middle finger has just screamed at me and the sound has been deafening. If we have anything left to say to one another, we will have to learn how to speak all over again.

The next week, two traveling lectures and one drizzly dig later, I'm a bit under the weather. I stay home from work one day and put on the vaporizer and soak my feet and read old *National Geographic* magazines. Women in a tiny island in the Pacific have a life expectancy of eighty-two years and half the body fat of the average American woman. I am not really as sick as I'd hoped to be. By the time Mr. Primavera calls in the afternoon, I've used three kleenexes, barely, and I'm hungry, with no food in the house.

"A cup of hot tea might do you good," he says.

"Why are we doing this?" I ask him the most tactful of my burning questions—why his voice trembles and what women see in him will have to wait.

"Why do we need a reason?" he says.

Why do we need a reason for anything that seems interesting, possible, harmless? I change my shirt and slip wool socks over my wrinkled feet. I wear beaded Chinese slippers and leave my hair hanging loose instead of winding it up into a bun and stuffing the end tips into the coil as I usually do. Taking a glance in the mirror, I see an odd and mythic creature—part empress, part sea dragon, part bag lady. Today, though, I have achieved some sort of softness, I think, some kind of grace. I am my most beautiful in profile, in mid-reach, the leans and stretches of me, sunk in a strange man's chair.

"You don't look very sick," Mr. Primavera says at the door.

"Sick is maybe too strong a word, Mr. Primavera."

"Come on. Make it Anthony. Let's have some tea."

"*Count Dracula was a vein man,*" reads my fortune. I laugh. Anthony pours himself a cup and joins me on the couch. I get up and turn Ludwig's angry face around. The Victrola sits silent. I have not moved Mr. Primavera to music, it seems.

"I wonder when Esther and Avery's marriage went sour," Anthony says out of the blue.

"I didn't know it had." I cough on too quick a gulp of tea, instantly glad that Esther and Avery have taken their secrets to the grave, that there will never be any proof that what Anthony is about to tell me is true.

"Before the mistress, or after?" The green rises in Anthony's eyes like floodwater.

"Mistress?" I say.

"Did Esther know?"

"She must have," I say carefully, swallowing my surprise, repeating myself. "Esther wasn't stupid."

"Avery and I used to talk out on the stoop. 'Just find a woman who understands you, Anthony,' he'd tell me. 'A square meal isn't everything. Find a greasy spoon if you have to, maybe a waitress.' Then he'd always say that Esther hadn't turned out to be the woman he thought she was."

"Who ever does?" I picture Rufus on that first day on the dig, so lively and full of smiles, so unlike himself. "Esther made the best of Avery," I say. "He could have done the same."

"I think he tried," Anthony says, rubbing the ear of a striped cat with a white patch over one eye. "But she made him crazy."

"Maybe he already was."

"Maybe." Anthony fiddles with his spoon. "What do you do, Elaine?"

"I'm a paleontologist."

"Come again?"

"I'm a geologist. Fossil and bone racket."

"You piece together the past?"

"That's a grand way of putting it, I guess."

The doorbell rings. Anthony puts the kettle back on. "Must be Alice," he says.

Laughing, I tip back my head and swallow the last sip of cold tea. I've become one of Mr. Primavera's tea ladies in spite of myself. "What do you do, Anthony?" I ask him as I put on my coat. "Besides drink tea and rescue cats?"

"Right now," he says. "I'm recuperating."

I am polite because my mother told me that rude little girls, along with little girls that picked their scabs, never got husbands—never got happy. And so I don't ask Anthony, recuperating from what? Alice is solemn, with thick, reddish hair, come with a limp and a violin case, as she does every Tuesday at six. I stand out on the sidewalk, looking up at Anthony's curtains. After a while, I hear the sweet desperate wail of the violin, and I understand for one cragged, flashing second, what Rufus has missed.

The next day, I get a call from Esther's daughter Camille in Chicago, asking me to sort through her mother's things.

"You mean that hasn't been done yet?" I imagine with horror the sour milk in Esther's refrigerator, the moldy shower cap, maybe even Esther herself, decaying, slumped over in some chair, teeth gleaming, fingernails grown into curling claws.

"I had to rush off on business right after Mother died," she says. I met Camille at the funeral. Small and slick like an otter, she bore no resemblance to Esther. "I'm in the thick of things just now, and my brother is useless at this sort of thing."

"Your mother was very kind to me," I tell her. "But I really don't think I'm the one. . . ."

"It was so sudden. She spoke of you so often, Eleanor."

"Elaine."

"Please, Elaine." Her voice self-corrects, stuck in a hard place, between a plea and a command. "We'd be grateful. I'm sure my mother would've wanted it this way."

Camille, I remember Esther saying, was used to having the last word.

The next day, I sit in Esther's apartment on the floor of her living room with a pile of papers I've taken from her desk. Even Esther has not managed to die cleanly, without a trace. I find the usual leftover business of the dead—some unpaid bills and receipts, a few lists. One reads, "Ajax, cottage cheese, cat food." Esther had no cats, only the dog that died. Another list must have been older; one of the items is "underwear for Avery." The thought of Avery dying in saggy, grey underwear drums up the nervous, slightly hysterical laugh of the living trying to grasp the dead, a laugh that used to burst from my throat at some of the worst misunderstandings Rufus and I had—a laugh that rose up in me unbidden, and shivered, dry and fishy tasting on the roof of my mouth before it spilled forth, a chute of dusty coal, making Rufus furious, misreading lips, fingers, scowls—socks for soul, headache for brainstorm, fuck for luck.

The lists are the most intimate things I come upon, the most revealing. Otherwise I am struck by the Jane Doe nature of Esther's things. There are no pictures, no souvenirs of trips, no matches from a favorite restaurant, nothing but generic aspirin and twenty-year-old epsom salts in the medicine chest, nothing to color it Esther's home except for the metal file box labeled, "STAR BOX," filled with the recipes of the stars, carefully clipped on the dotted line from the TV Guide. I replace the yellow tape that holds the label in place and I wish, maybe even pray, to a tiny wizened god I once saw in a tomb in Mexico, a mere box of bones, that the star box needed organizing. But it doesn't. Nothing here does. Without Esther, this is just a moldy, public place.

Midway through the pile of Esther's papers, I see the wavy fringe of an old photograph. I expect it to show two smiling children or Avery at the wheel of his truck, a young Esther in a wedding gown. But it is Anthony Primavera's face that stares out at me, Anthony at the age of fifteen or so, a terribly thin boy standing on a shore, his lanky hair windblown, the head already too heavy a burden on his thin neck. And it is there, the receding hairline, odd on a boy who is odd-looking to begin with. On the back are scribbled some words in Italian. I slip the picture into my pocket.

When the desk is orderly, I put on one of Esther's frilly aprons, with bitten cherries on it, and get ready to clean. The apartment is covered with a thin layer of stuck grime. I look for the Ajax that Esther never got around to buying, scrub as best I can with an old sponge and dish soap. I water Esther's parched plants, pick off the shriveled leaves and mist those that are left. I sweep all the cobwebs and dead flies from the bay window. Out on the grate of the fire escape, I find a cat dish, encrusted with bits of dry food. I soak the cat dish, put some tuna out on the grate as night falls, and lock the door. The next day, when I come back to Esther's apartment to finish up the cleaning, there is a knock at the door.

"I heard footsteps," Anthony says. "What are you doing here?"

"Cleaning," I say.

"Why?"

"Esther's daughter called. She wanted someone to take care of things."

"Things as in what things?"

"Everything. As in all things."

"Big job." Anthony looks at me strangely, maybe because I'm wearing a dress, one of several I've bought to wear to work—waisted, open-necked things with indescribable shapes and colors on them, soft, shimmery dresses that shift on my shoulders and show the shapes of my breasts. We had a visit today from a visiting Egyptian dignitary. After I gave him a tour of the museum, I took him to lunch. It is another me who performs these acts, not the digger in me, but the pleaser, the me who orders chicken salad and pays the check, makes transatlantic calls, smiles and gently removes the hand from my arm without offending the mind that has moved the hand, the one who locks the doors of the museum at the end of the day. "You look different today," Anthony says. "May I come in?" But he is already over the threshhold, taking everything in, touching things, hands sliding over surfaces and objects. "It never did feel like Avery's house."

"It's strange being here without Esther," I say. In the cupboards, I find no tea. "Will coffee do?" I ask him.

"Just some water," he says, sitting himself down in a hard backed chair. "Coffee has its way with me."

I pour Anthony some water and start on my third cup of coffee. "Esther talked about you a lot in the end."

Anthony sips at his water. "She made a movie character out of me, I think."

I nod. "Half saint, half pimp."

"Pimp?" He looks up at me in surprise.

"Just a joke. Who are all the women, Anthony?"

"Friends. Friends of friends."

"No men friends?"

"A few."

"Avery?"

"Avery was a friend."

"Do you collect women?" I ask him.

He shakes his head. "Collectors are hoarders. Finders keepers. They clean their finds and sort them and put them under glass. They are usually afraid of something. My father collected beer bottle caps. I wasn't allowed to touch them, the things that cut your fingers and littered the streets. He'd lay those bottle caps on velvet, but he'd hit me. I could never understand why you'd love something that wasn't even alive, and beat the daylights out of something that was." Anthony points to the row of fossil and bone pieces arranged along the window sill, things that I used to bring Esther as offerings for her company and her star food. "You are a collector," Anthony says.

"You can touch them," I say. "Go ahead."

Anthony picks up a seagull bone and runs his finger along its ridge. "I just never understood," he says. "What's the point of a collection after it's been collected."

"Crossing lines," I say. "Time zones, date lines, dimensions, going from one world to another. What about the cats?" I say. "You collect them, don't you? You feed them, brush them. You like their company."

"We co-exist," Anthony says. "They come and go as they please."

"The women, too?"

"Ha, ha. Of course."

"But they come to depend on you," I say. "For food and warmth. Bottle caps and bones aren't beholden."

"It's their choice," he says. "Cats aren't stupid."

"If you don't hold onto anything," I say, "then you have no past." I gesture around the empty apartment. "She left nothing. I'm having trouble remembering her."

"Who should she have left anything for?" Anthony says.

"Her children. Her friends. Posterity."

"You met those children," Anthony says. "Posterity is just as greedy. And you were only an acquaintance really, weren't you, just like I was?'"

"Why didn't you ever ask Esther up for tea?" I say. I want to get past the angry feeling I have for him and move onto something else—indifference, annoyance, even desire will do. "It would've meant a lot to her."

"I did," he says. "After Avery died, we met on Wednesdays. Her legs couldn't manage the stairs, so I came down here instead. We watched the soaps together. She had a crush on that vampire, Dr. Cranshaw, and I had a thing for, well, never mind."

"What did you talk about?" I ask him.

Anthony thinks. "Teenage pigeons. Where they hang out. Why you never see them." Pause. "Swollen ankles." Pause. "The nurses' uniforms on 'General Hospital.' How the hemlines haven't changed. They've stayed mini all these years, back in the sixties. I should've done the same."

"Why?" I ask.

"I'm only thirty-eight," he says, "but I feel like a fossil."

Collectors live day to day and call it sensible, gathering bits and pieces as they go, as gestures of time's goodwill, of apology. But they distinguish always between a past and a deep past. I look to the dark ages because my own short history reveals so little. I sidestep the future and ask it for promises it can't possibly keep. Rufus discounts the past, squiggle Z, and holds the future to nothing, understanding that they are one and the same, separated only by the dotted line of consciousness. Rufus will not be collected. He will not live in a glass case or be scrutinized in any other than natural sunlight. He will not be placed on velvet or led willingly into the rain. He will accept no labels, not even deaf. But unlike me and Anthony, he will take chances.

I know why the women climb Anthony's stairs, why they climb back down again. They bring no valuables here; they take no risks. Anthony takes nothing from them. He is the tea man, a gentle devil's advocate, the man in the black booth, the man with no childhood, no sex drive, no hair on his chin, no intentions. Curiosity may or may not have killed a few cats; it certainly is not enough, in the end, to keep people alive. Survival has to involve something that at least approximates love, and whatever that is, it is not easy or amenable. It comes neither in pieces nor in one fell swoop. Rufus takes blood every time I see him and I from him. We do not need more words, only more time to consider the ones we've already flung at one another.

"What are you recuperating from?" I ask Anthony softly.

"Call it whatever you like. A crisis, an illness. Love gone amok. A razor blade misused. Avery found me in my room. He bound me up and took me to the hospital. Afterwards, he sat with me out on the stoop and checked my arms, every night until he died. 'No more monkey business,' he'd say. He was my healer, the man on the stoop. I prayed for him when he was on the road. Now, I feel shaky some days."

I cannot touch Anthony and so I say, "I'm sorry."

"If he'd known the real truth about me," Anthony says, taking the last sip of his water, "he probably would have let me bleed."

"Esther would've mopped you up," I say.

"She wanted to find me a nice girl," Anthony says.

"Not really," I say. I take the photograph out of the pocket of my dress and hand it to Anthony. He looks at it silently, without expression. "That was my father," he says. "In Italy. His family moved here soon after. My grandfather died when I was four. After that, everything changed." Anthony's hand shakes ever so slightly as he slides the photograph into his shirt pocket. We sit in silence on Esther's sofa. What Esther thought we might offer one another, what we once shared—bits and pieces of the Brubakers—their food, their conversation, their comfort, is gone. Anthony rises, uncomfortable as a guest, cold without hot tea. He must be going. It is Wednesday, 4:30. He's out of Red Zinger tea and Meryl will be coming soon. Meryl is a botanist. I might like her, scientist to scientist. She's bringing an herb-and-shrub cure for his sinuses.

When Anthony's gone, I turn on Esther's TV and sit back down on the couch with the seagull bone and Esther's recipe box. A woman on "Merv" has proof that there is life after death. Sure enough, the couch pillows sink low and Esther is suddenly beside me.

"Turn to Channel 5, Elaine," she says. "It's a big day on

'Eden's End.'" Lo and behold, Deidre has just found out that her husband's brother is the father of her sister's baby and her mother's lover to boot and knowing Deidre, Esther says, one of them will be dead, crippled or in a coma before the week is out. I flip back to "Merv," and look in the recipe box under G for Griffin, to see what Merv may have had to offer Esther. Under G, there is only Jane Goodall's "Banana Delight."

"Oh, come on," I say to Esther. "It's got to be a gimmick. Jane Goodall would never write on a recipe card from her hut in Africa, an ape at each side, Dear TV Guide: Peel three bananas; rub two sticks together."

"Don't be such a cynic, dear," Esther says. "They're people, just like you and me. Don't you think Jane Goodall ever has bad dreams in that hut, a craving for peanut butter, a hankering for 'I Love Lucy,' any regrets at all?"

Esther takes out her knitting needles. I lean my head back and close my eyes. I smell Lucille Ball's Fried Halibut Supreme and I am suddenly starving. But it is not quite dinnertime, not yet time to do anything but sit beside Esther in the musty twilight and think—think lascivious and murderous thoughts with Deidre—plot, plan, keep busy, eyes wide, pulse thumping, chase Anthony to the health food store, wolf down the pack of oyster crackers I saved from lunch, push Rufus back into that supply closet and lock the door. The woman on "Merv" swears that she was a reptile in another life, eons ago, when the dinosaurs lumbered and the ice masses flowed. She ate leaves and bugs. To this day, she is a protein lover, a big woman. Life as a dinosaur was better. She had a new lover every year, and no taxes. The children left the nest early. There was only hot and cold, big and small. No good or bad, no deadlines, no PMS, no addictions, no guns, no TV, no offense, Merv. Merv laughs into his doubling chin. Esther's knitting needles click. By five o'clock, I'm dozing; the TV murmurs turn to the chatter of dreams. I have only this life, I tell myself, fighting sleep, and I will not rest except for this one moment. Rufus knows about time. He tried to tell me with his middle finger. Figure, at the Institute for the Deaf, the echo of Billy's basketball flings itself against a gym wall, and the leisure hour is not due for another hour and a half.

LOST IN CASABLANCA

My brother Edgar calls me one May day to tell me that our mother, Abigail, is losing her marbles.

"Dropping them one by one, Amanda," he says, "into the clear, blue sky."

I am in my kitchen eating a cold slice of pizza, a food we were forbidden to eat as children because it was foreign and fattening. "How can you tell?" I ask him.

"Episodes," he says. "Strange swings of character. Like today, I saw her walking downtown with a bag lady."

"Maybe she was walking *beside* a bag lady," I say for the sake of argument, but it's odd enough that Abbie was out and about, having long since decreed the streets of Boston fit only for hoodlums. "*Next* to a bag lady maybe. *Behind* a bag lady."

"They were talking, Amanda. I followed them to the Common. They fed the pigeons, talked to the Hari Krishnas, then bought some donuts for those kids who sing Irish songs in front of the subway."

"Maybe Abbie's just having some fun," I say. "There's no harm in that, is there?"

"Come on, Amanda," Edgar says. "You know Mother doesn't know the first thing about having fun."

"Maybe she used to," I say, starting to chew on the rubbery crust, "before she had us, before she met Father."

"Father," Edgar says, swinging my words into his as is his way, "would flip in his grave."

I hold the phone away from my ear and finish my pizza as he drones on. Although he is only eleven months older than me, I will forever be Edgar's little sister.

I don't see as much of Abbie as I used to since I moved out to the suburbs with my husband Alan and our two children. Edgar still lives downtown, not far from the townhouse in which we grew up, where Abbie has been hibernating since my father died four years ago. She has never liked the house, but it has become hers, and possession seems reason enough to stay. I don't often

170

go back to the city because it always makes me feel like a child again. My feet go pigeon-toed and the salesladies become impatient with me. Only some times and secretly do I creep down the slow lane of the Mass. Pike into town, to sit in the swivel chair of a man named Francois, who claims to be able to work miracles with even the most impossible hair like mine—straggly and limp around my pasty face.

But at 38 I have almost given up on miracles. I am not aging well, I think. None of the Sinclairs do, and I am a Sinclair like my father—not pretty and thin of hair, tending to overweight. Edgar once told me that I look like a toad. He, too, is rather reptilian—pudgy and balding, with beady eyes. We both seem older than our ages, have always seemed older than we are. Our father, Rhineheart Sinclair, once President of the Bay State Bank and Trust, expected great things of us, but lived long enough to know that we had both turned out to be only disappointments. Although Edgar became a banker to please my father, his real passions are birds and stark modern art. Consequently, he has never gotten "anywhere." I am a housewife, or, as my father started to say of me when I quit college to marry Alan and have children, I do nothing.

Summer comes early the year that Abbie's marbles start to tumble. I drive Hilary to gymnastics and play checkers with Adam, knit Alan a droopy vest. Francois gives me a permanent and because I am afraid to tell him I hate it, I pay a man named Giovanni to cut off all my hair. Edgar calls daily with more proof about Abbie; I suspect he may have spies. He tells me there is toilet paper trailing over the lampshades in her house and a blond wig on a mannequin's head in the bathroom, that there is music playing in a house long filled with only shadows and silence. I don't want to hear these things, don't know whether or not to believe them.

I let my garden go to seed and start spending more time with Abbie. We take in a show at the museum, go to the library, out for tea. Most days she seems herself—reserved and sad, dressed in one of the linen suits and matching veiled hats she's worn for years. But on some days I see glimpses of a new spirit. She wears a necklace or a purple scarf, hums to herself out of tune. The frail body long crippled with arthritis has a new grace, a new strength. And though Abbie has always been considered a handsome woman in a quiet sort of way, something of late has made her quite a dish, as Alan puts it. I watch her ruffle the hair of a strange child and flirt with the grocer, she whose stiff embrace I've only felt a few times in my life. She brings smiles to the faces of strangers. Cats follow her home.

"How are you feeling, Mother?" I ask her.

"Some days better than others," she says. No more.

The postman makes eyes at Abbie when she comes to visit. "That's some mother you got there, Mrs. Mullins," he tells me. "If I were only thirty years older. . . ." Something pricks at my heart as I take the mail from his hand and go back into the house to clean the ring off the bathtub. I have always had a crush on the mailman.

Edgar calls me one night while I am thawing TV dinners. Like Abbie, I am a terrible cook, used to worry as a child that my husband would leave me in disgust for someone who made souffles that never fell.

"It's Mother," Edgar starts out. "I just got a call from Angelo's Meat Market over on Charles Street. She's down there making a scene. She keeps asking for a pound of lion meat and says she won't leave without it."

"Oh, dear," I say. "She must be thinking of that store over in Cambridge, where Julia Child shops. They sell lion meat there."

"Amanda, that's hardly the point," he says with a sigh. It doesn't surprise me that Edgar has never married. There are no such women left in the world as he would require—demure, deferential, opinionless.

"Hurry, Amanda," Edgar says. "I have to finish up something here at the bank. I'll meet you down there as soon as I can."

Leaving Alan and the children to fend for themselves, I drive into Boston in rush hour traffic. I park in front of a hydrant and start making my way through the crowd Abbie has gathered. She is sitting on the floor in her stockinged feet. The butcher says, "Lady, please, enough is enough. Go home already."

"Not until I get my lion meat," she says, and gives him a sexy smile. He shakes his head, then shrugs at the crowd. For a moment, stunned, I stop and watch Abbie as I might a stranger.

She has put on some weight recently, and it becomes her. Her breasts are full and the dark spots and pouches are gone from her face. Her hair, once wispy and dull like mine, is now snowy white and puffed up in some new way. She is wearing a red dress, a color my father called cheapening and forbade us all. Her brown eyes are clear and dancing with a rising light. Just then, Edgar arrives. Together we make our way to the middle of the saw-dusted floor, gathering Abbie in a huddle.

"Come quietly, Mother," Edgar hisses. "You're making a scene."

"You have the wrong market," I whisper into her other ear. "It's Savenor's that sells lion meat."

Abbie looks confused, brings a wrinkled hand up to her face. I notice that her wedding ring is gone.

"Oh," she says, then looks back at Edgar, suddenly the old Abbie again. She buries her head in his shoulder as the crowd titters and the shame washes over her. He puts a stiff arm around her, leads her with dignity out the door. With a softening in my heart, I remember that it is Edgar's fierce loyalty that redeems him. I gather Abbie's coat and purse and we make our way out onto the sidewalk.

"Some dame," I hear a voice say as Abbie passes by.

"Hope I have as much moxie when I'm her age," says another.

"Not me," says the first voice. "She's nuts."

I rip the parking ticket off my windshield and take Abbie home with me in the station wagon. We ride in silence. I don't know what to say and Abbie feels no need. Alan is outside mowing our small patch of lawn in the summer dusk and waves as we pull into the driveway "Hi, Ma Sinclair!" he yells, pushing his Red Sox cap back on his head.

"Hello, Alan," Abbie says stiffly, always offended by his sloppy affection.

Hilary and Adam are eating popsicles on the sofa, eyes glued to the TV set. Abbie straightens her hair and tucks in her blouse.

"Do I look all right?" she asks in a whisper.

"You look just fine, Mother," I tell her.

"Hello, children," she says.

"Hello, Grandmother," they say in unison. I think how much more they might love Abbie if they knew she'd been hunting down lion meat or feeding pigeons with a bag lady. But to the children she is still the old Abbie, proper and not much fun, my father's other half.

"Grandmother Sinclair has come to sleep over," I tell them. "Isn't that nice?"

"That's nice," says eight-year-old Adam, never taking his soft eyes—Abbie's eyes—away from a talking horse on the screen. Hilary, who is working on a gum wrapper chain that's nearly 17 feet long, says nothing. She is nine years old and a glum child— like my father, I fear.

"You shouldn't let them watch so much television," Abbie says as I usher her towards the stairs. "They might go blind. I once knew a boy"— she goes on—"well, needless to say, Amanda, it didn't end well."

"It's Friday," I tell her, though I see she's not listening. "We let the kids watch an extra hour on the weekend nights."

Abbie grips the banister, her legs wobbly and sore. "Yes, yes, Rhineheart, I know," she mutters, "I burned the peas."

I see Hilary making the crazy sign around her temple as Abbie and I slowly climb the stairs.

Later, when Abbie is reading in bed and I'm downstairs working on a puzzle of Mount Rushmore, the phone rings.

"Well, Amanda," Edgar says, "I'd say it's time."

"Why don't you come out here and talk to me in person sometime, Edgar?" I say, slipping Lincoln's eyebrow into place. "Time for what?"

"The suburbs make me nervous," he says. "All those cricket noises and matching lawns. Time to consider institutionalization."

"We've been over this before, Edgar," I tell him. "Abbie doesn't belong in one of those places."

"I think she's gone over the edge this time, Amanda. There's no telling what she may do next."

"Abbie's not senile," I finally say it out loud, hoping it will sound convincing, hoping to God it is true. "Her brain's just crowded after all these years. She gets confused."

"Not senile?" Edgar's voice rises. "You saw her down at Angelo's, Amanda. A woman of Mother's breeding acting that way in public? Do you really think she should be allowed to roam the streets? Think about it, Amanda."

"Oh, Edgar," I sigh, "save it for the courtroom." But the dial tone buzzes in my ear and my eyes fill with tears. "Damn you, Edgar," I whisper. Once again, I have not been quick or strong or brave enough. Once again, I have let Abbie and me down.

As I hang up the phone, I notice Abbie perched on the stairs in her nightgown and slippers, staring through the railings at me. I motion her down and we tiptoe past Alan, who is dozing in an arm chair. I kiss his head, drinking in a whiff of the peacefulness that surrounds him, jealous because it's the one thing he can't share with me, or teach me. I put the tea kettle on the stove and Abbie sits down at the kitchen table.

"Edgar shouldn't call so late at night," she says.

"You know Edgar," I say, wondering why I always spring to his defense, even when I'm mad at him. "He's a worrier."

"I won't go to a home, Amanda," Abbie says suddenly. "Those places are just fancy bus stops where people wait to die."

"I know," I say, pouring the steeped tea into our cups. "I know."

Abbie gets up from the table, paces around it With new vigor, hands on hips. She picks up a wooden spoon and slaps it into the palm of her hand. Her voice is low, gravelly. Like the Abbie at Angelo's, she is changed.

"I'm not ready to croak," she says. "Edgar has no right." She slips her weight onto one hip. "I remember him from Paris," she says. "He can't be trusted."

"Edgar?" I ask, scalding the roof of my mouth with too quick a gulp of hot tea. "Our Edgar?"

"Yeah, that's the one," she says, taking a pack of cigarettes from her bathrobe pocket. She lights one up, offers one to me.

"I don't smoke, Mother," I say. "Neither do you."

She shrugs, puts the cigarettes back in her pocket. "Everyone in Casablanca has problems," she says. "Everyone."

I drink my warm tea as Abbie paces and puffs away—scared, mortified, to see her so different, so unmotherly. I wonder whether she's crazy or just old, whether she needs help or comfort or maybe to be left alone, if she's just happy at last, as Alan keeps saying. But I feel an anguish flood through me then, because at that moment, as Abbie puffs cigarette smoke in my face and talks like Humphrey Bogart in the movie "Casablanca," I know that Edgar is right—that we can't go on this way. And in that moment, as I accept my mother's old age, I feel the sad and irrevocable loss of my youth, which I have never once missed before.

Edgar's psychiatrist friend says it sounds to him like some form of schizophrenia and that Abbie needs professional help. He sends us a pamphlet about a place called "The Lagoon in the Pines."

"What a ridiculous name," I say to Edgar. "When's the last time you saw a lagoon out in Framingham?"

"A book by its cover and all that, Amanda," he says.

I read the brochure out on the porch after the mailman, Abbie's admirer, delivers it one morning with what I am sure is a disapproving look. FREE INTRODUCTORY WEEKEND, it reads. BRING A FRIEND, RELAX BY THE POOL. The cover photos show sprightly elderly people with silver hair, some sipping drinks with lemon slices on a terrace, others riding in a golf cart. It gives me a sick feeling because of the lies it tells with what it does not say. The swimming pool will be tiny and filled with bugs, and the grass will be planted in squares that never latch onto the earth. Idleness, purposelessness, pleasantness— things you relish for a week or two of vacation, but which do not grace the end of a life. I rip up the pamphlet and toss it into the trash.

But I have no better ideas, and in a vague, defeated moment, Abbie agrees to go for the weekend. I pick Edgar up on a cloudy Friday in September and we drive in silence to Abbie's house, where she waits, dressed in blue silk, perched on the stoop with her bag.

"Hello, Mother," Edgar says, helping her into the car.

"Ilsa," she says. "Ilsa."

We drive west to Framingham. The trees are still thick with green from the summer rains. Abbie talks in a velvety voice about drinking champagne in a cafe in Paris, the day before the Germans marched in. "The whole world was crumbling," she says. "We picked a crazy time to fall in love."

I sit helpless in the back seat, chewing my fingernails.

"Champagne makes me hiccup," I toss in an occasional non sequitur. Or, "I've never been to Paris."

We arrive in mid-afternoon. An arc of ornate wrought iron fit for the entrance to heaven hangs above us as we check in at the visitors' booth. Edgar pulls up in front of a huge concrete building and helps Abbie out of the car. We stand there and watch as he pulls away.

"Are you ready to go?" I take Abbie's arm gently.

"We'll always have Paris," she says to no one.

After being welcomed by a nurse, Abbie and I settle into our room, which is one in a long corridor of rooms just like it. The walls are painted a timid lime green. Two daisies in a vase sit atop a bureau, breathing a fresh breath into the stale air. I notice a lock on the door, a bedpan in the corner. As I open my suitcase, Abbie sits down on one of the narrow beds, smoothes the spread.

"I see they don't plan on my having any overnight guests," she says, her eyes full of the dancing light. "I may have to sneak Rick in the back way."

I laugh feebly. This is as close as Abbie and I have ever come to joking, or talking about sex. I remember that it was Edgar who explained the facts of life to me, and what an unusual thing that was for a brother of thirteen to do for a sister of twelve. I wish I could sit down and joke back with my mother. I wish I could defend and applaud this other Abbie, the one with such pluck. Because it is this Abbie, the one who wanders in and out of Casablanca, who could better survive. But I can only fold and unfold my clothes in my suitcase as Ilsa plots and reminisces on the bed. I am still too confused, too frightened, to do anything.

The weekend visitors gather with the residents and staff that evening for a LUAU UNDER THE STARS. I wear a tag saying, "Aloha, I'm Amanda." My tights droop at the crotch and my clogs make too much noise on the stone terrace. The staff is dressed in Hawaiian shirts and grass skirts. There is a table filled with food, a paper-mâché pig with an apple in its mouth. I go to the WAHINIS' room for a while to hide. Ukulele music follows me into the stall, trickling from speakers that I can't find. I flush the toilet and go back outside.

Most of the guests are Abbie's age and older. They come with sons and daughters and sisters and friends, the people—like me—who love them but will leave them here because they don't know what else to do. A man with a straw hat hands me two paper leis. "Pass one on to a stranger," he says. "Make a new friend." It's the kind of thing Hilary's nursery school teacher used to say; I give them back to him. A wispy young woman comes by with a tray of pineapple chunks speared with frilly toothpicks.

"Welcome to the Lagoon," she says. "We hope you enjoy your stay."

"Fat chance," mutters an old man with a houndstooth jacket, reaching over me to grab some pineapple. His companion, maybe a daughter or a niece, takes his arm. He breaks away, comes up to Abbie. "You thinking of coming here?" he asks.

"No," she says. "I'm just passing through."

"Smart," he says, but Abbie has already wandered off.

We shuffle around the terrace as darkness falls, exchanging desultory, dead-end conversation—name-swapping and talk about the weather. Abbie sips at a glass of wine and smiles to herself, talking to no one. She seems to be taking the whole thing in stride, as if it were one of Edgar's boring cocktail parties. But I'm worried because I know that as Ilsa, Abbie isn't thinking about why we are here, doesn't consider that some days it hurts just to get out of bed, doesn't remember that this is a place she may have to stay. I can't bear to have to come back here again with Abbie, so I try to coax Ilsa back into reality, or whatever the moment is.

"Let's walk over to the garden before it gets dark," I say, gulping down the last of my rumless piña colada. "I saw the asters from our window. Remember, Mother? You used to keep the most beautiful asters out on the back terrace." She looks at me as if she does not remember the flowers or the terrace or even who I am. I take her arm.

The grounds are lovely—acres of pine and apple trees and fields, not the patchwork lawn I'd imagined. Sweet smells wrap around us and I hear the rustle of an animal as we walk along a wooded path. Abbie starts to limp then, overcome by the pain that Ilsa manages to chase away.

"Your father wouldn't approve," she says suddenly, "knowing that his money might end up at a place like this . . . taking care of me."

"It's your money now," I say, "to do with as you see fit."

"Yes," Abbie says, picking a leaf from a tree. "But no one seems to think I see fit anymore."

We reach the asters, settle on a wooden bench. Abbie reaches down to pick one; the petals come off at her touch. She smoothes her dress and I see the bones in her wrist, the spots and veins. She has become thin again, too thin. Abbie looks down at her hands; they tremble slightly. She fights to keep them still.

"Piano hands," she says. "That's what your father once called them. Just once."

"Why did you marry Father?" I've never dared ask this question before. Now, there is nothing to lose.

"I was glad to be asked," she says.

I take one of her hands, feel the lumps at her joints and the cold that's crept into them. "This isn't such a terrible place, is it, Mother?"

Abbie looks up and around, as if for the first time. "If I've become a burden to you and Edgar," she says, "then I suppose I must be put somewhere."

"You're not a burden," I tell her, "but we worry about you. You're not yourself sometimes."

"What do you mean?"

"You've been taking on the characters of other people, fictional people even." I have never been any good at tact.

"Who?" she asks.

"One day you were Humphrey Bogart. Lately you've been Ingrid Bergman in *Casablanca*," I tell her.

"Really," she says, not with fear, but with curiosity.

"Everything about you changes," I try to explain. "Your voice, your manner, your reactions, your . . . judgment."

"Like the time I went to Angelo's?" she asks.

"Yes," I say. "Like the time you went to Angelo's."

"Sixty-nine years of beef, Amanda," she says. "I needed a change."

"I know," I say, and give her back her hand.

The man in the houndstooth coat is waiting for Abbie back at the luau. He comes up to her, offers her a glass of punch.

"So, pretty lady," he says. "What do you do?"

"Nothing," she says. "Anymore."

"Me either," he says, gulping down the last of his drink. They turn away from one another.

After the luau, we go back to our room. I brush my straggly hair, newly laced with grey, the same hundred strokes Abbie insisted on when I was a child. She puts on her nightgown and goes over to stand by the window.

"You have an appointment tomorrow with one of the doctors," I remind her. I told her this earlier, but am not sure who was listening. "Just to chat, before the Lagoon Ladies' Luncheon."

Abbie pulls back the curtains and pushes open the window.

"Did you hear me?" I ask gently, wanting to make sure there will be no surprises. "About the doctor?"

She nods. "I heard you, Amanda," she says, breathing in the night air. "I heard you all three times."

I wake up sometime later feeling chilled. The light of the moon streams into the room. The window is closed. Abbie's bed is made up neatly and the daisies are gone from the vase. I get up, go to the closet, find only my rumpled clothes still hanging. I run to the door and down the hall in my flannel nightgown, slipping in Alan's red socks. I see Abbie's small figure at the end of the hall, suitcase beside her, hand on the knob of the door. She is still. The daisies droop in her hair.

"Where are you going, Mother?" I ask. "Nowhere," she says, slowly turning around. "The door is locked."

I feel it all at once with a rage—the unkindness of old age, the slow abduction of dignity and strength, the loss of control, and freedom. The line between Abbie and Ilsa is not so clear; neither is really crazy. There is craziness here, too, in this fake lagoon in the pines, on these shiny, waxed floors. And who's to say when Abbie's last marble has fallen? It's just a best human guess, a finger pointed at a clock and why not mine?

"This can't be the only door," I say.

"We have to go past the security guard at the other end of the building," she says. "And what would we tell him?"

"The hell with him," I say. "Let's not tell him anything."

"Amanda!" she says. "The man is only doing his job." The dreamy look comes into her eyes and I hear Ilsa's low murmur. "I hate this war so much," she says. "It's a crazy world."

"Mother?" I say loudly.

Her eyes waver, the light dances in and out, her mouth rises and falls from a smile. She looks first at her suitcase, then back at me.

"It's you, Mother, isn't it?"

"Yes, Amanda, of course it's me."

"You don't want to stay here, do you?"

"No," she says plainly, a no full of weight and sadness and truth. "I can't stay here, Amanda."

We hear footsteps coming toward us and creep back to our room. Closing the door behind us, I put my finger up to my mouth. Abbie nods. We stand—the statues of naughty children—until the footsteps pass by our door. A moonbeam falls on my arm and I look up to trace the light.

"The window," I say. "You opened it earlier, didn't you, Mother?"

"Yes," she says. "It was stuffy in here."

"Then it's not locked!" I say. "And we're on the first floor." Running over to the window, I fling it open and see the broken latch flapping from its hinge. "It's a sign," I say, laughing. "A sign from somewhere." I throw my coat on over my nightgown and toss the rest of my clothes into my suitcase. Abbie makes up my bed as I pull on my shoes. "

"Please, Amanda," she says. "Try and do something with your hair."

I groan and pull a brush through my hair, clipping it back in one of Hilary's barrettes. Hiking up my coat, I climb onto the sill and slip out onto the grass. Abbie hands me our bags and then holds out her hands. She weighs no more than Adam; I ease her down onto the ground. The dew chills my feet and Abbie smoothes her hair.

"Where can we possibly go, Amanda?" she says. "It's dark out and we have no car."

"We'll walk," I say. "To the park, out for breakfast. Maybe to Casablanca."

A Note about the Author

Anne Whitney Pierce lives in Cambridge, Massachusetts, with her three daughters and their father, Alex Slive. Her stories have appeared in over a dozen literary magazines, including *American Fiction*, Number 2; *The Chattahoochee Review*; *Cimarron Review*; *Crosscurrents*; *Kansas Quarterly*; *The Massachusetts Review*; *The North American Review*; *The Southern Review*; and *The Virginia Quarterly Review*.